WHAT REMAINS

NICOLE REEVES

This is a work of fiction. Names, characters, places, and incidents are either the product of the author's imagination or are used fictitiously, and any resemblance to actual persons, living or dead, business establishments, events, or locales is entirely coincidental.

Published by Nicole Reeves

Printed in the United States of America

First U.S. Edition: January 2024

ISBN ebook: 978-1-7357037-3-2

ISBN print: 978-1-7357037-2-5

Author: Nicole Reeves

Editor: Melissa Frey

Cover Design: Joshua Reeves

For my Grandpa Dennis.
You mean the world to me.
I will always be your brown-eyed girl.

Chapter One

NOTHING SAYS "I'M DESPERATE to pretend my vacation plans weren't canceled" more than a frozen pizza, though I had serious doubts that even carb-filled deliciousness could make me forget we're stuck at school for the holidays. We're imprisoned here for at least another three months when we should be home with our families. It doesn't matter if the powers-that-be claim it's for our own safety.

It just sucks.

Period.

"Selena, will you grab the ranch?" Hanna yells over her shoulder. Dinner in the school cafeteria is so far from the turkey dinner smothered in gravy we've been dreaming about for weeks it might as well be on another planet. Thanksgiving is still a day away, but we only found out this morning we won't be going on break, and that calls for emergency carbohydrates.

At least I'd convinced the kitchen staff to prepare and freeze pizzas before they left for the holiday. Like we should have been—yes, I'm bitter about it—but I knew that wasn't going to happen. It's been almost a year since any of us have left campus.

Richard Franklin Academy, or "RFA" as we call it, is an off-grid, private school for gifted students. Although the only thing we're "gifted" with is rich parents who participated in a secret program to bring us into this world. Hence the undisclosed location, high fences, and posted guards.

How did my grandpa describe us? Oh, yeah: "Bioengineered test-tube babies. The future of our dying human race."

I'm not convinced they dropped anything special into those tubes. I mean, we don't look any different than any other kids our age. Not that I've ever been able to meet one.

The bright side is that we've spent our entire lives together. While we didn't have a traditional upbringing, we had each other, and we've made our own makeshift families within these walls. By chance, I was placed in a room with two girls who became my two favorite people in the world. I'm not sure I could have been any more blessed.

Evelynn and Hanna are my best friends and roommates. Kelly is our fourth roommate, but unlike the rest of us, she didn't return from break last Christmas. Something about a family emergency. *We should all be so lucky.*

Which means, it's only the three of us in our room for now, and honestly, we prefer it that way. Not that there was anything particularly wrong with Kelly—except the part where she didn't appreciate our late-night gossip sessions or the contraband we sneak into our room. Contraband in the form of sour candies, spicy chips, R-Rated movies, and caffeinated beverages. Yeah, we are true rebels. *Insert eye roll here.*

The rules at RFA are meant to keep us healthy, since our parents pay for us to eat meals that are tailored to our nutritional needs. That's a fancy way of saying they want picture-perfect kids in exchange for their money and troubles. We can't be fat or unhealthy; it would reflect poorly on the program. *More like it would reflect poorly on their parenting.* So we eat what we're told and exercise regularly, like the good little children we are... most of the time, anyway.

Over the last few years, I've started feeling as if the professors and staff feel sorry for us. The fewer of us there are, the easier it seems to break the rules.

I grab the ranch, pepper flakes, and a stack of napkins before joining my friends at one of the tables in the cafeteria. "Pass me a coke, would you?" I ask my friends. "I'm so thirsty." I flop down in my chair, scanning the room for other students.

Evelynn pops the top off the glass bottle and hands it to me with a grin. Her blonde ponytail swishes back and forth from the excited movement. "It's nice to have soda out here in the open for once. You'd think it was alcohol the way Kelly freaked out about it." She takes a giant swig of her cold drink, her long fingers covered in flecks of multicolored paint.

"Well, between Ms. Kay's secret wine stash and Mr. Mason's bourbon addiction, I don't think anyone is going to report us this week. I can't believe there are so few staff around. I really thought more of them would be stranded here with us over break—it's kind of creepy having the school all to ourselves." Hanna gestures to the nearly empty room.

What none of us is willing to admit is that our canceled break isn't the only thing that has made the building so empty. Fewer students have returned to the Academy every year. What started in kindergarten as a full school of one hundred students and even more staff has steadily dwindled to twenty-five students. Seventy-five percent of our original group have dropped from the program, but it happened so gradually, it kind of snuck up on us.

I'd always been under the impression that our parents were not legally allowed to pull us from the program, but I don't want to ask questions when I might not like the answers. Besides, the school does a good job of keeping us busy so we're too preoccupied to ask them.

"Well, we're not completely alone," I remind them, my eyes darting to the other occupied table in the room.

"Oh, yeah!" Hanna sneaks a glance at the table two rows behind her before looking back at me. "Garrett and Liam are still here. It's so weird; if anyone's parents were going to break them out of this place, I would have expected Garrett's dad to be first in line. He's more than our headmaster; he's like a majority shareholder or whatever my dad is always grumbling about."

While all the students at RFA are used to being away from home most of the year, we'd never been asked to go this long without seeing our families. Most of us hadn't left campus since last Christmas—a full year next month—and anyone who had been home in the last year hadn't returned to school. My parents hadn't even attempted to break me out of here as far as I knew. They always went along with whatever the program decided was best. Even our headmaster had been gone for months on an extended leave of absence, leaving his son behind with us.

Spring Break, Summer Vacation, and now Thanksgiving Break had all been canceled. The only contact we had with our families was through our tablets, and even that was limited and supervised. The more we talked to our families, the more homesick we became. We had quarterly scheduled calls now, which meant, if this kept up, we'd only speak to our families four times a year.

Christmas break had been cut short due to the harsher quarantine rules, and I felt like I'd barely been home at all. "Get back to school, and hunker down. It's for everyone's safety," Mom had said before hugging me a little too long. The way she'd said it hadn't felt comforting. It felt like a warning.

World leaders were demanding everyone quarantine in their homes for as long as possible. So much of our society had fallen into chaos in the last few decades. Virus after virus had obliterated the world population. Vaccines and cures were elusive, and not a single corner of the world had escaped massive population losses. As soon as it felt like one virus had finished taking lives, another more powerful one would hit.

Everyone followed the rules because no one wanted to be the next to die. Only those with the most essential jobs were still working. Food, medication, and supplies were dropped on doorsteps. Everything else was done remotely with as little human contact as possible. What little contact *was* allowed was limited to small circles, sometimes only a person's own household. I couldn't even imagine how lonely it would be if someone lived alone.

Except for us, quarantine meant returning to campus. School would continue but with limited staff and activities. This had always been the plan for us, even before we were born.

Students at RFA came from the most powerful and wealthy families in the country. When the viruses hit, healthy pregnancies were almost unheard of. Infants died at alarming rates, unable to build immune systems before being exposed. In their desperation, our parents had chosen to become part of an experimental birthing program. They'd trusted a private group of scientists to grow what they called "future babies." This program promised to make children with a fighting chance against the growing number of viruses. We were their last hope for the future, and it hadn't come cheap or with much explanation.

Highly classified. Need-to-know basis. Don't ask because we won't tell. Sign this dotted line, and we'll help you conceive a healthy baby. How badly do you want this?

The cost and stipulations didn't matter to our parents; they jumped at the chance to participate.

Our parents had agreed that when we were born, we'd be excluded from the general population. And once we were old enough to attend school, we'd be held at a secure academy—the location of which they were not allowed to know—and kept separate from our less genetically engineered peers.

Children and the elderly were always the first to go, and as there were so few left in the world, our parents would not risk losing us, too. So they'd signed their rights away, not knowing much about what they were getting into or how their babies would be altered but willing to risk everything for the chance to have surviving offspring.

A family.

The survival of a dying race.

If it weren't for my friends, this place would probably feel more like a science experiment than a home. It sometimes felt like a prison barred from the outside world.

"Hey, Garrett," Hanna calls to the boys across the room, pulling me from my somber thoughts. My face immediately heats, and I slap her thigh under the table, trying to get her attention. *What is she doing?*

"We have some pizzas, and there's plenty to go around if you and Liam are hungry," she calls in a cheery voice.

I glare at the back of her head. Despite the headband she's using to hold it back, her unruly red hair pokes out in every direction. I'm tempted to yank it off her head. She's always suspected that I have a crush on Garrett, but she also knows he only dates bubbly girls like Kelly.

I have zero chance and prefer to obsess over him from a distance. Maybe if I had access to boys outside of school, he wouldn't even be on my radar... I may never know. As it is, we have a limited pool from which to snag a fish, and Hanna is always ready with her lure.

I take a bite of pizza, hoping the cheesy goodness can distract me from my embarrassment.

"Seriously, the staff left way too many pizzas for us," Evelynn adds, laughter sparkling in her eyes when she sees my face. Pizza is a massive treat around here—we have to beg the kitchen staff well in advance so they can order the supplies to make them. Because regular frozen pizza won't do; it has to be specially made to be allowable. And since we were afraid this break would be canceled like the rest, we'd planned ahead this time.

"Nice!" Liam dramatically pumps his fist in the air. "Thanks, ladies."

Chairs scrape loudly across the waxed floor as the boys head over to join us at our table. Garrett kicks the chair out next to me and turns it around to straddle it. He hugs the back of the chair with his arms and grins at me. "Hey, Selena, how's it going?"

I immediately choke on the bite of pizza in my mouth. It lodges in my throat like a lump of uncooked dough, and I slap the table with my palm as I fight for air. *Real smooth, Selena.*

Garrett's large hand slaps me on the back, but the force is too strong, and I have to put both hands on the table in front of me to keep from face-planting. I reach for my soda and wash the offending food down the rest of the way. "Sorry—"

"Dang, are you okay?" He watches me closely, a mixture of concern and amusement on his face.

"Yeah, fine." The words come out on a wheeze. "Didn't go down right, I guess." My cheeks are flooded with heat. Leave it to me to choke when I'm face-to-face with Garrett.

"What are you ladies up to tonight?" Liam asks. His eyes move from mine to Hanna's. "We snagged the key to the theater room if you guys want to watch a movie or something."

"As long as it's not animated, I'm down." Hanna smiles. "I think we still have a few horror films to watch, if you two are into that."

I nod, finally recovering from my coughing fit. "We found one called *House of Wax* in Mr. Mason's stash last weekend. It's super old, so if anything, it might be fun to roast it."

"Oh, I think I've seen that one—it's got Paris Hilton in it, right?" Liam asks.

"Am I supposed to know who that is?" Hanna raises an eyebrow. "I'm guessing she's hot, why else would you know some old actress's name? That movie is like a hundred years old."

Liam laughs. "She's not hard to look at if that's what you're asking. And it's not like she was old when it was filmed."

Hanna wipes pizza grease off her fingers with a napkin and tosses it at Liam. "Well, should we go room to room and see if anyone else is interested in Liam's old-lady girlfriend? Make it an official movie night?" Heads around the table nod in unison. We used to have movie nights all the time when we were younger, but it's been a really long time.

We all agree it'll be fun with more people and plan to meet at the doors to the theater room at seven. Which means we have two hours to get snacks together and make sure Mr. Mason and Ms. Kay are both occupied for the night.

Maybe Thanksgiving break won't be a total bust after all.

After convincing Mr. Mason and Ms. Kay to treat each other to a date complete with pizza and a top-secret stash of ice cream, we headed to the girls' wing. Everyone was down for hanging out with the boys in the theater room—I could tell everyone felt bereft at the lack of fun family activities that usually accompanied Thanksgiving. Tomorrow, we will be getting a special supply delivery, but it won't be the same.

It hadn't been hard to convince Mr. Mason to turn a blind eye to our after-hours activities. I think he feels bad that our lives are far from the normal upbringing we read about in history class.

Mr. Mason and Ms. Kay are the only two unmarried teachers at our school. I'm pretty sure they'd voluntarily agreed to stay behind, but it's also possible that it was a "*volun-told*" situation. They are the youngest and least jaded teachers we have, unlike many of our teachers who are not fans of children. I'm not sure why they became teachers in the first place. Maybe, after so many years, some teachers are ready to turn into the witch from Hansel and Gretel and eat their students.

After rallying all the girls, the three of us head back to our room to change. Unlocking the door, I wait for the familiar scent of fruity body spray to engulf me. It's my favorite part of living with my friends, and I've learned to associate the smell with home.

I open the door wide and take a deep breath. Without Kelly harping on us, our room isn't quite as orderly as usual. Shoes and clothes are strewn across all four single beds tucked into every corner of the room, and a desk for each of us sits nearby. Since the room is designed for four, we have one of the larger rooms and our own shared bathroom. It's so nice to not have to walk the halls with shower caddies like we did in our younger years.

There are plenty of empty rooms now. If we asked, we could probably each have our own. None of us have, though—I think we'd be too lonely without each other.

We fix our hair at our desks in the mirrors we each hung over them so they double as vanity tables. We learned a few things over the years, tricks that make life a little easier.

I'm still trying to decide what to wear so I look around the room at what my friends have chosen. Hanna is going in an emerald-green shirt and a jean skirt that definitely wouldn't pass the dress code fingertip test. Lucky for her, no one official will be scrutinizing our outfits tonight, and the way the green pops vividly against her vibrant red hair proves it's the right choice.

Evelynn has poured herself into a simple black bodycon dress that hugs her thin frame like a second skin, but its long sleeves make it look sleek and sophisticated. She's added a braided crown to her ponytail and put on some red lipstick. Both look ready for a special dance or event, even though we are only heading to a dark room to watch a movie. I'm trying to get into the spirit myself, but every time I stare into our shared closet, nothing calls out to me.

"Selena, you need to hurry up and pick something out. You look amazing in everything you wear." Evelynn throws a pillow at me; it ricochets off my head and into the open closet.

"I can't decide what I'll feel comfortable in." I sigh, picking up the pillow and tossing it back at her.

Hanna shoves past me and pushes some hangers to the side, making her selections. "You look good in a true navy; it brings out the blue of your eyes." She tosses me a dark-blue skater dress. "It's mine, but it'll totally fit you, and you can pair it with those gorgeous blue heels you never let anyone borrow."

I thank her and change quickly. The dress fits me like it was made for my body. The t-shirt style top fits snug across my chest before flaring out at the waist. Despite my short legs, the dress hits high on my thighs. I fluff my dark hair a little, running a wide comb through the loose curls. This look is the perfect blend of casual and dressed up, and adding my coveted blue suede heels to the mix elevates my outfit to another level. I catch my reflection in the mirror, and with the amount of leg meat on display, I'm glad I chose to shave this morning.

"Are we ready now?" Evelynn grins. "Or are you really stalling because Garrett is going to be sitting with us?"

I try not to roll my eyes. "Look, I know I literally choked earlier when he was talking to me, but he's just a boy. I'll be perfectly fine. We've known him our whole lives; nothing has changed."

"Right, he's totally just a boy that you have the hots for." Hanna sticks her tongue out at me. "And Liam, who is probably looking for his latest conquest."

"Gross. Count me out." Evelynn shakes her head. "Maybe Kyle or Devin will come hang out—I'd much rather be in their company."

"You never know." I shrug. "Maybe they escaped with the staff."

"You're probably right; they're not orphans like we are. Their parents probably miss them." Evelynn flops back down on her bed.

Hanna sprays herself with body spray, making sure to spray each of us as well—we have her grandma to thank for the lifetime supply of bottles that have created a permanent cloud of fruity scents in here. Then she turns toward Evelynn with a scowl. "We are not orphans; speak for yourself. My parents don't want me to get sick, that's all. And there's nothing wrong with Liam, he's... confident."

I chew on my nails to keep from answering her with pessimism. I wish I could believe that my parents were only looking out for my best interests, but something feels off. Comments they've made over the years have started to add up. Would they let me come home if it were an option? Or do they truly believe it's not safe at home?

Hanna prefers to live in the land of blind ignorance. I wish I could live in that place; it'd be easier than these dark thoughts I keep having. In moments like this, I truly miss my grandparents. They have always been more honest with me, trusting me to know more about the realities of our world than the other adults in my life.

After that comment about Liam, I have a sneaking suspicion that Hanna thinks of him as more than a boy on a conquest. She always seems to stick up for him. I let her comment roll around in my head. Sure, he's cute—but he's cocky, too, and he's more than confident, persistent to the point of annoying.

I turn toward the door, ready to be done with the direction our conversation is heading. My heels click against the shiny concrete floor as I walk. I hope I won't regret not wearing something more practical. My shoes do look amazing—nothing like high heels to boost a girl's confidence, especially when she's short.

"Alright, enough talk. Grab the candy stash, and let's go watch this freakish movie," I say.

"Amen!" Evelynn agrees, and we head out to meet the rest of our classmates.

Chapter Two

The theater is my favorite room at the Academy. I'm a terrible actress myself, but there's something magical about watching a play come to life on the stage. The room is beautiful—our parents have always been generous with their donations to our school. Every classroom is equipped with state-of-the-art technology and expensive décor. Everything is sterilized and tidy, too, as the staff clean constantly for our safety. We'd be hard-pressed to find a single stain on the bright red carpet.

The room is bigger than necessary, with two hundred seats made of plush leather and equipped with power reclining chairs. The large projector screen comes down from the ceiling, much like the movie theaters we read about in our books. Never in the twelve years we've lived here have all the seats been filled, but it is a luxury we enjoy, and it's likely the closest any of us will ever get to the real thing.

When we finally show up, Garrett is leaning against the wall next to the main entrance of the theater, drawing something in his sketchbook. His outfit is casual, black jeans and a white t-shirt, but the boy looks like he belongs in a clothing ad. Hanna and Evelynn loop their arms through mine, and we step forward as a unit. He looks up from his drawing and smiles at us. "Ladies."

"Garrett," I say, a smile tugging at the corner of my mouth. I watch him tuck the small sketchbook into his back pocket, and I can't help but wonder what he was drawing.

"We'll go snag some good seats," Hanna says, grabbing Evelynn and rushing into the dark hall without me. *Well played.*

"Liam is saving seats for all of us." Garrett laughs. "But I get the feeling they were giving us some space."

My face burns. Even with my heels on, he's much taller than I am, which means I can stare at his chest and avoid looking into his eyes. He's not overly muscular, more like trim and fit. Like the rest of us, he takes his appearance seriously—years of scrutiny from our parents ingrained the habit into our DNA. His simple outfit probably cost more than the shiny new fitness tracker on his wrist.

I think our parents spend as much money on us as they can to balance out their physical absence in our lives.

I smooth my hands over my dress, suddenly wondering if I should have worn my jeans instead. Do I look as overdressed as I feel? When I look up, Garrett's eyes are following the motion.

"I like your dress. Is it new?"

I nod, finally finding my voice again. "It's Hanna's. I'm borrowing it." He's even more charming than usual. I always feel stronger about Garrett when he's near—something about the way he gives me his undivided attention makes me want to know more about him. Kelly used to say that having Garrett's attention on her felt like basking in the sun. Right now, I'd have to agree with that statement. My cheeks feel like they might get a sunburn.

"Looks more your style than hers," he says. "It suits you. I hope she lets you keep it."

"Thank you, that's sweet." The burn on my face intensifies.

I'm not boy crazy by any means; usually, they're barely a blip on my radar. But for some reason, it's always felt a little different with Garrett. We've grown up together, and whenever he's near, I feel a pull to him. I don't moon over him in his absence or bring him up in conversations with the girls, but if he's in the room, I can't help but take notice. He has good energy.

"Want to sit next to me tonight?" he asks, and I'm surprised by the shakiness of his voice. There's no way Garrett James is nervous about talking to me.

His invitation still has me screaming on the inside. He's been flirty lately, but he can't possibly be interested in me in more than a platonic way. Not because there's anything wrong with me, but because I'm not Kelly. He's probably just bored because Kelly isn't around for him to flirt with. We're friends, and that's completely fine with me.

Still, I am proud of myself when I answer and my voice remains calm and collected. "I'd love that."

A few more students file into the auditorium, and there's a rumble of chatter from inside the doors. "I think that's everyone. Shall we?" He winks, reaching his hand out toward me. I stare at his long fingers for a moment before giving him mine. His skin is warm and soft. It takes a lot of effort to focus on not tripping in my shoes as I allow him to lead me toward the front of the theater.

The lights are still on, but the overhead projector is running. Old previews from the early 2000s—when *House of Wax* was first released—flash across the screen, but the sound is muted. We were lucky to find a stash of old horror films in a box that Mr. Mason was throwing out. He'd asked us to take a few boxes to the dumpster before classes started, and we'd been too curious not to peek inside. The stash will keep us entertained for a while still. Thank goodness for the vintage DVD player that hooks up to the projector screen.

Idle chatter buzzes among the students who have come to watch, and it looks like the entire school is here, all twenty-four of us. I see Hanna and Evelynn right away—Liam is in the seat between them, chatting away.

Garrett pulls me gently down the center aisle toward our friends. I keep waiting for him to drop his hand so no one will see, but it remains firmly in mine. He stops when we get to Hanna's seat and smiles at her. "You want to sit next to Selena? Or is it okay if I sit here between you?"

Hanna makes a kissy face and then mouths the words "Bow-Chicka-Wow-Wow" at me. I shoot her a warning glare.

"Nah, you can sit by her. I get her to myself all the time." Hanna winks at Garrett, and he laughs, taking the seat next to her. I sit quickly, before the distance will cause him to let go of my hand. I am enjoying the physical connection. I can't remember the last time I held hands with a boy.

"Liam, start her up!" someone calls from a few rows back. Liam, never one to miss an opportunity for the spotlight, stands to address the crowd.

"Alright, Ladies and Heathens, tonight's movie is *House of Wax*. Keep your chitchat to a minimum, and if you have contraband, be sure to send some my way." He chuckles before hitting a button on the remote, sending the room into complete darkness. "Let's do this!" He drops back into his seat, and I stare at the screen, watching the opening theme begin.

Garrett leans in close to me, his breath tickling my neck as he whispers into my ear, "If you get scared, snuggle in close."

A laugh bubbles up in my chest. I love scary movies, so that's unlikely to happen, but I adore the offer all the same. I lean back, turning my head to reach his ear. "And if you get scared, feel free to do the same." He doesn't answer. He simply tucks my arm inside of his, our fingers still laced together. It's cozy, and I don't object to this setup at all. The movie is playing, but I already know I'm going to have a hard time focusing on it when Garrett is holding me this way. I'd much rather study him than some silly horror movie.

I know Hanna and Evelynn are going to tease me mercilessly after the movie and interrogate me for details, but for once, I'm more excited than annoyed by the prospect. I lean into Garrett a little more, and the heat from his body and his fresh clean smell envelops my senses. I feel relaxed and comfortable.

Even though it's not turkey and gravy, this might be the best Thanksgiving gift I could have asked for.

Chapter Three

An hour passes, snacks are shared, people are having quiet conversations around us, and Garrett is still holding my hand. One of the main characters in the movie gets a pole thrown at her head, but before it can make impact, the entire theater plunges into darkness.

Complete darkness. Not even the glow from a single floor light or exit sign to illuminate the room. A collective groan ensues, and murmuring about power outages starts. With our solar panels, it's rare but not completely unheard of during bad weather.

"What the hell?" someone calls out. "Very funny prank, you wanker!"

Cough. "Liam." *Cough.* can be heard from somewhere in the back.

"Who are you calling a wanker?" Liam snaps back. "I didn't do anything."

I let Garrett's hand fall and reach for the fitness tracker on my wrist, pressing the power button on the side to activate the touch screen. Nothing happens. My watch must be dead, but I could have sworn I had a full battery when we started the movie. I lean past Garrett to talk to Hanna. "Is your tracker working?" I can barely even see her outline in the dark.

"No, I guess it's dead."

I blow out a breath. "Mine, too, what the heck?"

"Anyone's tracker not dead? Can someone turn on their screen light?" Hanna yells into the darkness.

Garrett shifts next to me; I can hear his fingers tapping on the glass surface. "Crap, mine's dead, too."

"That's weird—even my pocket flashlight won't turn on." I hear Liam clicking the button repeatedly.

More kids complain about dead electronics, and I feel the first prickles of anxiety start to creep up the back of my neck. I sense someone moving in front of me and Garrett. "Dude, no one's trackers are working. I swear I had nothing to do with this," Liam says quietly.

"This prank would be too elaborate, even for you." Garrett laughs, but I feel him tense up beside me.

"Figures we'd lose power or whatever the heck this is when we're finally having fun in this crap hole." Liam's knees press against our legs. I'm guessing he dropped into a crouch. "How long do you think we have before Mr. Mason comes down to send us all to bed?"

"I give it less than ten minutes," Evelynn answers. "I say we go back to our rooms and hang out before he sees us. And by 'we,' I mean all of us."

"Scandalous! Evie wants to risk a purpling offense?" Liam's teasing tone makes me laugh. I imagine if I could see his face, his eyebrows would be bouncing up and down suggestively. I don't want to risk getting into trouble, but I am not ready for this night to end, either.

The Academy was built with five wings branching out from a central common area, our cafeteria. There's a green hallway for classrooms, an orange wing for the staff and teachers, and red for the auditorium, pool, and gymnasium. The girl's wing has a pink border, and the boys, in turn, a blue one. If a student is caught on the opposite side, they're considered purpling. *Never shall the two colors mix.*

When we were young, this threat was a serious deterrent. No one wanted to get caught and be forced to sit on the large purple bench at the entrance to the classroom hallways for everyone to see. The older we got, the more of a rite of passage it came to be. The boys especially would hoot and holler at each other, congratulating the offender for their brave trek into the girls' bedrooms. The girls were more reserved, usually red-faced with embarrassment. The teachers would shake their heads at all of us in their disappointment.

As a card-carrying member of the virgin squad, I have never been caught crossing that line. I've never really been invited to cross, either. But the thought of purpling hasn't stopped some of the girls from venturing there over the years. As far as I know, Hanna and Evelynn haven't ever been over there. The most shocking offender has been Kelly.

"Almost everyone is gone, anyway. Who cares? I'm pretty sure Mr. Mason is planning on purpling with Ms. Kay tonight," Evelynn adds. It's not like her to be the one to suggest breaking the rules. I think Hanna is rubbing off on her.

"Your room or ours?" Liam whispers.

I think about the mess waiting for us back in our room and how peeved Kelly would be if she found out we had boys in our room. Even though I don't know when or if she's ever coming back, it feels wrong to go against her wishes.

"Yours," I answer quickly.

Garrett leans in, and I feel his breath on the shell of my ear. "Really? If you're worried about getting caught, don't feel like you have to."

The comment makes me pause. I suddenly wonder if Garrett doesn't want us to come to his room, that this is all Liam, but my worries are quickly silenced when he reaches for my hand and squeezes it gently.

"I'm giving you an out because I know how you worry..."

I bite back a smile in the dark. "I think it'll be okay. We'd better get moving before Mr. Mason gets here, though."

"Alright, everyone, the party's over! Head back to your rooms, and if anyone asks, we were never here!" Liam shouts over the noise in the room. No one even groans this time. Instead, we all grope around, grabbing seat backs and each other to find our way to the exit doors. Even while we're fumbling around in the darkness, everyone is still laughing and having a good time.

Once we're outside the theater, the common area windows provide some faint moonlight. I can at least see the silhouettes of my friends.

I turn to Hanna and take her by the arm. "Are we really going to their room?"

"Heck yeah. You don't turn down an invite to the blue wing—not from Garrett and Liam, anyway. It'll be fine. Mr. Mason is probably too drunk to even notice." She shrugs as Evelynn comes to join us. Technically, they didn't invite us, Evelynn took that upon herself, but I don't correct her.

"Hey, are none of us concerned about this weird power thing?" Evelynn sighs. "They'd better get it all figured out before our calls home. We were supposed to get that special call tomorrow with our parents. I even double-checked with Mr. Mason earlier. I want to ask my mom to send me more paints since I doubt they're even going to let us escape for Christmas with the way things are going."

I stare at the watch on her wrist. Only the slight reflection of the moon and a few dry flecks of paint are visible on the otherwise black screen. "The fitness trackers all going out at the same time is really weird. Unless they only work if the computer that tracks our information is still on, but that seems unlikely." I shrug.

A simple power outage wouldn't have affected flashlights and trackers—and why hasn't the emergency generator kicked on yet? Without the generator, we won't have internet on our tablets, either. For any internet use, we'll need permission and supervision from Mr. Mason or Ms. Kay, and as of right now, they seem to be out of commission.

Anxiety swirls like a vortex in my stomach, pulling my mood down with its weight.

"Let's not worry about things we can't control," Hanna scolds. "We have a golden opportunity here, girls—let's not waste it."

We nod at her, but I can tell that Evelynn is concerned about the strange power situation. It sucks that in times like these, we can't even count on our parents.

The common area is quickly emptying of bodies, and Liam comes out of the theater room last, locking the door behind him. "Come on, we gotta get moving!" He doesn't wait for us to respond, so we fall in behind him. There's no sign of Mr. Mason or Ms. Kay, and I almost wish they would appear out of nowhere and tell us this was an elaborate prank or a test to see how we'd react in an emergency.

I look around for them one last time and then surrender myself to our plans for the night. I sincerely hope we don't live to regret this decision.

Cedar and mint—that's how I'd describe the smell of the boys' room. With only the moonlight to see by, it appears organized and spotless, nothing like I'd imagined in my head. It's identical in size to our room, but only two of them occupy the space meant for four students. They've clearly lucked out on room assignments.

"Liam, light one of those girly candles your mom is always sending us," Garrett says, digging in his desk for something. Evelynn, Hanna, and I stand awkwardly near the door, none of us quite sure where to stand or what to do.

The blue side.

We've never been on this side of the school, and despite the fact that both wings are identical in architecture, the boys' side has a completely different feel.

Liam disappears into the closet and comes out with two large glass candles, which Garrett lights quickly, placing them on a small table in the center of the room. The room fills with a warm glow, and my eyes search Garrett's face. He's smiling at me as he walks over and drags a hand down my arm. "Come in, ladies; don't be shy. We can play some cards at the table or something until the power comes back on."

I'm not so sure the power is going to come back. Something feels undeniably wrong, but I don't want to ruin the moment, so I nod and let him lead me to a chair. There are only four chairs at the little round table, so Liam drags his desk chair over to join the rest of us as we pile around it.

"What are we playing? Quarantine? Maybe Slap Deck?" Evelynn asks, picking at the dry paint on her fingers as she looks over the card options.

"Ew, Quarantine? Who wants to play that? We live enough of that already." Hanna shivers. "And I don't want to play Slap Deck with boys—it hurts if you get caught by one of their big hands."

Liam laughs. "Already sure you'll lose, Hanna?"

"Not likely, but why risk it? We'll just have to play something else so you can keep your hands to yourself. All the slapping in that game... so unnecessarily violent. No, thank you."

Liam rolls his eyes in response. "Well, we could play something vintage... what about Go Fish?"

"Uno sounds fun; my grandma loves that game!" Hanna squeals, grabbing the weathered deck of Uno cards from the table. She's always the first to offer to deal, showing off her self-proclaimed shuffling skills.

I sneak a glance at Garrett's side of the room. A thick blue comforter with matching pillows rests on his bed, and posters of what look like snowy mountains and trees grace the walls. I can imagine him on a mountain, cutting lines in the fresh powder on a snowboard or skis. Things people did before the world was crippled with sickness.

Everything he owns is neat and in its place. I'd love to thumb through the small shelf of sketchbooks under his nightstand, see whatever it is that he's always drawing. I've always been envious of Evelynn and anyone who can take mental pictures and turn them into beautiful artwork on paper or canvas.

The room is cool—the heat must have stopped pumping when the power went out. I cross my legs against the chill in the air, rubbing my free hand over the goosebumps freckling my arms.

"Are you cold?" Garrett asks, instantly reaching behind him to grab a small blanket from the end of his bed without waiting for my answer. "Here."

He wraps it gently over my legs, and I'm thankful for the kind gesture. It's soft and smells like him. I tuck it tightly around my legs, kicking my shoes off under the table. It would have been smarter to wear the jeans and thick socks I'd originally thought of wearing, but at least I can snuggle under this blanket now.

"Anyone else need anything? We have plenty of hoodies or whatever," Liam offers.

Hanna and Evelynn shake their heads, so we start our game of cards. Garrett scoots his chair closer to mine, and I let myself lean on him a little as we play. As much as I am enjoying the attention from Garrett in the middle of a night that should feel fun and exciting, the little voice in my head refuses to be silent.

Something is wrong.

Living here at the Academy, we sometimes forget there is a whole world suffering beyond our walls. Our parents do their best to keep us separated from the depressing realities, but what if that's doing more harm than good? What if they're setting us up to fail?

"Uno!" Hanna says, slamming a red six down on the top of the deck and doing a little dance in her chair. "Get out of your head, and play a card, Selena. Stop being such a worrywart; the power will be back on in no time."

I play my card and pray she's right.

Chapter Four

Thump. Thump. Thump.

The loud knocking pulls me from my sleep. I struggle to open my eyes, forced to squint against the onslaught of brightness from the sunlight streaming through the windows.

"Oh, crap!" Evelynn whispers quietly, grabbing onto my arm. We're still in the boys' room. I remember us climbing onto one of the spare beds and telling each other old stories but not falling asleep.

Evelynn squeezes harder, her voice now a strained whisper. "What do we do?"

I press my finger to my lips and point toward the closet door, and she nods. We drag a half-conscious Hanna along with us.

"Boys, open up!" Mr. Mason calls from the hallway. Garrett sits up in bed and sees us climbing into the closet. He nods briskly at me before shutting us inside.

"Coming, Sir."

It's pitch-black in the closet, but there is plenty of room for us. We sit down, and I press my ear against the door, struggling to hear what's happening on the other side.

"Good morning, Mr. Mason. Is everything cool?" I hear Garrett ask.

"Actually, no. Something happened last night, and I would like everyone to get dressed and meet in the cafeteria. Please hurry; I expect you out there in less than twenty minutes." His voice is steady, but I don't trust it.

"You got it, Sir," I hear Liam answer. "We'll be there."

"Thanks, boys."

"Happy Thanksgiving, Mr. Mason," Liam calls. I hold my breath until I hear the door click shut.

Garrett is smiling when he opens the closet door. "Hey, I guess we crashed at some point. Sorry, I meant to wake you up and get you out of here before morning."

I shake my head as I take his offered hand to help me to my feet. "Not your fault, but we need to go before someone catches us here."

"It sounds like the adults have bigger worries than purpling. Like why the heck the power is still out and why the generators haven't kicked on. I'm freezing!" Evelynn rubs her arms as she steps out of the closet behind me.

"Mind helping us get to the common area? Be our lookout in the halls so we can sneak by?" Hanna directs the question at Liam over Garrett's shoulder.

"We need to get back to the room ASAP and change clothes; it's pretty obvious that we've been out since last night." I smooth my dress down where it's wrinkled from sleep.

"We could easily argue that we were too lazy to change our clothes before we went to bed last night. But I'm with you—I want something warm and snuggly." Evelynn laughs.

I doubt anyone would buy that we slept in dresses, but I don't want to argue with her. I push my way toward the door with a growing sense of urgency. "Let's get moving."

Everyone is too preoccupied with the power situation to notice the three of us sneaking back through the hallways. The boys leave us in the common area, and we rush back to our rooms to change clothes.

With the curtains closed, it's still dark in our room—I pull them open so we can see what we're doing. We're silent as we touch up our hair and slip into casual outfits. I pull my jeans on like the security blanket they are and reach for my thickest hoodie. The temperature in the school continues to drop without the heat on. Even with my hoodie and jeans, I'm shivering. I slide into a pair of thick slipper socks and my favorite hiking boots. I'm tempted to climb into my own bed and snuggle down in my comforter, but I don't.

I'm brushing my teeth in the small bathroom when I hear the knock at our door.

"Girls? Are you up?" Ms. Kay calls through the thick wood. Evelynn swings the door wide, allowing her to come inside. Hanna sends me a conspiratorial wink—somehow, we've gotten away with our shenanigans.

"Hey, Ms. Kay, what's up? Any news on this power sitch?" She motions to the light switch.

Ms. Kay looks around our messy room and shakes her head softly. "As of right now, we have no way to get in touch with the custodian. We're meeting in the cafeteria in a few minutes, so please hurry. We'll talk about it together so we don't have to keep repeating ourselves. Besides, I could really use some coffee."

I wipe my face with the towel and step out into the room. Thankfully, it's a clear day, and the sun fully illuminates the small space. I can see the worry on Ms. Kay's face, though, so I hold myself back from throwing her the barrage of questions running through my mind.

My stomach grumbles, making me wonder what time it is. We're usually up by five on weekdays, but since there were no alarms and the sun seems high in the sky, it could be much later.

"Any idea what time it is?" I allow the one question to slip out.

Worry flashes across Ms. Kay's face. "I think it's around nine, but I can't be certain. Come along, girls—let's go to this meeting. You're the last of the hall to get moving this morning. And after the meeting, might I suggest you clean up around here? It's not like you ladies to have such a messy room."

I get the feeling she knows we didn't sleep here last night. Unlike Hanna, I'm not sure we completely got away with our sleepover. I wonder if she tried knocking on our door earlier this morning, but I can't worry about that now. I have too many other things competing for my attention.

We follow Ms. Kay down the empty hallway toward the cafeteria. I can hear the animated voices long before I see anyone. Everyone is amped up and curious about the situation. I can feel the nervous energy like charged static in the air.

Garrett waves us over to their table. I see some of the other students watching curiously—Garrett and Liam don't invite someone to sit with them every day, if ever. The gossip will be rampant, and if Kelly hears about this, she will not be happy about the situation.

"Hey—you made it undetected?" Garrett whispers, pulling out the chair next to him. I nod and take the seat. Mr. Mason is already up on the small stage in the cafeteria, and Ms. Kay speed walks to his side. They lean their heads together in an intimate proximity, talking too low for us to hear.

"This is nuts. The power should be back on by now, right?" I ask the question, but I don't expect anyone at the table to have an answer.

"I didn't hear the supply truck yet, so maybe it's not as late as Ms. Kay thinks?" Evelynn chews on her bottom lip. I can sense it; we're all confused and concerned.

"Well, whatever is going on, I hope we get to eat soon. I'm starving." Hanna plops down in the chair next to me, pouting.

Liam tosses her a protein bar. "Here, this should hold you over. I never leave my room without a few of these in my pockets." Hanna frowns at the bar on the table before shaking her head and ripping the package open.

"Okay, kids." Mr. Mason clears his throat to get our attention. The buzz in the room immediately quiets, all of us eager for information. "As you're probably all aware, the power went out last night and, for an unknown reason, has yet to be restored. It must be a rather large outage, as we have no working phone lines or internet. We are due to have a big supply refill this morning, so hopefully when the trucks get here, they'll have some more information for us.

"As only Ms. Kay and I are on campus, we don't currently feel comfortable leaving to get information. We will sit tight and likely have some news in a few hours. I know that it is Thanksgiving and you are all looking forward to our special activities today, so while those are delayed for now, we welcome you to eat whatever you can scavenge from the dry pantry. But do everyone a favor, and clean up after yourselves, okay? Mr. Ramey, our wonderful custodian, isn't due back until Saturday, and I do not want him to return to a complete disaster. You're more than capable of cleaning up. Be sure that you do."

A few kids laugh, but we all know he's right to remind us not to be jerks. Some of us need the reminder more than others.

A couple of hands are raised in question, and Mr. Mason sighs before calling on one of the students. "Yes, Jack, did you have a question?"

Jack stands up from his seat, his small voice barely reaching the front of the room. "If it's only a power outage, why are our trackers not working? I know mine was charged, but it's so dead it won't even turn on." His cheeks turn the same shade of red as his t-shirt, and he tugs on his watch band. He asked one of my biggest questions. A power outage does not explain everyone's trackers going out.

Mr. Mason takes a seat on the edge of the stage. "I don't really have an answer for that. It's possible there was a power surge that damaged nearby electronics. I'm not big on technology, and I am not a science teacher. I wish I had more answers for you."

"What about the backup generators?" I don't mean to speak out of turn, but the question flies past my lips. "Has anyone gone to check and see why they're not turning on?"

Ms. Kay and Mr. Mason share a look. She places a hand on his shoulder, joining him on the edge of the stage. "That was our first task last night. We took some candles to the boiler room and tried to figure out what the issue was. It has plenty of oil and gas, and we can't see a reason why it shouldn't be kicking on, so whatever is wrong with it is beyond our abilities. We're going to have to wait for our deliveries today and hopefully get someone out here to fix it. In the meantime, dress in layers, and we'll try to get a fire going in the library."

Liam stands up as well. "So we don't know anything, and we're free to do whatever until we find out more?"

Mr. Mason nods. "Yes, that's all we've got. I'm sorry."

"Okay, then." He pumps a fist in the air. "I call first dibs on the cereal selection!"

Laughter erupts from the students, and I wish I felt even the slightest bit of humor. I watch as Evelynn and Hanna follow Liam to the kitchen, laughing at his jokes. Garrett knocks my knee under the table. "Hey, are you okay?"

I sigh. "I'm worried because this all seems really weird. I already feel so closed off from the world with all the sickness, but now... now, I really feel like a prisoner." I chew on my thumbnail. I hate to admit it, but I wish I could call my parents and have them tell me that everything will be okay.

"I'm sure once the delivery comes today, we'll know more. Maybe there was a solar flare or something. I learned about those in science last year—they can knock out all kinds of things." He shrugs, and I appreciate him trying to calm my nerves. "Are you hungry? I can grab you some fruit or something from the kitchen if you want."

"Sure, one of those fruit parfaits sounds good." I'm not hungry, but it won't do me any good to start skipping meals.

He nods, standing up from the table. He's still wearing the same clothes from last night, but they don't even look wrinkled. The only sign that he's not put together is his slightly rumpled hair.

As soon as he's out of sight, I head over to talk to Mr. Mason myself.

"Selena, how can I help you?" Mr. Mason runs his hands over his black slacks. He looks tired and nervous, and I try not to read into any of it. Ms. Kay has left his side, probably to supervise the kitchen situation, and without her for backup, he looks even more flighty.

"Do you really think it's something simple, Sir?" I try not to fidget, folding my hands together in front of me.

Mr. Mason's dark-green eyes finally meet mine, a smile touching his thin lips. "You know, you've always been one of my favorites, Selena. You never accept things on a surface level, and that's rare these days. You'd make a good leader if you were interested in being seen." He pushes off the stage to stand in front of me.

"You didn't answer my question." I hold firm. Some of the students start to filter back into the cafeteria with their breakfast choices. Mr. Mason lowers his voice and leans in close to me.

"No, Selena. I don't think this is something simple, but until we have more information, it doesn't make any sense to get everyone riled up. Can I trust you to not cause a fuss for now? If I have anything to share, I'll make sure you're the first to hear, okay?"

I nod, but his answer makes my stomach churn. Mr. Mason has always been real with us, so if he feels the need to hold back right now, this can't be good. He is right, though; mass panic has never helped solve a problem.

"Okay, I get it." I sigh, biting on the edge of my thumbnail again.

"Don't bite your nails, Selena. Let's stick to our hygiene rules—we don't want anyone getting sick on top of everything else. Make sure you wash up before breakfast and try not to worry too much. I'm sure things will work out fine." He pats my shoulder before walking away. The worry in his eyes betrays his words.

It's easy for us to forget about the threat to our health, tucked away from the rest of the world as we are out here. Seeing everything from a distance and filtered through the school and our parents, it's hard to get a clear picture of what the rest of the world is going through. And yet, as far as I know, none of the students here have ever officially caught a virus.

In the early years, we'd been more scared, washing our hands until they were dry and cracked, cleaning doorknobs and desktops and wearing masks in the hallways. But as the years passed, we'd stopped wearing the masks on campus—after all, it's not like we're permitted to leave. The only people coming in and out are delivery people, and they have strict protocols for safety. We never see them ourselves, and the professors and security have quarantine rules when they come back from breaks. In so many ways, it is exactly like a prison.

"I got your parfait." Garrett bumps my shoulder as he walks by, putting the tray down on our table. Evelynn and Hanna are not far behind, carrying croissants and fruit. "Power might be out, but the refrigerator is still cold for now."

I swallow back my fears about the power situation and sit with my friends, stirring the blueberries, strawberries, and oats down into the vanilla yogurt. I won't do anyone any good if I don't eat, so I take a bite of the sweet fruit and close my eyes. These yogurt parfaits always remind me of spending summers with my grandparents picking strawberries, cherries, and apples from their fruit trees and using them to make all kinds of treats. Grandma was always so proud of her garden. I wonder if she's out there this fall, missing my company.

"I stashed two boxes of the good cereal behind the flour in the pantry," Hanna says between bites of a banana. "Until that supply truck comes, I'm not willing to risk my favorites. Figured we should eat the fruit first before it all goes bad."

"And the bread." Evelynn winks, taking a big bite of her flaky croissant. No one is worried about our nutritional plans this morning, and we so rarely get free rein of the kitchen. Pizza and sweets and now a free-for-all breakfast? My inner voice reminds me I should go for a run this afternoon to burn off some of the extra calories.

"Anyone feel like running after breakfast?" I ask the group.

"You're joking, right?" Hanna scoffs. "I'm going back to bed. No classes, no Thanksgiving dinner, no calls home? I am so sleeping right through this nightmare."

Evelynn fiddles with her braid. "Sorry, girl, I'm with Hanna."

We turn our attention toward Liam and Garrett, who are chowing down on huge bowls of cereal. "Either of you feel like going for a run in a little while?" Hanna asks them, sending me a wink.

"Naw," Liam says through a mouthful of food. I try not to cringe as I watch milk dribble down his chin. "I'm taking full advantage of the free time and starting up a round of poker with some of the guys."

"I'll go for a run." Garrett smiles at me. My heart pounds a little faster in my chest.

"Okay, awesome," I say, trying to be chill. Hanna squeezes my leg under the table. My friends might be trying to kill me, but I'm not that mad about it.

After doing our breakfast dishes and helping tidy up the kitchen, we head back to our separate rooms. I wash last night's makeup off my face and pull my hair up into a neat ponytail before brushing my teeth again and slipping into my running clothes, black athletic leggings and a slouchy pink running top that my mom sent me in my last care package. It's cute and has a small heart-shaped cutout on the back of it. The last of my summer tan peeks through the hole.

"I can't believe we have a real day off and you're going running," Evelynn says, snuggling down into her fluffy green comforter. "You could not pay me to go out in the cold and burn calories today. I'd rather stay here and risk a diet regimen next month."

"I'm going to take a shower, and then I'm putting on my warmest PJs and going back to bed." Hanna laughs, pushing past me into the bathroom and slamming the door in my face.

"She's loads of fun today." I chuckle. "I feel like I have all this nervous energy to burn off—"

"I probably would, too, if I was all wound up over Garrett James." Evelynn giggles.

I think about telling her that I'm not wound up about him at all, but the truth is, I'm thankful for the distraction he provides. I've almost been able to silence the little voice in the back of my head that says I'm a convenient replacement for Kelly. *Almost.*

"Yeah, well, since the two of you are too lazy to join me, maybe we can at least pick up this room when I get back?"

"Ha. Unlikely, though you're welcome to do it if it's bothering you." Evelynn tugs her eye mask down over her eyes and waves me off as she burrows deeper into her blanket. The two of them will be no help later, but I know a run won't be enough to dispel all my nervous energy.

Chapter Five

Garrett is waiting for me by the main entrance of the school. He's stretching his legs against the bench by the front door, his shorts showing off the strong lean muscles of his tan calves. He's always been athletic, and though the Academy rules mean we can't have competitive team sports, he's been the captain of the cross-country team for a few years running. Granted, there are no teams we're allowed to compete with, but if we could, I know he'd win.

I've always preferred to exercise on my own.

"Hey, are you ready for this?" he asks, his perfect teeth flashing in a wide smile. The braces he wore during our middle school years paid off spectacularly. While he finishes up, I do a few stretches of my own.

"How far are you thinking we'll run?" I'm not opposed to a long run, but I'd like to know what I'm getting into before we start so I can pace myself accordingly. I roll my shoulders and my neck as I wait for his reply, loosening everything up.

"Actually, I have an idea." His eyes flash, and he takes my arm, pulling me outside through the entrance doors. "How do you feel about sneaking off campus?"

My curiosity flares hot. How far "off campus" does he mean? With our teachers preoccupied with student safety and unwilling to go check things out themselves, this could be our chance to get information. "I don't know, Garrett. Even if we can get around the guarded perimeter, how far can we make it on foot? Maybe we should take the bikes? How will we even know what direction to go?"

Garrett gently squeezes my arm, pulling me around the school toward the recreation building. "So many questions. I already got them ready and packed a backpack with some water and lunch for later. I was hoping you'd say yes."

I put my free hand on my hip, but a smile breaks through my false defiance. "But I didn't say yes."

"But you're going to, I can tell."

I shake my head, laughing. "How'd you get Mr. Mason to let you have the keys for the bike locker? He's not suspicious?"

"Actually, I didn't ask. I just snagged the key off his keychain after breakfast. I doubt he'll notice there's one missing. He seems really stressed out—I bet he would have given me the front office keys if I'd asked for them."

I fake my most scolding voice, fighting back laughter. "Garrett James, you stole the keys?"

Garrett laughs, turning the key over for me to see. "Technically, I only borrowed *one* key."

"And you're sure this is a good idea?" Some of the laughter leaves my voice.

Garrett shifts on his feet. "I'm sure. Ms. Kay seems to be the one with her head on right now, but she's only worried about waiting for someone with more authority to show up. I don't think that's going to happen. I don't want to wait around when there are alternative options."

I freeze in my tracks as reality rushes in. Something in Garrett's tone tells me that he is as concerned about this "power outage" as I am. There's more going on here—the school phones should be working, the backup generator, too. Too many questions are unanswered. *I'm glad I'm not the only one worried about what's happening.*

I've never been outside of campus grounds. We've always been bussed in and out, and even the buses have blacked out windows; I've never seen past the gates. All the precautions are to keep the location a secret, even from the students whom it's meant to protect. Maybe especially from us. We could be hours from town, or it could be right around the corner. My money is on the former option.

It's marginally warmer outside in the sun than it felt inside, and I take a deep breath of fresh air. "Gare, have you ever gone outside the gates?"

Garrett stops walking a few feet from the rec building as the smile falls from his lips. "A few times. There's a small pond about twenty minutes outside the guard post that Kelly showed me. I've taken Liam there recently."

Kelly. How had I missed what a rule breaker she'd become? They'd been close, and even though Kelly never shared the details with any of us, I had a feeling that they were more than friends. I'm willing to bet he's the reason she was caught in the blue hallway. It was hard to get away with that here on campus, but I'd seen them stealing moments with my own eyes. I think all of us had.

"Do you think she'll come back?" The question leaves my lips, and I immediately wish I could take it back. Garrett runs a hand over his jaw, shaking his head slightly.

"I think you already know the answer to that question. Anyone who isn't coming and going as part of the group never comes back. I think you just don't want to admit you know." His jaw ticks, and I can tell he's clenching his teeth.

The words hit me like daggers, burning my chest and leaving bleeding wounds behind. He's not wrong, but I wish he would let me pretend for a little while longer.

I've always suspected that students didn't leave the program. Grandpa had explained it to me too many times to believe something so simple. I've seen the way our teachers and staff look at us, like they feel sorry for us for so much more than the sheltered life we are forced to live.

"You think they all got sick?" My voice shakes. "That they're..."

I can't make myself finish the sentence, but Garrett nods. He brushes a hand over my cheek, wiping away a stray tear as it falls. All those students, all the staff members. Did they lose their families, too?

"I don't think it, Selena. I know it. They're gone."

I want to ask him how he knows. How he's absolutely sure that they're dead and that everyone is keeping it from us. No one ever officially said a student caught a virus... But his body is so stiff, his hands flexing into fists, that I know even this small exchange has cost him too much. So I swallow back the questions and open the door to the rec building.

Instead of pushing him, I ask my other burning question. "You're sure we won't be caught by the border guards? My parents will kill me if I get caught breaking Academy rules."

Garrett lets out a breath, looking both surprised and relieved that I've dropped the topic of Kelly and our other missing friends. "As far as I can tell, there haven't been any guards for a long time, and your parents would have to come get you to kill you."

His attempt to make me smile works, and I'm thankful for the gesture. I want to say I'm surprised that the guards are gone, but the shock doesn't come. We're on our own out here, in more ways than one.

We load up and take the bikes out to the trail. It's a mile to the gate, but if Garrett is right about the guards, at least we won't have to try to throw the bikes over the fence. I thank him for the backpack he hands to me and take a small sip from the water bottle in the side pocket.

"I brought us masks, gloves, and goggles. I'm not sure if the stores will still require all those things, but I don't want to get somewhere and then find out we're not prepared." He shrugs. I'm impressed that he got so much done in such a short amount of time and that he's decided to include me in his investigation.

There's no way he came up with all of this in the hour since breakfast. Was he planning an escape all along? "Seems like you thought of everything."

"I hope so."

"Alright, I don't know what time it is, but we should probably get going if we want to explore and get back before dark."

Garrett nods and hands me my helmet. I push off and start to pedal, and I feel calm for the first time all day. At least we're finally doing something besides twiddling our thumbs.

The ride is pretty smooth for the first few miles. As Garrett predicted, the guard post was not an obstacle. Not only were there no guards, but the gate swung open without so much as a padlock to keep it secure.

It's not the most beautiful ride ever—the scenery is mostly flat, fields of long grasses blowing in the breeze. Past the school perimeter, I don't even see any trees. We follow the paved road that leads from the Academy to an old highway, and I keep track of mile markers on the side of the road as we ride. Five miles from the school, we turn onto an old, rutted highway, and I switch my bike into a higher gear to make the ride easier.

The two-lane highway looks old and unused. I'm not surprised when we don't pass a single car on the road. The sun is our only clock for now, and I wish we had one of those old sundials to check the time of day. Not having numbers on a screen to measure the time passing feels weird. If my tracker would turn on, I'd know for sure how far we'd traveled, if it even worked this far from the school.

Finally, a green sign on the side of the road signifies that we're three miles from a town. Nine miles down, and I don't feel tired at all.

I guess that an hour has passed at our comfortable pace. The cool breeze feels good against my slightly sweaty skin. I'm surprised at how comfortable the silence feels, and Garrett and I only break it occasionally. Without music playing through my tracker, I've been happily serenaded by the sounds of nature.

"Feel like a water break?" Garrett asks, and I nod, happy to get a reprieve from the less-than-comfortable bike seat. We pull our bikes to the side of the road, leaning them on their kickstands in the gravel.

"It's so quiet," I say, stretching my legs and using my shirt sleeve to wipe the sweat from my forehead.

Garrett takes a drink from his water bottle and peers down the road. "I feel like we should have seen someone by now. Wouldn't the supply trucks come this way?"

I shrug, because even though I've gone to the Academy for most of my life, I'm still unfamiliar with the area. I feel like we're in a whole other world when we're at school. We've never been permitted to go off campus for leisure. Even when we're home with our families, the rules for us have always been clear: Don't go anywhere that's not necessary; don't take the risk of exposure.

I've heard rumors about our classmates sneaking out in their parents' cars to visit the city, but I've never been brave enough to even think about risking something like that.

Part of me wonders why I let Garrett talk me into this bike ride so easily. Surely, I'll be in as much trouble as those students had been if we're caught, and my parents won't forgive me as easily as others might. Most of the parents of my fellow students threw money at any problem that came up. Our headmaster was not immune to the depths of the Academy parents' pocketbooks or above a good bribe. I'd be lying if I said I never imagined sneaking off to see the real world, though.

I take a drink from my own water bottle, and I know that I would have found a way to come out here with or without Garrett eventually. If Mr. Mason and Ms. Kay are not going to take this seriously, someone has to be brave enough to look for answers.

I finish a quarter of my water and put my bottle back on my bike, hesitant to drink it all too soon and get a side cramp. "I'm ready if you are."

Garrett laughs. "In a hurry?"

"I mean..." I look away sheepishly. While I'd love to sit here and enjoy the company of a cute boy, the longer we go without seeing another human, the more my anxiety increases. I'm not sure what scares me more: Running into another person, or not finding any people at all. "If you need some more time—"

"No, it's fine; I totally get it." He wipes his mouth with his shirt sleeve and puts his own water bottle away. "I'm eager to see what's going on, too."

I smile at him. At least one other person is on the same page as I am.

We climb back on the bikes and increase our speed. The road winds softly downhill, giving us an advantage, and we make it to the town in what feels like no time at all. We stop at the edge before turning onto Main Street. A crossing signal for a train is down, but there are no flashing lights and no train in sight. Cars are parked in the street, seemingly abandoned by their owners. It's strangely quiet, not a single engine or voice to break the silence.

Except my own. I step off my bike, letting it fall into the street. "What the heck?"

"Where is everybody?" Garrett asks, letting his bike fall as well. "This is nuts."

Of the dozen or so storefronts on Main Street, not even one has an "open" sign illuminated. The buildings don't all look abandoned or in disrepair, though; a few still look cared for. If it wasn't the middle of the day, the entire street would be pitch-black and still. Whatever this power situation is must be affecting more than the school. But why are the cars still in the streets?

Garrett's whole body is rigid, and I know this isn't the scene he expected to see, either. Somehow, that doesn't comfort me much.

"What should we do?" I don't know if I'm asking Garrett or myself, but I feel the familiar hands of fear creeping in under my skin. I shiver against their icy fingers.

"Let's mask up and see if we can find anyone in these buildings. There has to be someone around here—better to be cautious."

I opt to wear all the protective gear we have. Latex gloves, face mask, and goggles. Garrett hands me an extra hoodie. I pull it over my head, thankful for its warmth now that the chilly air has settled in my bones.

Everything we've been told about the viruses leads me to believe that being unprepared is deadly. I look over at Garrett who has chosen to wear everything as well and burst out laughing.

"You look like you're from another planet." His hair is slightly damp from our brisk ride, and the sun reflects off his goggles, giving them a mirroring effect.

Garrett's head snaps up, and he laughs with me. "Well, if I look like you do, then I totally understand why you're laughing."

"Hey!" I toss a bottle of hand sanitizer at him. "I'd watch what you say to me, Mr. James." He catches the bottle and stuffs it into his hoodie pocket.

"Alright, let's start with this pharmacy on the corner. If anything, they should still be open. People will need medicine, right?" He reaches out his gloved hand, and I gladly take it. As brave as I am trying to be, I'm terrified of what we might find here. The warmth of his hand reaches me through the layers of latex, and I focus on that as we duck under the railroad crossing and head toward our uncertain destination.

Chapter Six

An old hand-carved wooden sign reads: *Welcome to Hidden Maples, WA.* Just reading the name of the town feels strange. All these years at the Academy, we've never even known exactly what state we were in. The old pre-virus maps were useless, as most of the cities have fallen over the past sixty years. Grandpa said that when people grouped together, many smaller towns were abandoned or looted and then destroyed.

This town seems to have survived at least in some ways. Someone has taken the time to water and care for the flower beds that line the sidewalks along the street. While some of the dozen or so storefronts are boarded up, more than a few appear to still be in business.

The red brick pharmacy building says *McAllen's Pharmacy: Established 1928* on a large wooden sign above the frosted glass door. It's so similar to the town sign, I suspect they were crafted by the same person.

The main window is decorated with fake snow and has a Christmas tree on display with little pill-bottle-shaped ornaments hanging from the branches. The "open" sign light is off, but Garrett pushes on the door and it swings inward with ease. The tinkling from the tiny bell makes me jump. Everything is eerily quiet, and the little sound is almost too loud for my ears, but it smells like cinnamon inside. A large metal box of scented pinecones sitting inside the door is the likely source of the wonderful aroma.

"Hello?" I call out, eager to hear a friendly voice answer me. Garrett pauses, and I strain my ears for any kind of response. Nothing. Absolute silence greets us. I pull my hand from Garrett's and approach the register to our right, peering over the counter, looking for any signs of life.

Everything appears in order, but no one is behind the counter to help us. "Maybe in the back? Over where the pharmacist would be?" I ask quietly. I don't know why I'm whispering. The silence just makes everything feel too loud.

Garrett heads down the closest aisle, salty snacks on one side and candy on the other. Little stickers that say 2 for $1 rest on vintage candy displays. But fewer items are in the store than I expected. It looks like they need to restock almost everything—it's even more empty than the school pantry. Maybe it's because everything comes delivered? But even then, wouldn't they need to get items in to fill those orders? Do so few people physically come to the stores now that nothing needs to be locked up? Somehow, that doesn't seem like the right answer.

This little pharmacy would be a fun trip under other circumstances. Part of me wants to let myself pretend Garrett and I are out for a date. I've never been into a store, even with my parents. I can count on one hand the number of times I've been out in the real world, and never when there were other people involved.

I wish we were here under better conditions and could take the time to enjoy this new experience. I want there to be lively groups of people milling about and making purchases, like the old movies we watch at school. But no carefree shoppers walk the aisles here, this is not a date, and we have a job to do.

I follow closely behind Garrett, unwilling to be left alone in the eerily silent store. Afraid even he may disappear into thin air like everyone else in this town.

When we reach the counter, I see that a metal gate is down over the pickup and drop-off window. It's dark beyond, where there are no windows for sunlight to reach. "Hello?" I call again into the darkness.

"If they took the time to lock up the back, why is the front door unlocked and no one here?" I ask, feeling even more frustrated. I play with the ends of my ponytail, anything to keep from pulling my gloves off to bite my nails.

What is going on?

Garrett calls out a few more times, his loud voice booming through the silence, but still, we hear nothing.

"Well, there's no one here. I guess we will keep trying buildings for now. We're bound to find at least one person, right?" Garrett looks as desperate as I feel. So I nod, though I'm not confident we will find anything but disappointment in this town.

Three buildings later, I'm losing hope that we'll find any answers, and I'm confused why all of the doors are unlocked. Do they have no thieves in this area? I know I've never been to a store myself, but locked doors for unmanned stores seems like it would be a minimum standard. I need to use the restroom, but I'm too scared to leave Garrett's side, especially to fumble around in the darkness of an unknown space. This place feels so creepy without any people in it.

We head out of the clothing store we've cleared, and I let out a long breath. A blue truck is parked in the road ahead of me with *Jesse's Construction Co.* written in white block letters across the side of it. I cross over the sidewalk and peer into the passenger side window. It's empty—no personal belongings or groceries or anything on the bench seat.

As I'm about to turn around, a flash of sunlight shines into my eyes, catching my attention. I pull hard on the door handle, and the door swings open easily. The cabin smells dusty and old, reminding me of the sawdust-and-oil smell in my grandpa's shop, but I push it away to search for the shining objects I'd seen from the window. And there, twinkling in the sunlight, I find them, still hanging from the ignition.

"Garrett, the keys are still in this truck!" I yell, unable to keep my voice even. I slip back out, slamming the door closed. I run across the street to a red sedan that is half in the road and half in a parking spot. I try the door—also unlocked—and again, the keys are still in the ignition. "Here, too!"

Garrett comes up behind me, his brows furrowed. "Okay, that's really strange," he mumbles, climbing into the driver's seat to inspect the car.

"The driver didn't even put it in park," he says. "Looks like they pressed the e-brake." He turns the keys, and nothing happens. Not even the telltale clicking of a dead battery. Grandma once left the lights on in her car, and when Grandpa had tried to start it, it made clicking noises, and the lights had flickered on the dash as it tried to start. This car remained completely lifeless.

"How do you know how to drive?" I ask. I vaguely remember playing pretend driver behind the wheel of my parents' car, but I've never actually driven a vehicle.

Garrett nods. "My dad taught me when I was twelve. He used to let me drive up and down our private road. He told me every boy should know how to drive."

Another rite of passage that most of us have never experienced. People took many things for granted in the world before the viruses. Will I ever learn to drive a car? Will there ever be a reason for me to know how to? So far, I've been a passenger my whole life. Always someone else telling me what to do or taking me where I needed to go, never asking my opinion on the matter.

Will I ever get to sit in the driver's seat of my own future?

I race back to the truck, repeating the process I'd seen Garrett do in the car. Foot on the brake pedal, I turn the keys, and again, nothing happens. "This one's dead, too. Like our trackers, and the generator..."

Something is going on, and I know it's way more than some silly power outage. I rub my hands over my arms, leaning back in the truck seat as I take deep breaths, willing myself to breathe through my fear.

"Hey, are you okay?" Garrett pulls his goggles and mask off, tucking them into his hoodie pocket. He leans into the truck and gently helps me remove my own mask and goggles, adding them to his pocket, before turning me in the seat to face him.

I try not to let him see the tears that have gathered in my eyes. I'm probably overreacting, but it's been such a crazy day already. He tucks a stray curl behind my ear and smiles at me softly. "I know it's freaky, but we'll figure something out."

More tears leak down my cheeks, and I watch Garrett take one of his gloves off and use his thumb to brush them away. I never cry in front of anyone, and now I've done it twice in a few hours.

"I don't get it. Where could everyone be?" My lip trembles. I'm too upset now to pretend I'm out on a secret date with Garrett, no matter how much I wish it were true.

"Selena." His arms wrap around me, the warmth coming off his body a welcome reprieve from the chill in my skin. I let my arms wrap around him, tightening our embrace. As I press my cheek against his chest, he leans against me, and I feel him kiss the top of my head. The gesture is sweet, and I sigh against him. At the sound, he pulls back to look at me, his brown eyes pinched.

"Do you want to head back to school or keep going?" He takes my hands and pulls me from the truck bench to stand with him. I don't know how to answer him. I want to find answers, but I'm feeling more and more hopeless with each building we enter.

I open my mouth to respond, but I'm interrupted by the melody of church bells ringing in the distance.

Both of us turn our heads in the direction of the sound. Searching the tops of the buildings, I easily spot the bell tower. A tall white church stands a little above the other structures, weathered from time but still a beacon for weary travelers. We're only a few streets away from the swinging bells, and my heart leaps into my throat.

"Let's go check that out!" I say quickly, pulling Garrett with me down the street. This could be the break we need.

At the street corner, we take a left, and I still keep a firm grip on Garrett's hand. I scan our surroundings for any signs of life, but I am only met with fallen leaves scuttling down the street in the wind. The trees are a rainbow of color in the afternoon sun, a beautiful picture that I wish I could stop and appreciate. But both fear and anticipation keep my feet moving, begging for life to appear.

Garrett slows down, and he tugs on my arm, motioning for me to stop. "Let's mask back up, just in case." He pulls my protective items from his pocket and hands them to me. I comply quickly, feeling my impatience grow. I know he's right, that we should approach this situation cautiously, but my impatience is at war with my intelligence.

"Don't forget you need a new glove," I say, remembering the way his thumb felt against my cheek. My face tingles at the memory. We've known each other for years, but we've never spent this kind of one-on-one time together. This is different.

He digs in his backpack for a fresh glove, and I study the church from the side closest to us. The wooden building needs a fresh coat of white paint, and some of the black window shutters are missing from the second floor. It's still pretty, even if it could use some love.

I don't see any people milling about outside the church, but that doesn't mean there aren't people inside. Someone rang those old bells—it's clear even from the street that they're operated by pulling on a rope.

Once he's ready, Garrett takes my hands in his, our latex gloves making a funny noise when they connect. "Listen, let me go in first, just to be safe."

I think about telling him that I'm a big girl and can handle myself, but the truth is, I'm happy to let him take the lead. "Okay. Be careful." I'm not sure what I'm warning him for, but I feel the warning is warranted regardless.

"If we don't find what we're looking for here, we'll head back to the school, okay?"

"Deal." I nod at him, and his returning smile doesn't quite reach his eyes. Nerves are getting to us both. I squeeze his hands firmly, lean forward, and place a soft kiss on his cheek before securing my mask over my face. "Thank you."

A real smile reaches his eyes before he puts his own mask on. The moment is over too quickly as he turns to lead us to the front of the old white church.

The big black double doors are closed. We take the cement steps two at a time, and Garrett gives my hand one last squeeze before letting go and pushing against one of the doors.

It swings open easily, and instantly, the old-church smell hits my face. Even through my mask, it's pungent. Dusty old carpet, ancient books? Whatever the smell, it reminds me of melted crayons.

Everywhere I've been in my life has been sterilized and clean, yet nothing about this old building is new or sterile. I'm not sure what the smell is, but it's unfamiliar and strong.

"Hello?" Garrett calls, his voice loud in the small entryway. A large cross hangs over another closed set of doors ahead of us. I nod at Garrett to continue, and he nods back before pushing through the second set of double doors.

He stops walking halfway through the doorway, and I bump into his back. A man's voice breaks the silence. "Why, hello there."

I stand on my tiptoes to peer over Garrett's shoulder. A handful of people are huddled together at the front of the church. A few more are scattered on church pews. There are less than a dozen people here, but I feel myself exhale in relief. We're not alone in this town.

We're not the last people on Earth.

"Come, come, children," the man calls out to us, his curly blond hair bobbing as he nods in our direction. He looks like he might be the pastor in a light-blue sweater vest and matching tie. His smile is kind, and I pray that he has some answers for us.

Although everyone else in the room is wearing masks and goggles like us, the pastor is free of any protection. It's nice to be able to see his friendly face. I can't guess the ages of the others, but the pastor looks close in age to my own parents, somewhere in his fifties, perhaps.

It's hard not to stare at the people gathered here. I haven't seen strangers since my first days at the Academy. I want to study all their faces and their movements, ask them questions. The excitement battles for attention inside of me.

We walk to the front cautiously, getting a feel for our surroundings. The maroon pews are worn from years of age, but the rest of the room looks slightly more up-to-date and inviting. Sunlight streams across the gray carpet in rainbows of color, tinted by large stained-glass windows. I haven't been inside a church before, but this looks like the ones I've seen in movies.

"I'm Pastor Driscoll, but you may call me Ben," he says softly, the others around him quietly finding their seats in the pews. "We were gathering to discuss recent events. Was there something I could help you with?"

Garrett's voice is quiet. "We came to town to see if anyone had any information on the power situation—"

"Ah, yes. Of course," Ben says, interrupting him. "So this is happening over at the Academy as well?"

Garrett and I share a look. How does he know the Academy exists or where it's located? With all the efforts the program has made to make sure we're hidden, we never considered anyone nearby would even know it was there. We hadn't intended to tell anyone who we were or where we were coming from, but maybe we should have known that in a town this small, and with so much loss, we'd stick out like sore thumbs.

"How did you..." I start to ask but think better of it and close my mouth.

Ben laughs softly. "I've lived in this town my whole life. Not much goes on around here that I don't know about. When they came to town looking to buy land for the school, my parents were happy to sell it to them. My father was an architect, and he helped them plan out that very interesting shape himself."

I don't know what to say to that, and Garrett stays silent as well. It seems like he knows more about the school than our own parents. The near asterisk-shaped building would be hard to forget even if someone only saw it once.

"Don't worry; I don't think too many others know about it. I only suspected it because you have a look about you, even with the masks and goggles. You're too young and certainly too clean to be from the outer parts of this old town. We don't have any young people around here these days. Not for many, many years."

My stomach feels uneasy knowing that our friends at school aren't as hidden away as we've always thought. Does this Ben also know that the guards are no longer manning the gates?

He doesn't seem bothered by our silence and continues to talk softly to Garrett. "Most of the remaining members of our little town have gone to shelter in their homes until we know more. Not too many of us are left after the last round of viruses. New events cause quite the stir in our little community these days."

That explains the deserted storefronts, though it doesn't explain why they'd leave everything unlocked and vulnerable to thieves. Unless they have some kind of unspoken agreement with each other.

"We're glad we heard the bells. We were starting to think no one was around." I shrug like I'm not completely terrified.

"Glad you heard them as well." He pats my shoulder with his hand, and I resist the urge to knock it away. "Have a seat, then, and we will get started with the meeting."

"Thank you," Garrett says. I follow him to the nearest empty pew, and once we're seated, he takes my hand in his again. I watch his knee bob up and down nervously, and I can't blame him for feeling that way. Even though we're in a church and Ben seems like a kind man, this entire situation is unnerving. I press into Garrett as close as I can, comforted by his proximity.

"Okay, then, Ladies and Gentlemen, let's talk about the situation, shall we?"

They don't know anything.

Nothing more than we knew, anyway. Last night, around seven-thirty, the power went out. Not only the power, but anything electric immediately stopped working. Cars on the streets, radios, telephones, cell phones, you name it. Backup generators refused to start, and somehow, in a matter of minutes, we'd been plunged right back into the dark ages.

Their small hospital had taken the worst hit of all. Without power, backup generators, or any way to call for help, some of the patients had died overnight. The latest viruses had left so many patients in need of respirators or extra oxygen, and without access to power, those had failed.

I feel Garrett stiffen beside me, and I wonder if he is worried about his family. But I stay quiet, intently listening to every scrap of information being shared. I bite the inside of my cheek to keep myself focused on what Ben is saying. It won't help anyone to cry, though I certainly want to.

"I tell you, this has got to be a terrorist attack!" a man yells out from one of the pews behind us. I turn a little in my seat to look at him. He's pacing the small space, sweat beading on his forehead above his goggles. "Why else wouldn't the government have warned us this was coming? Where the heck is the cavalry? Who is going to come save us, and why is it taking so dang long?"

"Now, Jacob, let's not start a mass panic over speculation. If we were under attack, I'm sure someone would be coming through here to let us know," Pastor Ben says, but I can see from his expression that he has no idea what is or isn't happening. He motions for the man to have a seat.

"Could have been an EMP attack or a solar flare—those can cause massive outages. Even our vehicles are toast, so there's no way to go for help! But they know when solar flares are coming; they could have warned everyone." Jacob's voice is painted with agitation as he continues to pace.

"Sit down, dear," the lady next to him says sternly, smoothing her hands over her pants. She reaches out and takes him by the shirttail, pushing him back into the pew. "It doesn't do any good to panic or yell."

I can't see the man's mouth or his eyes, but his body language screams annoyance as he sits next to who I assume is his wife.

While I agree with the woman, I do feel panic seeping into my skin again. If no one knows what's wrong, and not a single car is working in the town, it could take us days to go anywhere and see how far this outage reaches. Part of me wonders if that man is right. What if this is some kind of attack? Would our government send people out here to help us? To warn us? Wouldn't they be here already if they could be? Is there even any government left?

"What should we be doing, Pastor Ben?" a small voice from the front of the room asks. From here, I can't tell if it's a woman or a person with a soft voice, but their inflection makes them sound kind. "Are there any people in town that we might need to check on? I know the hospital is having issues and some have gone up to lend a hand, but is there anyone we might be forgetting about?"

I consider raising my hand to say that there's a whole private school out of the way that could easily be forgotten, but something makes me pause. None of us has any medical reason to be worried that I know of, and we have some supplies in the kitchen and the school nurse's office. There are bound to be people who need more help than we do. Besides, this town doesn't know any of us personally, so how helpful will they really be?

My mind races with worst-case scenarios. I think about the mass hysteria that happened when the first viruses first broke out. The looting and rioting, the fighting in the streets, attacks on government buildings and law enforcement. I hadn't witnessed those things myself, but my grandparents had. I'd seen the footage; it was certainly not something I wanted to experience firsthand.

How long will it be before people start to feel desperate and get hateful? How long will we remain safe?

Pastor Ben walks the length of the room, back and forth, rubbing his jaw. His brown loafers bounce lightly, and his khaki pants are wrinkled where he continually pulls at the leg. "Because of all the sickness, we must be careful how much interaction we have with each other. However, I'd like everyone to know that they're welcome here at the church if they need a meal or some company. I have a few cots in the back if anyone needs to stay here. Mostly, we should all be extra kind to our neighbors, keep our eyes and ears out for anyone who may be struggling, and try to be patient. If there are any further developments or I have any more insight to share, I'll ring the bells to signal a town meeting. Does this sound agreeable to everyone?"

Although the room is barely occupied, the buzz in the room grows loud quickly as everyone tries to talk at once, shouting over one another to be heard. It doesn't sound like anyone is happy with his plan. A few people storm out through a back exit beyond the pulpit, and Ben tries his best to calm the remaining people down.

He raises two hands in surrender. "Please, you'll all be heard if you take turns speaking—"

"What are we supposed to do for food? None of our bank cards are going to work with no power. Who will make deliveries? Is there even enough to go around?"

Someone else yells louder. "We'll need firewood; it feels like it'll drop below freezing tonight."

Another man stands, nodding his head. "Yeah! What about those of us without a fireplace? Are we on our own?"

The questions fire off one after another, and Ben doesn't have a chance to answer any of them before more are thrown out. This is the kind of energy I'm afraid of. The kind where people turn on each other and get hurt.

I pivot to Garrett, who is watching the situation unfold with a calm I don't feel. He leans in close, speaking softly in my ear where no one else can hear him. "Things are about to get crazy here. We should probably sneak out now while no one is paying attention."

"You think they'll say anything if we try to leave?" I ask him, scanning the room slowly, making sure no one is watching us.

"I'm not really sure, but if more of them do know about the school, they might think we have more supplies up there than we do and start demanding things from us. I could be wrong, but I'd rather not stick around and find out. Clearly, they don't have any idea what's going on, so we're not learning anything new by staying." His line of thinking while Pastor Ben was talking must have been similar to my own.

"Okay, you're right." I sigh, my shoulders slumping slightly under the weight of defeat. We will have to return to the Academy having learned nothing helpful about our situation. Well, except that we won't see any supply trucks today—no one in town is capable of making any deliveries, and if they were expecting deliveries for themselves, too, none of them will arrive.

Anything that used to power on no longer works. It's anyone's guess how far this thing stretches.

Garrett's fingertips touch my lower back, and he gently pushes me toward the end of the pew. We walk slowly but with purpose to the back of the room before slipping out through the double doors. With everyone still shouting and fighting, I doubt anyone even turned their head in our direction.

Back on the street, it's still full daylight, but I have no idea what time it is. During the school day, I am constantly keeping an eye on the clock to make sure I'm on track to finish assignments before the period ends. It's a strange, disconnected feeling, not knowing what time it is. I've been without my tracker before—that's nothing new to me—but with the wall clocks in every classroom and in varying parts of the common areas, I always have a good idea of the time.

I follow Garrett back around the corner and toward the street where we started, but as we get close to the shopfronts, my fears are realized. A few residents are running in and out of the stores, screaming and yelling at each other. An old man runs past us, his back hunched over the large bag of dog food in his arms. Two women push a shopping cart down the street filled with random dry food items. Then a loud commotion comes from the pharmacy on the corner as Garrett and I run closer, and I pull us wide, out into the street.

"Break the thing down, then!" someone yells. "I need my medicine, and I'll get it one way or another!"

BANG!

The unmistakable sound of a gun firing makes me jump. Two people nearby scream in response, running out of the pharmacy. I trip over my own feet, and Garrett grabs the back of my shirt to keep me from falling to the ground. Our eyes meet, and I see my own fear mirrored in his. We don't stop to see what happened there; we just keep running.

Despite the cold weather, sweat pours down my face, around my goggles and into my mask. I can hardly breathe, my panic and the sweat in my mask making it hard to get enough oxygen.

We duck back under the train crossing and heave our bikes up from the ground. I'm thankful they're still where we left them—in the future, we'll have to be more careful. If history has taught me anything, it's that when people get desperate, they'll steal anything not nailed down.

We pedal fast and don't speak. As we ride, I pull my mask and goggles down to hang around my neck, gulping in the fresh air. I smell a hint of smoke, but I don't give myself a chance to wonder where it's coming from or what it could mean. I tell myself it's someone's fireplace, that they're warm and safe in their house like we will be in an hour or two back at school.

I tell myself that over and over, praying that I'm telling myself the truth.

Chapter Seven

Not until we are back to the private highway that leads to the school do we finally slow down. My clothes are drenched in sweat, and I'm pretty sure the adrenaline got us back to this spot in half the time. It's nice to know there are only five mile markers between us and the school now.

"Take a break?" Garrett asks, and I slowly ride to the side of the road. I flip the kickstand on the bike and let my body drop down to the ground, pulling the mask and goggles from my neck before turning over to lie down. I take deep breaths as I stare at the sky.

The sky is a brilliant blue with little streaks of white clouds dusting it here and there. It's cool, and now that we've stopped moving, the brisk wind feels heavenly on my sweaty skin.

"That was scary," I say. Scary is probably not a strong enough word for what I felt, but I'm too tired to search for a better one.

Garrett drops his backpack and lies down beside me. "Yeah. I'm glad we left when we did." We lay there together, both of us trying to catch our breath from the ride. "I'm sorry. We should have stayed at the school. I let my curiosity get the best of me."

"Don't apologize; I was a willing accomplice. And now we know this isn't only happening at school. Who knows how far this thing goes?" I motion to the sky and realize that I still have my gloves on.

I peel the rubber gloves off my hands, wishing I'd thought to take them off sooner. My fingers are wet and pruned, the gloves slick and dripping with sweat. I watch as Garrett does the same. Both of us scrunch up our noses.

"I have that sanitizer in my bag," he offers. "I don't know how much it'll help, but it might make us feel a little better. We should probably eat a snack and have some water, too. When we get back, it might be awhile before we get a chance to do much besides update Mr. Mason."

"What do you think we'll do next? Wait it out?"

Garrett stops rustling through his backpack and meets my eyes. "I don't know what Mr. Mason will want to do. I have a feeling this might go bad quickly, but I don't intend to let anyone tell me what to do. I'll do what I think is best. I've spent my entire life under someone else's control—I won't die that way, too."

I never thought of Garrett as a rule breaker before, but in some ways, it makes all the sense in the world. He takes little things wherever he can. He's brave in a way I've never been strong enough to be. I hope that someday I can be as fearless as he seems now.

For some reason, I trust him to make the right choices. Maybe it's because I've known him for such a long time, or maybe it's because he seems to be on the same wavelength as I am. Whatever the cause, I'll follow his lead. I can't allow myself to be paralyzed with fear, so I'll lean on his courage until I can find my own.

We share some teriyaki beef jerky and water as we sit in the middle of the deserted road. I still see no sign of any other cars or trucks. It's unnervingly quiet—even the birds from this morning have gone mute. I stretch my legs out since they're stiff and sore from the long ride. I'm in good shape, but we pushed ourselves to the limit to get out of town.

"Legs hurt?" Garrett nods at them as I rub my calves. "Going to be okay to get back?"

"Oh, yeah. They're sore, but I'm okay. I was feeling a little lightheaded, but the jerky helped. Good snack choice." I smile, taking another chewy bite.

Garrett grins, "I always bring jerky. I have a huge supply in my room, which might come in handy." He finishes off his water bottle and gathers up our trash, zipping it and our discarded gloves into a plastic bag before tossing it into his backpack. He's so efficient, definitely someone I want to lead us.

Mr. Mason and Ms. Kay are capable enough. They're both excellent teachers, but neither of them strikes me as the take-charge type. Ms. Kay is good at organizing people for tasks, so that would be helpful, but Mr. Mason has more of a wait-and-see type of personality. I could see him sitting on his hands and hoping that someone else would show up to take over.

I can't wait to see Evelynn and Hanna, but part of me wonders if they've even left our room today. They didn't seem even the slightest bit concerned about the situation. None of the other students had seemed too bothered, either. They'd only been angry about missing our calls home.

We're teenagers—what can we do? That had been the consensus. Part of me wishes I could feel that same level of detachment from the situation, but if things get bad, and I have a feeling they're about to, I will have no one to blame for my predicament but myself.

"You sure you're okay, Selena? You're really quiet."

I stand, wiping my hands on my pants before responding to his question. "I'm worried. I don't know what to expect, and we're out here alone. I'm trying to come up with a clear plan that everyone will rally behind. I don't do well on the fly—I need information. I need to know all the possible outcomes so I can make an informed decision. But I know that's not a possibility here, and I hate it."

Garrett slings his backpack on, securing it on his shoulders. He walks over to me, placing one hand on each of mine.

"It *is* scary, but we can figure this out. We need to stay calm and take this one step at a time, okay? I promise, you don't have to make all the decisions alone." He pulls me into a hug, and I return it, squeezing him tightly. We stand that way for a while, holding on to each other.

I nod against him, unsure what he means but not ready to ask the question. Does he plan to pack up and leave the Academy on his own? Where will he go? He's from the Portland area, like me—it's not exactly walking distance. Without a map, it's hard to even know which direction to go or how far it really is. But I'm too tired and stressed out to ask him any more.

We finally let go, wordlessly climbing back on our bikes and heading toward home.

Mr. Mason is standing outside the front of the school when we finally get close enough to see the building. He has his hands on his hips, his feet are wide, and his face is almost as red as the Academy shirt he's wearing. I'm pretty sure he's seen us and is about to lose it, but then I see Ms. Kay a few feet away yelling and flapping her hands in his direction. He turns back to her, and they appear to be fighting. Garrett and I slip around them to the recreation building, stowing the bikes in the bike rack and hanging up our helmets.

"I wonder what that was about." I motion toward the front of the school. Garrett lets out a loud chuckle.

"Lovers' quarrel, maybe?" He shrugs with a smirk. I love the sound of his laugh; it's such a welcome sound after the trip we've had. It's deep and smooth, the kind of laugh that I hear and can't help but feel jovial, too.

My own laugh joins his. "Whatever it is, they're really not going to like the news we're about to share with them. Do you think they'll bust us hard for leaving campus?"

Garrett shrugs. "What can they do to us? We don't have much they can take away at this point."

He's right, but the thought of getting in trouble still makes my palms itch. "I wish we didn't have to tell them the bad news at all."

Garrett kicks the ground. "Yeah, well, it has to happen. We can't all sit out here with our heads in the sand."

I nod my response. I know he's right, but it doesn't make me feel any better. Bad news is not what I was hoping to return with today.

The two teachers are inside the school doors, sitting on the bench we'd used to stretch this morning. "Hi, Mr. Mason, Ms. Kay." Garrett nods a greeting at them. They seem to have sorted out whatever they were fighting about, but Mr. Mason's face is still as red as a tomato. Even the top of his head is red where I can see his scalp through his light-blond hair.

"How was your ride?" Mr. Mason asks. I scrunch my eyebrows together at his calm tone. Shouldn't he be screaming at us?

"Actually—" Garrett starts.

"Where did you two just come from? And were you on your own?" Ms. Kay sits taller, studying us closely and shooting daggers at Mr. Mason. "Just the two of you? No chaperone or group for accountability?"

If we hadn't been through that nightmare today, the question would have made me laugh. From the tone of her voice, she clearly thinks we've been off doing inappropriate things. I can see why she might think that, but really? Right now? Maybe she'd need to worry about some of the other students, but doesn't she know me better than that by now?

"We needed some exercise?" I offered, my voice trembling. Mr. Mason frowns at us.

"Alone?" Ms. Kay's eyes burn a hole through my weak excuse. "I get that outside you're technically not purpling, but you know you're still not allowed to mix without supervision. The last thing we need right now is a teenage pregnancy—"

"We rode into town." I quickly spit the words. I'm not aware of a single pregnancy in the school's history. I'd rather be in trouble for leaving campus than accused of being inappropriate with a boy, and I'm embarrassed she'd even consider me a risk for that. What we did—spending time together without an adult—could still get us put on the purple bench. Even without crossing into pink or blue, we should have known they'd have something to say about it.

"Town?" Her shriek hurts my ears. "What town? Outside the gate? Who let you out?"

"It's about twelve miles. There are signs if you follow the old road." Garrett ignores her other questions, impatience written on his face. He's not in the mood to be interrupted or answer her pointless questions. I know, because that's how I feel, too.

"It's not that far on a bike, but the thing is, this situation is worse than we thought." I sigh, trying to collect my thoughts and figure out how to tell them what we've seen.

"The outage has reached that little town and maybe even further. No one can communicate with all the electronics out. Cars don't work, either." Garrett motions to the one old utility vehicle on school grounds. "Everything has stopped working. The townspeople said even the hospital is completely without power."

Ms. Kay's hand flies up to her mouth, the information hitting her hard. I watch as her other hand grasps onto Mr. Mason's shoulder. "You shouldn't have gone by yourselves; it was dangerous and reckless and—"

"What else did you find out?" Mr. Mason asks, giving Ms. Kay a silencing look. His face is still flushed crimson, and he's pissed—no one can mistake that in his tone.

"Not much; there was a pastor at the church holding some kind of town meeting. We left when it was clear they didn't know any more than we did, and the people were getting restless. The thing is, when we went back through town, the looting and violence had started. We heard a gunshot and—"

"What? Guns? Do you have any idea how irresponsible you two have been?" Ms. Kay sounds like she's been running, her breathing coming fast and hard. She points a finger at us, jabbing it with each word. "You two can't be off playing hero. We need to stick together. We are still in charge, and you have to let us know what you're doing and where you're going at all times."

Mr. Mason grinds his teeth. "There will absolutely be consequences for your actions today. How did you get bikes in the first place?"

Garrett silently hands Mr. Mason the key he *borrowed* earlier. "I knew you wouldn't let us go if I asked, and someone had to get answers."

"I need to take a breath before I say something I'll regret." Mr. Mason raises his hands and then gently puts them back at his sides. "I will deal with both of you when I've calmed down."

Ms. Kay steps in front of him. "Until we decide on your punishment, we're going to full accountability. Everyone will stay in their rooms unless they have an assigned duty elsewhere. Right now, we need to gather everyone up and take attendance, make sure no one else has wandered off irresponsibly." She purses her lips so hard they lose their color.

They're angry, and I expected that much, but they're not saying anything about reporting us to our parents or the headmaster, so I tread lightly. Maybe if I pretend to be sorry and make myself useful, they'll go easier on us later.

"I'd like to rinse off and change my clothes, if that's alright. If you can give us a few minutes to regroup, Garrett and I can help get everyone together in the common area for you," I say, not feeling half as confident as my voice sounds.

"That would be good," Mr. Mason says. "Run along. Ms. Kay and I will discuss some things and gather everyone shortly."

As soon as we're out of earshot of the professors, Garrett pulls me into the alcove of a closed classroom door.

"Listen, whatever we agree to or say to the group, know I have my own plan, okay? I can already tell that our teachers are going to be useless. Don't let anyone know you have food or supplies in your room. We might need them soon."

"You think it's going to get bad, don't you?"

Garrett nods, his jaw flexing as he grinds his back teeth. "Pack a backpack, and think about survival out in the elements while you're packing. Nothing unnecessary. Hide it but have it where you can get to it quickly if we have to jump."

"How much trouble do you think we're in?" I chew on my thumbnail nervously.

"Like I said before: What can they take from us? Don't worry about those two. They're outnumbered, and they know it."

I swallow hard, tears threatening to leak from my eyes. I'm scared and angry. I wish we were home with our parents and not forced to fend for ourselves here. I'm glad to have Garrett since he seems to have a handle on what to do next. But my anxiety is already listing all the reasons we should stay put.

"Okay," I say, swallowing back the bile in my throat. "I trust you. We can hook up in my room after the meeting. Think you and Liam can sneak over without being seen?"

"Oh, I know we can." He winks, and I'm not sure the butterflies in my chest are from anxiety.

Chapter Eight

I KNOCK ON OUR door before I open it, because I never know who might be naked. We've all grown so comfortable with each other over the years that we don't even think twice about changing out in the open. I always make sure the door is locked, but the girls have a hard time remembering to lock up if I'm out.

"Come in!" Evelynn sings out, giving me the all clear.

The cloud of body spray hits me as the door swings in, and I take big gulps of the familiar air. I'm still riding the adrenaline high from earlier, but I can feel a crash coming soon. I glance around the room, surprised to see that they have actually cleaned it up like I suggested this morning.

Evelynn rushes over to me, slamming the door closed behind me and locking it. "You've been gone all day—what the heck is up? I want all the details."

"I'll fill you in on everything in a minute. Where's Hanna?" I scan the room looking for her, but her side of the room is quiet and empty.

"Oh, she's off with Liam. They got stuck on kitchen duty."

"Kitchen duty?" I ask, sitting down to pull off my running shoes. My back is wet from sweat, and I'm sure I smell. Stress sweat is always terrible for me. I peel off my running clothes next, looking forward to some more comfortable clothing.

Evelynn flops down on my bed, staring up at the ceiling. "We were ordered to clean our rooms and sign up for chores. Ms. Kay is on some kind of weird power trip. I got lucky and only had to wipe down the door handles for our wing. Hanna is supposed to figure out what kind of dinner we can put together using the outdoor grilling space and no power. Liam volunteered to help her with that." She wiggles her eyebrows suggestively.

I toss my dirty shirt at her; it lands in a heap over her face.

"Ew!" She laughs, throwing it back at me.

"We have to meet Mr. Mason in the commons soon, but I need to rinse the sweat off really quick." I talk to her as I start the shower in our bathroom.

Evelynn rolls on her side, facing the bathroom door. "Be quick; the water is freezing. And I'm pretty sure that I heard Ms. Kay saying eventually we'll run out of water because it's fed by gravity or something. And we only get what's left of the water in the emergency tower, and when that runs out, that's it. But they think someone should be out here to help us long before then."

I shake my head and step into the cold spray, washing my hair and body as fast as humanly possible. I'd skip it altogether and simply rinse off, but there's no telling how long it will be before I get another shower. I close my eyes and press my forehead against the shower tile, letting the spray pelt my skin like icy blades. This is so far from how I'd hoped to spend my holiday—some Thanksgiving this is turning out to be.

Evelynn hands me a towel when I finally shut the freezing water off. She stares at me expectantly while I dry my skin. "I feel like you know something. But, like, something bad. You're never this quiet. You'd better spill and quickly, before the drama llama gets back from her chore."

Hanna can be a little over-the-top sometimes, but I was hoping to only have to tell my story once. Evelynn's expression tells me that I'm not going to get off that easily, so I put up my finger, motioning for her to wait a minute, and dig through my dresser for my favorite matching bra and underwear set. They're comfortable and durable enough that if I end up running for my life, I can live in them happily for a long while. Garrett's voice rings in my head, and I pull a backpack out of the closet, stuffing a few extra pairs of underwear and a spare bra into the hidden inside pocket.

"Listen, Evie," I say softly, unable to stop moving. "Get a backpack and pack whatever you'd take with you if you had to run for your life. Think cold weather and comfort over fashion. And if you have any snacks or food items, grab those, too."

Fleece-lined jeans and my thickest hoodie go into my backpack next. After that, I slide into my most comfortable pair of jeans and a plain cotton t-shirt. It's low cut and hugs my curves in a flattering way, and the cotton material is soft and practical. Then I throw on a thick wool sweater that my grandma sent me, the kind of wool that keeps me warm but doesn't itch.

I look up to find Evelynn still standing in the bathroom door, her face white and her mouth slightly open. "Hey, did you hear me? Make a backpack!"

"What the heck is going on, Selena? You can't tell me to," —she pauses to make air-quotes with her fingers— "'Pack up and run for my life' and not explain yourself. Where were you today? What exactly happened?"

I sigh. We don't really have time for this conversation, but I can see that she's not going to cooperate until I fill her in. "Garrett and I rode our bikes off campus, and we found a little town. This thing goes so far, and it's so much more serious than Mr. Mason and Ms. Kay make it seem. They don't know what to do, and they don't want to cause a panic, but listen: We *should* panic. People were freaking out; riots and looting were starting. Remember all that stuff we learned happened at the beginning of the viruses? You know, like, decades ago? It's happening now; I saw it for myself. People were shooting at each other over prescription meds—"

"What?" Evelynn snaps from her frozen state. She rubs her hands over her pink sweater, biting her lip before moving into action. "What do you mean 'it goes further'?"

I'm thankful that she's finally moving. "The entire town is out of power, but it's more than small things. Even cars aren't working. The hospital lost power. When I say everything is down, I truly mean everything."

I toss socks and my travel kit into my backpack. I thought it was such a silly gift last year when my grandma gave it to me for Christmas. It has a set of mini items: a toothbrush, a tub of toothpaste, a small first aid kit, nail clippers, a pair of small scissors, a mini hairbrush, soap and hand sanitizer, shampoo, and conditioner. It had seemed so out of place that I'd almost left it in my room at home. In the end, I'd chosen to bring it simply because it came in the cutest little purple bag.

They were all things I never thought I'd have a use for since I have the full-size items both at home and at school. But now, I silently thank my grandma for her foresight. And Grandpa's doomsday fear that led to their obsession with being prepared for anything.

"Gunshots? Were you terrified?" Evelynn stuffs our stash of food into her backpack, chewing her bottom lip again. Her paint-splattered hands shake as she pulls the zipper closed.

"It was scary, but we were out of there quickly. Garrett is really good under pressure, so I'm glad he's taking us under his wing. I don't know how well we'd do on our own." I dig under my bed for my best sneakers, the ones that aren't too tight but provide good traction and support. I'm not sure if we'll have to leave the school today, but I am too afraid to wait for a signal to completely prepare for the moment it happens.

"I'll start a bag for Hanna. You should probably pat your hair dry real quick, Selena—it's too cold outside to get caught with wet hair. Can't use the hair dryer, of course, but you can towel it off a lot more."

Evelynn is taking the news in stride and making herself useful, which soothes my nerves a little. I run to the bathroom and squeeze as much water out of my hair as I can before furiously drying it on a clean towel. I grab a stack of hand towels from the cupboard above the toilet and add them to our supplies.

I throw our used towels into the shower first, drying out the tub itself so it won't get our things wet. Then I take my now full pack and hide it behind the shower curtain. Evelynn brings the other bags to the tub as well.

Garrett seemed sure that we would be forced to share our resources, so it's better to be safe than sorry. I watch Evelynn as she fills her water bottle at the bathroom sink and then reaches for mine to fill as well. I feel guilty for being the one to tell her the bad news, but we can't run from the truth now. I tell myself it's better she hears it from me than to be blindsided by the information when we have less time to react.

"Our sleeping bags from the astronomy camping trip are still in the closet—I'll throw them in with our backpacks. Do you think you could dig through the closet and find each of us some kind of winter coat?" I ask. Evelynn is in full task mode now, and I'm glad that I don't have to convince her that this is serious.

Bang! Bang!

I nearly jump out of my skin when someone knocks loudly on a door nearby. My nerves are still shot from earlier. Evelynn's hand grips my shoulder, a frown on her face. "It's okay, Selena. Take a breath."

I can hear Ms. Kay telling the students next door about the meeting in the commons. She must have gotten tired of waiting for me to rally the girls, so we're out of time for now. I run to the door and open it, pulling Evelynn out with me. I double-check that it's locked up tight before turning around.

"We can get the coats after; I'd prefer Ms. Kay not come into our room. Especially not when she's already peeved at me for being out alone with Garrett." At least I'm clean and dressed in layers—I've accomplished something in the time allotted.

"I wish you had been up to what she thinks you were." Evelynn sighs, and I squeeze her fingers as we round the corner to the commons. I wish that was all I'd been up to today, too, but something tells me we're lucky we found out when we did.

The commons is a mess of nervous chatter. Everyone is speculating about what the news will be, but I doubt any of them have the slightest idea how serious the situation really is. We're in our normal seats again, girls on one side and boys huddled together on the other. Hanna has yet to emerge from the kitchen, and I'm tempted to go hunt her down myself.

I want eyes on all the people I care about.

I'm about to leave my seat when I see her and Liam come out of the kitchen doors together. Hanna is laughing at something Liam is mouthing to her and pushing him away. They're obviously flirting, and I feel a small smile touch my lips. Leave it to Hanna to be flirting when the world is crashing down around us. I see Garrett across the room waving Liam over, and Hanna finally disengages from him and heads over to us.

"What the heck? I thought we were on chore duty! What's this—round two?" She laughs, plopping down into the seat beside me.

"I wish that's all it was," I mutter, taking her hand in mine.

"Why are you being weird?" She pulls her hand back. "Did something happen with you and Garrett or something?"

Mr. Mason speaks loudly over everyone's chatter. "Quiet, please."

Hanna rolls her eyes. "Fine, tell me after Mr. Mason gets his five minutes."

The students all quiet down, and I bite the inside of my cheek to keep myself from responding. I know Hanna would take the news better in private, but the time for that has gone.

"Earlier today, we expected a delivery of food and other supplies. We also thought we'd hear from the headmaster and the rest of the teaching staff. However, it has now come to our attention that this power outage, whatever the cause may be, extends far beyond the school. It is unclear when we will have contact with anyone, and as of now, there will be no deliveries."

A collective groan vibrates around the room.

"So we aren't getting power back? Can't someone fix the backup generator or something? We don't even have hot water." Mandy from my biology class clicks her painted nails on the table. "I'd like to call my parents and request they come get me. Someone needs to figure out how to make that happen."

Mr. Mason's tomato face returns, and I watch Hanna's eyebrows rise with the volume of his voice. "I don't think any of you are hearing me, so let me dumb it down for you. There is no power. There is no power anywhere nearby. No one is coming or going anywhere. You can't call your parents because the phones don't work. The hospital doesn't even have phones or power, so why are you any more special than those people who actually need it to survive? This is a crisis. We already know people are sick and dying all over the world—adding this power situation on top of that means catastrophe for some people. I think all of you will be fine without your internet and Mommy and Daddy's coddling for however long this takes. Until we can get help or speak to someone who outranks me in your care, I suggest you get your priorities in order. We are on our own, kids, and we are all going to have work to do. Do we understand each other?"

His outburst is met with silence. None of us make eye contact with each other. He's summed up our situation in a way that doesn't really warrant the asking of questions or complaining. It simply is what it is: the harsh reality of our current truth.

Ms. Kay steps up behind him, her eyes sharp and serious while she scans each of our faces as if daring one of us to complain again. "I am going to take attendance, and then we are going to talk about the rules. The first rule is that no one leaves here without implicit instructions to do so. We cannot have you running around in such an unsafe situation." Her eyes turn to my table, and I feel her gaze searing into my skin with laser focus. She's calling me out, and she wants that to be clear.

I shift uncomfortably in my seat and resist the urge to look for Garrett. It's better if I don't draw unnecessary attention to our friendship.

Ms. Kay finally releases her gaze from me before continuing her speech. "We will work out a way to keep a schedule, and we will each have daily chores to do. The food situation will have to be analyzed, but I'm sure we'll get it all sorted quickly and effectively. We need all of you to cooperate and be part of the team. This only works if we all work hard to keep it together."

We all nod, but I have no intention of letting them dictate how we survive. Their plan still seems to hinge on someone finally coming to our rescue. My gut is screaming out that no one is coming. We're on our own now.

Mr. Mason hands Ms. Kay a clipboard, and she takes out a pen. She tells us it's time for full accountability and then begins to call us out by name, one at a time.

Twenty-four names later, and we are all accounted for. We're asked to stay seated while they have a short conversation about today's expected duties. This seems to appease Ms. Kay, and I watch her shoulders relax as she slumps down into a chair next to Mr. Mason. Their heads tilt together as they discuss what they'll say to us next.

I bet they wish they hadn't drawn the short straws and were anywhere but here. Maybe they wish they'd snuck out with the staff when everyone but us got to leave for break. It doesn't really matter now; they are stuck here with us, for better or worse.

Hanna hisses in my ear. "Alright, I think you had better start explaining! What the heck is going on?"

I lean in to tell her about this morning, careful to keep my voice low enough to not be overheard. I recap the trip into town and the conversation with Garrett. The packed bags waiting in our room and the escape plan. I hold my breath when I've finished, waiting for Hanna to do her typical freak-out and expecting to have to talk her back from the edge.

Hanna's full pink lips fall into a pout as she twirls strands of her wild hair around her index finger. "My parents will come for me; I know they will. It's better if we stick it out here and wait for help. We're not all exactly outdoorsy or whatever. Where do you expect to go exactly?"

"Garrett is supposed to meet us later with Liam. We're going to work out a plan."

"Oh, I see. We're going to trust the two biggest players we know to protect us from whatever or whoever is out there lurking in the wild?" Hanna glares at me. This is not the response I was expecting. Tears maybe, but not this chilly attitude.

"I don't think it's safe to wait around here for help, Hanna. If the cars in town aren't working, it's possible our parents couldn't drive here if they wanted to. And they wouldn't even know exactly where to drive to. I think we need to try to get back home to them. Maybe if we get far enough out, we can find somewhere that hasn't been affected—"

"Maybe? You're going to risk all our lives on a *maybe*? What if, in a few days, everything is back to normal, and you've risked everything for nothing? I bet they would expel you—you're already in trouble for leaving campus. We're so close to graduating and getting out of here that I'm not risking it. This is my home. My life is here."

Evelynn and I share a look, but I can already see the stony resolve in Hanna's eyes. I'm not sure we'll be able to change her mind. I don't want to leave any of them behind, but I also feel in my bones that no one is coming to help us. Certainly not any of our parents.

Evelynn pleads with her quietly, reminding her that we should stick together, that we are closer than family. I tune them out, suddenly feeling very tired. Hanna isn't wrong; we're not used to having to physically fend for ourselves, and there is a possibility that I'm wrong and things will be better in a few days. But what if they aren't?

Why would the people in town be so desperate already if this isn't likely a very serious situation?

No. Whatever happens, whatever choices we make, of one thing I am certain: None of it is going to be easy.

"Okay, kids." Mr. Mason stands, rubbing a hand over his stubbled jaw. "We understand that a lot of you are probably scared and overwhelmed right now. We're going to ask that you head back to your assigned rooms and observe some quiet hours. Clean your space, read a book, study, whatever will help you relax. For the time being, resist using water unless absolutely necessary. When it starts to get dark, Ms. Kay and I will grill some frozen meat out in the courtyard and throw some produce together for everyone. We'll eat the perishables before they're unsafe to eat. We may not have power, but we do have good old-fashioned fire to work with."

When no one says anything, he continues. "Mostly, try to stay calm. We will get this all sorted out soon. And please, feel free to come find one of us if you need to talk to someone." He pauses, taking a long breath. "Any questions?"

Silence permeates the air.

"Okay, then, head on back to your rooms," Ms. Kay adds from her chair. I watch her face for any sign of hope, but all I see is defeat in her expression. They don't have any idea what they're doing, either.

I find Garrett's gaze across the commons. He nods at me, letting me know the plan is still on. I barely manage a weak smile back at him. Evelynn grabs my arm and pulls me back toward our room. Hanna is already gone; she didn't wait for either of us.

From down the hallway, we see Hanna stepping inside our room, the door falling shut behind her. When we reach it, Evelynn turns and presses her body against the solid wood before I can grab the handle.

"I don't know if we can turn her around," she whispers to me. "If we can't get her to come with us, maybe I should stay behind, too, keep an eye on her. She'll lose it if she's here alone—"

"I can't ask you to do that, Evie. I don't think it's going to be any safer here." My heart races. I don't want her or Hanna to stay behind, but if they both stay, I could lose my entire family in one fell swoop. "What if the townspeople come here looking for supplies? It's not clear how much they know about the school, but at least one of them knows we're here. They don't know that we barely keep enough to feed us—they could think we have everything they need here. They don't know that the nurse is gone, and we don't have any access to medicine or first aid—"

"Selena, stop." Evelynn smiles at me, stepping forward to tuck my damp hair behind my ears. "I know you think you're responsible for all of us. You've always been the mom of our group, but you're not really our mother. Whatever happens, no matter what you decide to do—or who stays or goes—we all have to make our own choices here."

I nod because I know she's right, but I don't like it. I want to keep them safe; I want to stay together. I could stay behind, too, if they don't want to go—we could wait this out, stick together. But deep down, I know I can't stay. My fight or flight response has kicked in, and all my instincts are telling me to run. *Get out.* Head in the direction of home and look for help. The plans in my mind are unraveling at the seams, and I want to stomp my feet and pull my own hair like a petulant toddler.

The bedroom door flies inward, and Hanna glares at us. "Are you going to stand out here all day and talk crap about me? Or are you coming inside to talk this out like the big girls we are?"

"We're not even talking crap." I push my way past her. "Garrett and Liam will be here soon. Leave the door unlocked so they can get in quickly."

"Encouraging purpling now, too, are we, Selena? Oh, how the mighty have fallen." Hanna's snarky tone rubs me the wrong way, but I stay quiet.

"Shut up, Hanna. What's your problem?" Evelynn shuts the door behind her, and I sit down on the edge of my bed. This day is relentless, and we don't have anything figured out yet.

Evelynn pulls Hanna closer, and they stand an arm's length in front of me.

"Listen up, both of you," Evelynn starts. "I understand where each of you are coming from, but we can't be fighting right now. We have no idea what is going on, but we're never going to make the right choices if we can't even talk to each other without getting nasty. Agreed?"

Hanna rolls her eyes, and I swallow the rude comeback that flits through my mind. I'm trying to keep us safe.

"Sure, yeah," I say, picking at a loose string on my sweater. Evelynn blows out a frustrated breath, and I agree with her sentiment. We stew in silence, none of us speaking or moving.

I count to three hundred in my head before our bedroom door swings open and Garrett and Liam shuffle in.

Liam shuts the door behind them, locking it securely with a grin. His voice cuts through the silence like a knife. "We've still got it, Garrett—no one saw us!"

"Don't pat yourself on the back too hard," Garrett says softly. "We still have to make it back without getting caught." His eyes meet mine, and he gives me a reassuring smile.

Hanna takes Liam's hand and leads him over to her bed; they sit together, and I wonder again what happened today in the kitchen that has them acting like a couple now. Evelynn joins me on my bed, and Garrett grabs my desk chair, straddling it between all of us so he can talk to the whole room.

"So what's the plan?" Evelynn asks, tucking her knees in under her chin. Her lips quiver a little, and I'm thankful that at least one of my girlfriends seems to be taking the situation seriously. I glare at Hanna across the room.

Garrett clears his throat. "Well, we have a few days' worth of food and supplies between the two of us. Liam reminded me there are tents in the recreation shed—"

"But you gave the key back to Mr. Mason, so how will we get back inside?" I ask.

"No worries. I left a window unlocked today when we returned the bikes so we can easily borrow them again. We need to get away from the school; it's too big of an area for us to defend if anyone gets crazy and comes here for supplies."

"Why would they do that, though?" Hanna whines. "It's not like we're anywhere near their town, and we don't have that much at the school."

"They don't know that, Hanna. They think we're pampered rich kids, and in their minds, that could mean we're prepared." I am getting more annoyed by the second. Our parents have never made us want for anything aside from their physical presence. I don't trust them to be worried enough to come looking for us now.

Hanna has always tried to pretend that her parents are different, but they didn't keep her home, either. We might be pampered and even spoiled, but we've also been highly educated. We know better than to expect anyone else to take responsibility for us.

"I'm not coming." She crosses her arms over her chest, letting Liam's hand fall back into his own lap. "You're gonna have to leave me behind."

"We're heading back to Portland, Hanna." Liam shakes her knee lightly with his hand. "We can find your parents, and if we can find my brother, maybe he'll have some answers for us."

"Your brother?" I ask, suddenly wishing I knew Liam better. As loud and wild as he is, he usually keeps the intimate details of his life to himself. It's weird how we've all lived under the same roof for twelve years, and even though we're closer to each other than our own blood families, we don't know much about each other outside of our school lives.

Siblings are so rare they're almost unheard of. He'd have to be quite a bit older than Liam, or what use would his family have for the program?

"Yeah, his name is Chase. He's in the military. He's stationed at a special weather station in Portland. He might know something or at least know someone who might be able to find out." The first real spark of hope blooms in my chest. At least this sounds like something we can work toward.

Evelynn bites her lip. I know she's thinking over the task and compiling her questions. "How many miles is it from here to Portland? We don't even know where *here* is." She throws her hands up in the air.

"Washington," I tell them. "The town we found was called Hidden Maples."

"We're a little south of a bigger city called Kennewick," Garrett offers.

Hanna stands, pacing the bedroom floor. "How do we know any of those places are still there? How do we even know which way to go?"

Garrett pulls a map out of his pocket. It's old and wrinkly but still legible. I watch him trace over the state of Washington with one finger before stopping on the spot he's looking for. "Here. This is where I think the school would be if we were marked on the map."

Hanna crosses the room to get a closer look. "That looks so far from home. How many miles is that?"

"I used the map scale. If the roads I chose are still passable, it's about two-hundred-and-forty miles. Under perfect conditions, it's about nineteen hours of riding. We'll have to camp out—there's no way we're making it all in one day. But we can take highway 82 to Umatilla and then follow the Columbia River almost the whole way. If we hit bad weather, we might end up ditching the bikes and walking, but if we stick to the roads, there should be at least a couple of towns we can stop in for supplies."

"We've never even been shopping alone before, and you think we should ride hundreds of miles across two states by ourselves?" Hanna huffs and returns to her spot on the bed with Liam.

"Do you think it's safe to be so close to cities, Garrett?" I ask.

My mind replays the shooting at the pharmacy today. No plan will be foolproof or safe. What I wouldn't give for a running vehicle—even a sweaty, sardine-packed bus sounds better than the trip ahead.

"Obviously, we should avoid them as much as possible, but they'll be there if we need them."

"I really hope it's only this area. Maybe everything beyond here is normal. Maybe they don't even know there's a problem." Even as the words leave my lips, I know I don't believe them. I can't put my finger on why I'm so certain, but I am. My best-case-scenario attitude is on hiatus.

"That would be nice." Evelynn hums beside me. "Let's hope for that but be prepared for anything."

"Good plan," Garrett agrees. He looks over at Liam and Hanna, who have their heads down, whispering among themselves. "You guys got anything to add?"

Hanna's head lifts up slowly, her eyes watery with unshed tears. "I guess I'm coming. But for the record, I think this is the wrong decision."

Chapter Nine

THE SCHOOL IS COLD and dark now. We ate dinner in the commons by candlelight—each of us were assigned one personal candle and a pack of matches. Then we were sent back to our rooms for the evening. We agreed to meet Garrett and Liam behind the recreation building once everyone had gone to bed for the night, which had taken a lot longer than we thought. Ms. Kay walked up and down the halls for what seemed like hours.

When we feel we've waited long enough, I check the hallway to make sure the coast is clear. "I think it's safe. Are we ready to do this?"

Evelynn nods, handing me my backpack. Hanna doesn't speak but tightens her own backpack on her shoulders.

We sneak through the hallway, taking the emergency exit down the classroom hall, hoping to avoid waking Ms. Kay. Even though I am sure we could still go if the teachers caught us, leaving without alerting the other students seems smarter. And all of us leaving as a huge group seems more dangerous.

The moon beams its bright light on us, illuminating our path. While it's great for visibility, the light makes me feel exposed.

My full backpack slaps against my back softly when I pick up my pace. Evelynn and Hanna are behind me, letting me lead the way. Then I hear a crash inside the rec building and pause, holding my breath. The girls knock into me from behind at my abrupt stop.

"What was that?" Evelynn whispers.

"Geez, Liam, be careful." We hear Garrett's voice, and I exhale. We're far enough from the main building that no one should have heard the crash, but I'm still on edge. It won't do us any good to get caught before we've even started.

The three of us hurry around the corner and see the door is ajar. At that moment, Garrett comes through the opening carrying a tent bag and carefully steering one last bike; four other bikes and helmets are already lined up outside the door. Liam comes out behind him, candle in one hand and massaging the back of his head with the other.

"Sorry, man, I thought I had it. I didn't mean to knock myself in the damn head with the camping supplies!"

"You found the tents?" Hanna asks. I hear a little bit of excitement in her voice. Maybe she'll feel better about all of this when she realizes that Garrett is preparing us for the worst the best that he can.

"Tent," Liam says. "There's only one left. The rest of them must have been thrown out after that skunk incident."

"Will we all fit in one tent?" Hanna crosses her hands over her chest, pleasant tone forgotten. So much for her excitement.

"It's a four-person tent; it'll do," Garrett says, throwing her a helmet. "Besides, we have to be careful not to carry too much with us."

I try to fasten my helmet, but my fingers shake, and I fumble the nylon strap. I've been ready for hours, but now the fear is settling in.

Garrett gets his own helmet on and then turns to me. The moonlight reflects in his dark eyes as he reaches to fasten mine. "You good?"

I nod. I *am* good—I'm filled with adrenaline and praying we're making the right choice. Once we're all on our bikes and heading toward the highway, I sneak one last glance at the school that has always felt like my safe place. I half expect to see someone running after us or candlelight flickering in one of the windows, but it's quiet and dark.

Ready or not, we're on our way.

We sneak through the town of Hidden Maples, careful not to make any unnecessary noise. If we're lucky, we can get onto the main highway without anyone ever knowing we've been here.

The commotion from this morning has long passed, and all the storefronts are dark and quiet. There are items strewn across the roadway and sidewalks, likely abandoned in haste during the shootout. There is also a suspicious dark spot on the ground near the pharmacy, and I'm thankful it's too dark to investigate it any further.

Garrett leads the way, Evelynn and I are paired behind him, and Liam and Hanna take up the rear. None of us has said a word since we left campus, but we're keeping a good pace and have yet to stop for any breaks. All of us are amped up with fear and anticipation, but we have days of riding ahead of us, and I refuse to be the first one to ask for a water break or to stop to go to the bathroom.

The wind has picked up a little over the last few miles, and it's so quiet that the leaves blow across the road and make strange rustling sounds. The sound reminds me of a memory from kindergarten. We had this little brown gerbil that would wait until quiet time to rustle around in her cage. The sound always made falling asleep at nap time impossible, which irritated me and made me feel anxious.

The sound of the leaves has the same grating effect on me now. How will we hear danger coming if that sound doesn't stop?

It's so dark without any streetlamps or light pollution from cars and buildings. The stars and the moon cast a nice glow that allows us to see the road but not much beyond that. A blanket of blackness is upon us, which I suppose is fitting.

As we leave the town limits and make the final turn onto the highway, I feel myself sigh and relax. We've made it through the first step; only two-hundred-plus miles to go.

A handful of cars are abandoned on the highway in the beginning, but not as many as I expected to see. I imagine as we get closer to some of the bigger cities, we'll find more of them.

A little red sedan sits with all four doors hanging open, but it doesn't appear to be occupied. Liam's voice booms from the back—it's not really any louder than normal, but after so much silence, hearing someone speak at all feels jarring.

"I gotta take a piss. Can we stop for a second? I'll walk to the side real quick," he says.

"Sure," Garrett answers him, coming to a stop ahead of me. Evelynn and I stopped as well, careful not to bump into him. "We should all take a little bathroom break and drink some water. We'll ride until first light and then try to get some rest."

"Ugh, we're going to ride all night long?" Hanna asks. "I'm so tired already and sweaty, too. Isn't that bad? Being sweaty when it's cold out?"

"Well, it's not ideal," Evelynn says. "Maybe take off the sweater under your coat for now. Tuck it in the top of your backpack in case you feel cold later and need to put it back on."

I take a few sips of water from the bottle on my bike before setting the kickstand and heading behind the nearest car to squat and pee. I'm careful to go on the side opposite Liam. I'm not trying to flash the boys while I relieve myself. "Don't come over here. I'm going to pee!" I yell over my shoulder. Evelynn laughs and tells me she's coming, too.

"Do you think Hanna is still mad at me?" I whisper to Evelynn when we've finished our bathroom break.

"Yeah, she probably will be until we get to Portland. Then she'll forget all about it. She's scared."

"We're all scared. I hope she knows I'm scared, too. I want to do something. Anything. Sitting around waiting seemed like the worst option available to us."

"Babe, you don't have to convince me. I'm in, okay? Let's get home." Evelynn gives me a side hug, and I squeeze her back with force. We have a long way to go, but hopefully she's wrong and Hanna will come around sooner rather than later. I hate knowing she's upset with me.

"Let's get going, ladies! We have a lot of ground to cover," Garrett yells, and we rush back to our bikes. The sooner we can get this over with the better.

At the first sign of the sunrise, Garrett finally lets us stop. We've ridden so many miles, my legs are screaming and my butt hurts from the uncomfortable bike seat. Normally, I'd try to keep my butt off the seat, but the added weight from my pack makes it almost impossible to sustain that position.

So much of this part of the ride is flat—farms and vineyards as far as I can tell. I don't see anywhere for us to hide from view by the roadway, so we move off the trail about a mile to set up the tent. At least this way we might see someone coming before they're right on top of us. *If anyone is even out here.*

We have to walk our bikes through the farming soil to get far enough away from the main road. The air smells like farm animals and wet earth. We trip over old corn stalks and uneven ground as we go before finally dropping our bikes and bags with loud relieved sighs. We don't waste any time unloading the tent on the flattest spot we can find.

While the sticker on the side does claim that it's a four-person tent, I'm not sure what four people they mean. Four hobbits, perhaps? The tent looks surprisingly small once it's set up. Add the fact that there are five of us, not four, and it's a really tight fit. But this is what we have to work with, and it's better than being fully exposed to the elements.

We are all tired, sweaty, and sore by the time the tent is up. The sky has exploded with pinks and oranges, rising behind us as if to say it has our back.

The last road sign we passed said we were still 150 miles from Portland. Riding uphill in some places slowed us down significantly. If I had to guess, I'd say we've ridden for somewhere around eight hours, which meant we were averaging less than ten miles an hour—a lot slower than we had originally thought we would be moving. But the weight from our gear, the cold weather, and the hills have slowed us down considerably. Two-hundred-and-twenty miles is a big commitment, but we've made our choice now. There is no turning back.

None of us have talked much since we stopped riding. Not that we talked much while we were riding, either. We kept a steady but often slow pace, trying not to burn ourselves out right out of the gate. I worry that the longer we are out here, the worse the mood will get, but I can't see us picking up the pace much without a fight.

We take off our shoes and unroll our sleeping bags. If the girls all sleep one direction and the boys sleep sideways at our feet, we can make it work without being too uncomfortable.

"Should someone stay up and keep watch?" Liam asks, looking up and down the road in both directions.

"I thought about it, but we haven't seen anyone, and we all really need to rest," Garrett answers. "A couple hours, and we're out of here, so we need to make it count."

Garrett looks defeated. We all do. The weight of our situation is hard to avoid once we're out in the middle of nowhere. We don't have any way to defend ourselves, and Garrett and I saw firsthand how quickly things could turn violent.

I climb in the tent behind Evelynn. Hanna is already on the far left, so I take the far right, the most possible space I can give her. Evelynn naturally takes the spot in the middle, giving me a reassuring arm squeeze when she sees me frowning.

It's cold, so I leave all of my layers on and climb inside my sleeping bag. With our bags in the tent, we have even less room, but we're too afraid to leave them out in the open. Leaving our bikes out there is scary enough.

Garrett piles our bags up in a line just inside the tent door, and he and Liam squeeze in. None of us have much room, but we're all too tired to complain or care. I close my eyes and feel sleep taking me right away.

If only sleep could fix everything.

Chapter Ten

Far too soon, Evelynn is shaking my shoulder and telling me it's time to get up. I'm the last one in the tent, and apparently, I was out cold. My limbs feel stiff and tired, my mind is hazy, and my vision is clouded with sleep. I want to stay here and sleep all day, but I know that's not an option, so I hurry from my sleeping bag and roll it up neatly.

I won't be the last one ready to go. Hanna will call me on that for sure.

Outside, everyone is eating a quick breakfast of granola bars and fruit. Hanna glares at me, sitting cross-legged next to Liam. I try to avoid her gaze as much as possible, sliding my shoes on and eating my breakfast quickly.

Garrett sits beside me and drapes his arm over my shoulders. "Good morning, sleeping beauty." He laughs. "You want to help me take the tent down?"

"Absolutely." I smile back, thankful for his playfulness. *At least one person isn't mad at me.*

"Pull up the stakes on that corner, and lean the tent pole out toward you. Then you can easily fold it up." Garrett points to the far corner of the tent as I follow his directions.

I watch him do the same from the other side, and the tent collapses easily. "What's the plan today?" I ask quietly, staring at the ground. "We're not nearly as far as I hoped we'd be."

Our bodies have left a distinct spot behind, a square imprint in the dirt—the only evidence of our overnight stay that we'll be leaving behind. I focus on the pattern, trying not to feel overwhelmed by the large task ahead of us.

"We have to stick with it. Keep pushing forward. I don't want anyone to get too tired, but we should keep a steady pace. The longer we're out in the open, the more likely we are to run into people, and you can never predict how that will go. As we witnessed in town yesterday, it can get bad fast."

"It's crazy to think that was yesterday morning. It feels like weeks ago already."

We fold the tent into a small rectangle, and Garrett stuffs it back in the storage bag with the poles. "Thank you." He pulls me close, resting his chin on top of my head. "And, Selena, don't worry about Hanna. She'll come around."

I don't answer him, because I don't know if he's right, but I do appreciate that he's trying to make me feel better. I feel the weight of his arms around me, and I press my hands into his back, bringing him a little closer. His clothes still hold a hint of his cologne, and he feels warm and solid in my arms. We've known each other most of our lives, and I always felt like our friendship could grow, but I never imagined it would quite like this.

"Hey, lovebirds," Evelynn calls out from behind the pile of bikes and backpacks. "Let's get moving!"

Garrett laughs, and I reluctantly let him go, throwing a sheepish grin in Evelynn's direction. I refuse to have a bad attitude today.

We rejoin the group. I reattach my sleeping bag to my backpack, and Garrett uses bungee cords to attach the tent to the outside of his. It looks like it could fall off with very little effort, but he made it work all day yesterday. I sigh. This would all be so much easier if we had a car, but then, if cars and electronics were working, would any of this be necessary in the first place?

We resume our ride in the same order we rode before: Garrett leads the way, Evelynn and I are right behind him, and Liam and Hanna take up the rear. I glance behind me to see how far back they are and notice their two helmets reflecting the sunlight back at us. They're not close but still close enough for me to see the daggers Hanna's eyes are throwing at me. *Seriously?* We're all out here together; she's going to have to be a team player at some point. I didn't force her to come with us.

I turn my head back around and try to ignore my hurt feelings. She'll get over it eventually—at least Garrett and Evelynn both seem to think so.

Evelynn sings old pop songs as we ride, and I watch the landscapes go by. I'm too stuck in my head to sing along with her; even Taylor Swift can't pull me out of my thoughts. I simply stare at farmland, vineyards, small rivers, and creeks.

The further west we get, the greener everything becomes. We pass by some small towns, and the houses we can see all look dilapidated and unoccupied. Sheltered in the Academy, we haven't seen the reality of the pandemic like others have, only the slowly disappearing student body and whatever we could gather from the limited news we were allowed to see.

I remember hearing on the news that more and more people were dying. First, the elderly people with weak immune systems and other underlying health problems, but then healthy, younger people were dying, too. Everyone had seen it over the last few decades, and in some ways, we'd become almost numb to it. We wore our masks, followed the protocols, stayed quarantined at school, but how much of it had been downplayed and hidden from us? From the looks of things, a lot.

The viruses had multiplied and mutated, each time becoming stronger, more resilient to vaccines and treatments. Young, old, healthy, rich—no one was spared. It went after humans, equally affecting all genders, ages, and races. It didn't discriminate.

The year before last, before they started canceling our breaks and keeping us from going home, millions of people all over the world seemed to perish overnight. No one had any answers. Nothing seemed to slow the death rates down. Even the people who didn't believe in the beginning couldn't argue it away anymore. Not when everyone had lost someone.

Seeing these complete ghost towns with my own eyes, knowing that the lockdowns and quarantines hadn't been enough to stop our world from collapsing, sits on my chest like a heavy weight. As much as I want to be upset with my parents for leaving me at the Academy when we could have been together through all of this, I can't blame them.

We're taking a risk with the viruses even now. Being out here, we could be exposed to any number of viruses, but without power, without a way to contact anyone we love, what is the alternative? To sit and wait and hope that everything turns out okay? *No, forget that.*

We'd go crazy doing that. Most of us were already stir crazy. Frustrated, scared, and alone.

Garrett slows down to ride beside me. "Penny for your thoughts?"

I see Evelynn push up in front, giving us some space to talk. She looks back at me for confirmation before pushing even further ahead. "I was thinking about all the people we've lost. Everywhere I look, I see empty houses and boarded up businesses. It hits harder when you're seeing it for yourself."

"I know what you mean. Being at school made me feel protected, like I was inside this bubble of denial. We were some of the lucky ones."

I imagine a giant dome over the school, protecting us from the outside world. It did feel like that sometimes. At least at first. "Yeah, until some of the kids stopped coming back. And the teachers."

I sigh, thinking about my favorite teacher, Mr. Hamrick. He'd been one of the first to leave despite being a former professional athlete and arguably the healthiest adult in the school. It happened so fast. One day, he was sniffling in class, and the next, he was escorted off campus for medical treatment. By the following Monday, he had been removed from the school directory completely.

When I felt at my lowest, Mr. Hamrick had always been the one to turn me around.

He'd pulled me aside on a particularly hard day, and we'd shared wheat crackers in his classroom. When I told him I felt lost and wasn't sure the direction my future was heading at school, he'd let me cry it out. But then he'd said something to me I'll never forget.

"*You can decide what to do on a rainy day, Selena. Grab an umbrella and stay dry, or go dance in the rain. There's no such thing as bad weather or a bad day. There are only choices on how to navigate your circumstances. And there's always more than one path to happiness. If the first path isn't right, choose another one."*

I'd felt his loss deeply, but I'd held it in, afraid to put a name to it. Afraid to admit, even to myself, the true weight of our situation.

We hadn't even had time to mourn his leaving before the next teachers disappeared from school. I think, deep down, we knew they were sick, that they didn't come back because they were no longer breathing. But if we didn't admit that, we could convince ourselves they'd gone on to new jobs.

"But we were lying to ourselves, weren't we? They were sick, and we ignored it." I shudder, ashamed of myself for being so selfish. So eager to push away the truth.

"They left the school; we didn't actually watch them deteriorate like we would have if we were out here and not secluded at the Academy."

I tighten my grip on my handlebars. "I guess you're right. I don't know if I'd call us lucky, though. We lost a lot of good people: family, friends, teachers…"

I think about Kelly, and I wonder if Garrett knew when she left that she wouldn't be coming back. She was our roommate, but her circle of friends was different. She tolerated us, but Evelynn, Hanna, and I were the last people she'd call her confidants.

I open my mouth to ask him but close it just as fast. If he wants to talk about Kelly, he can bring her up himself. I'm not torturing him with that subject again, at least not so soon.

Garrett lets out a long breath. "But we're still here. And we owe it to the ones who aren't to keep fighting. We can't hide anymore; we have to find out what's happening and try to fix it."

I nod, because I like the sound of what he's saying. Deep down, I can't help but remind myself that we're a bunch of kids—what the heck are we going to do? I want to get home and hug my parents and have them tell me everything is going to be okay. That they'll fix it. I hold on to that picture in my head.

It's not even close to dark, which means we have a lot of good riding time left in the day. My bike tires make funny noises as they scrape against the road, and I let the noise lull my brain into silence. The elevation changes slightly as we ride, up and down, curving around the road.

Soon, we should run into the bigger interstate, the one that will follow the Columbia River west to Portland. We will cross the river when we can and take the 84 the rest of the way. I think Evelynn said the town where we cross over is called White Salmon. I'm looking forward to getting across the bridge. It's a landmark that will prove we're getting closer to our destination.

We stop a few times to take bathroom breaks and drink water and once to eat a small lunch. We're close to the town of Maryhill when we stop, but we're careful to stay out of sight of the town. If our calculations and the road signs are right, we've gone about thirty-five miles so far today, giving us a total mileage of around a hundred miles for the two days since we started. We have so much more to go.

This close to the river, the area should be getting more populated. I'm worried about the fact that we haven't seen another human since we left the school. A few more broken cars litter this area, and I swear I see a corpse in one. Part of me wonders if the whole world is dead and we're the last of it.

My muscles hurt, and I'd give anything for the pain in my backside to ease. The bike seats are not meant for such a long trek or the weight of our backpacks. Despite that, today the ride is physically a little easier. If we make it out of this, I'll have to thank our fitness instructor for keeping us in fighting shape.

As strong as I feel physically, emotionally, today feels much harder. Hanna still won't make eye contact with me, but she did pass me an apple earlier without saying anything snippy. I consider that progress. Evelynn rode with her and Liam for a while, so at least one of us is talking to her.

Garrett and I chat on and off about school, avoiding any talk of our current situation. We remind each other about our hilarious French teacher from a few years ago and how she'd come to class every day in a different pair of rubber boots, always with googly-eyes and a matching umbrella. She'd sit at her desk like that, boots up, her umbrella open inside the classroom and attached precariously to the back of her chair. We laugh until I feel tears leaking from my eyes.

"Yeah, but she had nothing on the Spanish teacher!" Garrett laughs. "Remember her wigs? What was up with those women?"

"Maybe they had a secret club?" I smile, but it doesn't hold. Both teachers had been taken from us. Garrett gives me a knowing look and sighs. Everything, even the funny memories, lead us back to this depressing situation. We simply can't escape it.

"Hey, I'm starving. Are we almost done for the day or what?" Evelynn's voice breaks through my sad thoughts. I agree with her on the hunger pains—my stomach has been growling for miles now.

"We haven't made it quite as far as we did yesterday," Liam protests. "I feel like we should keep riding until we're ready to stop."

Hanna whines. "What if some of us are already there? I have blisters on my blisters, and I could really use a break. We have so far to go. Are we on some speed-demon schedule or something?"

Liam points at a sign up ahead that reads: *Hidden Canyon Trailhead: 2 miles.* "I've been to this trailhead before!" he says excitedly. "Personally, I think we should ride more, but if we really wanted a safe place to stop, that could be it. It's off the road and has trees and some waterfalls and creeks where we could refill our water bottles. It's still light enough that we could make that work in our favor. And we're not that far from the bridge now, so first thing tomorrow, we could be crossing over into Oregon!"

"You've been here before?" Hanna eyes him.

"Sometimes, my brother would do special training for the military. He let us tag along, and we would turn the training time into family camping trips. Since it's outdoors and not very populated, they allowed it." His eyes light up as he looks at each of us in turn. "It's a good place to stop."

I agree that we should keep riding, but seeing the relief on Evelynn's and Hanna's faces by the suggestion makes me cave. What's the harm in having a safe night's sleep? We should probably be careful to conserve energy. And we *are* almost out of water.

"What do you think?" I ask Garrett quietly.

"We have to keep morale up, so I think we should stop. It's not the best plan, but it is a solid one. We've covered around 120 miles, but at least so far, the weather has held."

It does make sense; we have to keep everyone getting along, and it won't help us if someone gets too tired to keep going. We can't afford any injuries, either. I can admit when I'm overruled.

"Okay, Liam, lead the way!" I yell behind me and watch as he speeds up to take the lead. I'll feel much better tomorrow when we're back on Oregon land. Even if nothing looks familiar to me, it helps knowing we're one step closer to home.

The sun hovers above the horizon to the west, the sky exploding into cotton candy pinks and blues. We busted our butts and finished setting up camp faster than we anticipated. I am sitting on the ground watching the sunset when Garrett nudges me from behind. "Hey, wanna take a little walk with me?"

My face instantly heats at the idea of spending time alone with him, even if it is only on a trail in the woods.

Our solo trip to town had been more about the mission than spending time together, and the movie night had been a fiasco of its own. Neither of those things were actual dates, were they? Are we even dating? We haven't even discussed whether we are a *we*. Nothing about us getting together has been normal. Maybe that's what he wants to talk to me about? Butterflies flutter in my stomach.

Would he try to kiss me?

Kissing the top of my head aside, he's only ever been friendly with me.

I stand and dust the dirt from my hands onto my pants. "Sure, sounds good," I say. My voice comes out much calmer than I feel.

He takes my hand in his. It's clammy, and I hold back a laugh. Maybe Garrett is feeling as nervous about this as I am.

It seems silly to be worried about a boy when the world is falling down around us, especially a boy I've known for most of my life. I don't know when I stopped seeing Garrett as the little kid who liked to steal all my pencils and started seeing him as someone that I might invite to a school dance, but it was changing. It had already changed.

"We're going to look for some more firewood. We'll be back," Garrett says to the group.

"Get a lot of it; take your time." Evelynn laughs. She's taken it upon herself to find rocks to make a firepit. Liam and Hanna have their backs turned to us. They've piled up all our food supplies and are working on sorting them out to divide them equally between us. A somber mood has settled among everyone, and I'm relieved to sneak away from the doom and gloom and be a teenage girl for a minute.

It's beautiful up here, away from the road. From our vantage point, the small lake below looks like an untouched sheet of glass. I take deep breaths of the fresh fall air. The dirt beneath my feet feels uneven, and my legs are wobbly from riding, but being out in nature and not cooped up at school or sweating on the back of my bike feels healing.

Garrett tugs me along, holding back the long tree branches for me to pass by without getting smacked in the face. When we're out of earshot of the group, he finally turns to face me, taking my other hand in his and holding them both loosely.

"I know we haven't really had any alone time since before we left the Academy, and I wanted to talk to you."

My tongue feels too big for my mouth, so I nod instead of trying to respond. He looks up at the sky and then back to me.

"I like you, Selena. I have for a while. And this seems like the worst time to come out and say that, but maybe it's the only time we'll have. So there it is." He squeezes both of my hands.

Twelve years we've lived at the Academy, from kindergarten to now, and so much has changed. Garrett's eyes are still the same familiar shade of deep brown, but the boy inside seems more like a stranger to me than before.

I'd always seen him with someone like Kelly. No, not someone *like* her, with Kelly herself. Perfectly poised and put together.

Granted, they'd never come out as a couple officially, and I'd never seen them do anything that would say they were together in that way, but it was one of those things we all knew. *Wasn't it?*

But Kelly isn't here. Hasn't been for an entire year. All that time, I've ignored the signs that Garrett and I are teetering on some kind of tightrope. And here he is, taking a leap. Am I brave enough to follow him? Do I want to follow him?

Garrett bites his lip. "Please say something, Selena."

His timing is awful, but I think of Mr. Hamrick and his quote about rainy days. I smile, but the smile quickly morphs into a full-on laugh. "Wow, Garrett. It took the end of the world for you to tell me you like me?"

His laugh is deep and full. The rumble of it sends vibrations of happiness through my chest. "I guess it probably seems that way, but I wanted to tell you before. I couldn't decide if I thought you liked me back or not."

"Seriously?" My eyes narrow at him. "I've been an awkward mess around you for as long as I can remember. I thought for sure you were trying to let me down gently." *And there was the whole Kelly thing.*

Garrett's jaw drops open. "Um, you are not an awkward mess. You're adorable."

My cheeks flame with heat, and I thank him. He pulls me into one of his tight hugs. "We don't have to figure anything out right now; I just wanted you to know," he says.

I nod against him. He's right—there's no reason to push anything now. But it does feel nice to have the words out there.

"When this is all over, I'll take you out on a real date. What do you say?"

I hold up my hands, a hysterical giggle leaving my lips. "Only if you promise it won't require a bike ride."

"Definitely no bike rides," he agrees, his chest heaving with his own laughter. We smile at each other, taking a moment to revel in the small happy corner of the world we've created, stealing a minute more.

Before we can get too comfortable in our little bubble, though, Garrett motions back toward the camp. "We should get some wood for the fire and head back; the sun will be down soon."

Reluctantly, I help him gather the wood, letting the reality of where we are sink back into my mind. But all the while, my brain won't let go of one simple fact: Garrett wants to take me out on a date.

It's such a silly thing to even consider when we're on the adventure of our lives and everything is hanging in the balance. We have so much to figure out, far too many miles left to navigate. Hanna isn't even talking to me because the stakes are that great.

I'm trying to ignore the very real possibility that the date Garrett wants to take me on will never happen. That the bitter end of everything we've ever hoped for is all that awaits us at the completion of this journey.

At some point, I'll have to ask Garrett to tell me about Kelly. Did he know she was leaving school before the rest of us? Were their trips to the lake more than friendly? I'll have to unravel the mystery of what they were to each other. Especially if we're going to have any chance of starting something real of our own. For now, that feels like it can wait.

Despite the storm raging around me, I feel like I'm dancing in the rain.

Chapter Eleven

Garrett and I bring plenty of wood back to camp, and once we have a good fire going, Liam passes out dinner. A lemon protein bar and a fruit cup for each of us do little to satiate our hunger, but none of us complain. We know we have to ration our food to be safe. While we have a little stash of food between us, it won't be enough to make it through to Portland, especially if we get delayed or keep up this slower pace. Tomorrow, we will try to find a store in White Salmon before we cross the bridge. I have nerves just thinking about it.

Evelynn leans into me, placing her head on my shoulder. "I'm so tired. Do you girls want to come lay with me in the tent?" she asks quietly.

"Sure, I'm tired, too," I say, leaning my head against hers.

Hanna glares at us from across the fire. I see more than the flames reflecting in her eyes. "I'm good. I'll stay out here with Liam and Garrett for a little longer."

She's still mad, but I'm not letting it get to me anymore. I sigh and follow Evelynn into the tent. She's already pulled my sleeping bag out for me and placed it in my designated spot.

"Thanks." I smile, climbing into the welcoming cocoon that is my sleeping bag. The ground is hard and bumpy here with little pebbles in the dirt making patterns across the tent floor. The tent smells like plastic and feet. I'd give anything to be back in our room in the familiar cloud of body spray.

"Sure thing." She sits up, hovering over me. Her whispers seem too loud. "Now, tell me what you and Garrett got up to in the woods!"

"Shh." I laugh. "There's not much to tell. He said he wants to take me on a date when this is all over."

Evelynn frowns, her blue eyes flooded with confusion. "Seriously? That's it?"

"What did you want me to do—launch myself at him?" I lift my arm and push her over onto her own sleeping bag. She snorts with laughter.

"I can't believe he didn't try to kiss you. What is the boy waiting for? He's not as smart as I thought he was. I was sitting back here imagining all the trouble you two were getting into in the woods. I thought for sure your hair would have twigs in it or something."

She's ridiculous, but her words make me wonder. "I don't think we've had anything close to that moment yet. Maybe it's not really like that between us. Yeah, he says he likes me, but what does that even mean? Maybe what he had with Kelly was... more."

"Promise me something?" She's quieter now, and I roll on my side to hear her better.

"Within reason—"

She clicks her tongue at me. "Next time you're alone with a cute boy that you clearly have feelings for, don't let him get away without kissing you."

I roll onto my back and stare at the top of the tent. It hadn't felt like the right time to kiss Garrett. In fact, not once when I've been alone with him have I felt the overwhelming urge to kiss him. I obviously like him; I've had a crush on him forever. But it doesn't feel like the books I've read. I don't feel sparks flying between us. I get butterflies from the attention, but I'm not overwhelmed with attraction or anything like that. We're friends. I thought that was how it was supposed to start.

"What's it like? Kissing someone, I mean." I'm embarrassed to ask the question. I'm the last one of us to kiss a boy. Hanna was the first, and Evelynn joined the ranks two summers ago. I feel like the Academy stunted my growth in the relationship department. Or maybe it wouldn't matter where I went to school. Maybe I just haven't been ready for that.

Evelynn sighs. "Honestly?"

"No, lie to me." I push her shoulder playfully. "Of course, honestly."

"It's a little underwhelming. At least, it was when I kissed Tyler Adams. It was slobbery and weird. I think maybe it has to be the right guy at the exact right moment." She gets quiet, and we both lie there in silence for a while. Evelynn had been infatuated with Tyler since the moment he'd sprouted up to six feet in the seventh grade. Before that, she'd hardly noticed him. But he was too big to ignore now.

When we came back from summer break that year, she told us that she'd finally kissed him. But as much as we tried, she never gave us the details. Now, I realize she was saving us from her own disappointment.

"Maybe I take back what I said before. Maybe only kiss a boy if you're ready to be disappointed."

The monotone way she says it makes me laugh. "But you really liked Tyler. I'm surprised."

Evelynn smiles. "I still like him, only now I know we're better off as friends. I didn't feel what I expected to. I want sparks, fireworks, the whole deal."

"And you think that exists?"

"It has to. I feel this pull when I'm painting. It's like my whole body is taken over by a warmth I've never known, like I'm floating in the sky. I've felt it often enough through my art to know that passion truly exists."

I nod, wanting to feel what she's describing. "You think a person can make you feel that way?"

"People write whole novels about it. Songs, paintings, giant monuments... I definitely believe in it. We only have to find it. Find them."

"I'd be content with finding our way home for now." This trip is wearing me out, and we've barely gotten started.

"We'll get there." She yawns. "This is what we get for asking for an adventurous senior year."

"Are you scared of what we'll find?" I ask the question, but I don't know if I'm asking Evelynn or myself. The only response I get is Evelynn's soft snoring. So I roll over, close my eyes, and wait for sleep to take me, too.

Chapter Twelve

We're pros at breaking down camp now, which means we are quickly back on our bikes this morning. Before too long, we see homes and businesses pop up along the interstate as we enter the small town of White Salmon, where we will cross the bridge to Oregon.

Liam and Hanna are leading today. Evelynn and I ride next to Garrett behind them, bobbing around obstacles in the road.

"Hey, let's take this exit," Liam calls out. "There's a sign for a drugstore right off the road—maybe they'll have some supplies left."

My stomach lurches, fear bubbling inside like carbonation. So far, we've been blissfully alone on the road. We haven't had to talk to anyone or worry too much about people and their motives. I know we need food, but I'd almost risk starving over going into another store after the scene Garrett and I witnessed.

We follow him, taking the off-ramp and weaving through the side streets to the large drugstore. I see broken glass in the parking lot, and it's clear we're not the first ones to stop here. I'd hoped we'd find a happy, bustling town, with both electricity and life, but the outage has clearly made it here as well.

We carefully hide our bikes behind a couple of long-forgotten movie rental machines near the front door. The store appears empty and abandoned, but someone could be inside.

"We should mask up." I drop my backpack and pull out my mask and goggles. Evelynn nods and does the same. The others quickly follow. Having one of us get sick out here won't do us any good.

One more thing for us to worry about.

"I'll go in first, make sure no one's lurking," Liam volunteers.

"I'll go with you. The girls can watch the door while we make sure it's clear." Garrett pats my arm. "We'll call out when it's safe to come inside."

"Be careful," I say, squeezing one of his gloved hands.

Hanna joins me and Evelynn at the doors, and the boys slip in carefully, avoiding the jagged glass left behind. My heart hammers hard in my chest. It's not dark in there—the skylights allow for plenty of sunlight to get through—but I still feel nervous.

"If they die, it's on you," Hanna huffs, turning her narrowed brown eyes on me. "You talked us into all this after all."

"Alright, Hanna. I can't take it anymore," Evelynn interjects. "You can lay off Selena; she's trying to get us home." I watch the two girls square off at each other and feel sick to my stomach.

I throw my hands up in the air. "Listen, I love you both, okay? I'm doing what I think is best. You didn't have to come, Hanna, but here you are. I think Garrett is right, that this is our best chance. We need to get home, find our parents, and hopefully figure out what to do about all of this." My voice wavers with emotion. "I'm scared, too, it's just... I can't sit around and wait to die. At least this way, we're doing something."

Evelynn starts to cry; she pulls her long blonde hair into a ponytail with shaky hands. "We're all scared, but we can't turn on each other."

Hanna stares down at her feet. "I'm sorry, but I really think this is a bad idea. And it hurt my feelings that you took Garrett's side without even talking to me about what I thought we should do."

"What do you think we should have done, Han?" I ask softly, all the fight draining from my limbs. "I could have asked you, that's fair, but what other options are there?"

"I think we should have waited for help to come. We're a bunch of stupid teenagers, Selena. What the hell are we supposed to do? We can't get the power back on or cure anyone... we probably would have been safe back at the school, waiting for our parents to come find us. Not the other way around." She crosses her arms over her chest. "But it's whatever. Liam says I'm the only one who feels that way, so here I am. I don't hate you, Selena; I'm just scared. It's easier to blame you than to think about how terrified I am all the time."

"I don't understand why you blame me for any of this. What the heck did I do?"

Evelynn reaches out to touch Hanna's wild red curls. "I'm scared, too, Hanna; we all are."

"Yeah, well, Selena never looks scared. It makes me furious." She sounds angry, but she winks at me when she says it.

I feel a smile touch my own lips. "You think I'm not scared?"

She nods. "Would it kill you to *pretend* you're terrified, at least?"

"Oh, I'm freaking beyond terrified. Why do you think I agreed to leave school so fast? I need to be doing something so I don't go crazy."

Hanna sighs, crossing her arms over her chest. Her shoulders slump, and I feel like I can see her angry façade slipping away muscle by muscle.

We haven't had any real beef between the three of us in a few years. I can't even remember what the last fight was about because we usually work through whatever is bothering us before it can become a big issue. That's what makes this fight seem extra hard. We're like sisters... no matter what is going on in our lives, we still love each other; that never changes. Only this time, the realization feels heavier than it ever was before. The stakes have never been so great. But now that Hanna is finally talking to me, I feel the slightest shift in that weight.

Evelynn sighs loudly, as if the weight is lifting from her shoulders, too. "Can we promise to get along from this point on at least?" She thrusts her pinky out for our standard pinky-promise.

"I'll even promise to whine about how scared I am if Hanna will be nice to me again," I say, offering my pinky.

The three of us nod in agreement, linking pinkies in surrender.

Hanna finally smiles. "Now that everything is settled, please know, if either of you say anything about me and Liam, I'll punch you in the throat."

Evelynn's eyes go wide with mock surprise. "There's a 'me and Liam'?" She gasps.

"Well, not officially, but there will be." She grins. My heart squeezes with relief that, for now at least, we seem to be back on track.

"You'll have to let me paint your first couples portrait when we get back." Evelynn laughs. "I've been dying to try out this new red-orange paint combination for your hair."

A crash sounds from inside the store, and we all turn to see what's caused the commotion. Liam is standing up on top of a cash register counter doing a victory dance, his arms in the air as he whoops and hollers. "Coast is clear, girls. Let's make this quick!"

I bump Hanna with my hip. "That's your man? You're claiming him?"

Hanna rolls her eyes, and the three of us break into giggles. At least it seems I finally have my friend back.

We enter the store together, careful not to make too much noise in case anyone is nearby.

Clearly, we're not the first group to come through looking for supplies. Most of the shelves and clothing racks are empty. Hangers and packages litter the floor, and it smells like a bottle of vinegar must have spilled at some point. It's a giant mess, but no one is here, so we hurry to grab whatever we can.

We scavenge, packing as many cans as we are able to find into an extra backpack Liam found. It's a red kids' backpack with a happy blue dinosaur on the front, and unfortunately, we can only find peas and beans in cans to stuff inside it. Hanna makes a good find: a box of fiber bars in the mostly empty vitamin section.

Evelynn nudges me in the side. "Will you help me find some pads or tampons or something? I'm supposed to start my period any day, and I don't want to be out there with nothing to use." I nod at her, pulling her around the corner to the family planning aisle.

We catch Liam stuffing his pockets with condoms. He jumps when he sees us. His mask hides his face, but I can guess it's a dark shade of red. "What? You never know! It's the end of the world; gotta be prepared!" He grabs another box before running in the opposite direction.

Laughter breaks through my fear, though I wonder what Hanna would think about his shopping choices. Evelynn shakes her head.

I manage to find a single box of tampons in the mess of boxes that have been shoved to the floor. I toss them to her, and she thanks me before shoving them into the dino backpack. We hurry back to the front of the store.

I shiver involuntarily. "We should get out of here; this place gives me the creeps."

"Yeah, I second that," Evelynn says. Garrett nods behind her. "The sooner we leave, the sooner we get home."

We load our backpacks with our scavenged supplies. Because we're now slightly overloaded, I have to loop my sleeping bag over my bike handles. But it's better than being caught out in the wilderness with nothing.

The sun is bright today, and the air is slightly cooler than yesterday. We're all bundled in layers with our thick coats on. We must look ridiculous, so overloaded on our bikes, but we don't have much choice.

Garrett and Liam take over the lead with the three of us girls riding in silence together. It's a comfortable silence at least, now that Hanna is actually talking to me again.

We reach the bridge that we need, and I grip my handlebars even tighter when the boys venture onto it seemingly without a care in the world. The bridge is made of grated steel, and as we make our way across, I can see the water far below through the tiny holes in the metal. I feel sick riding along the bumpy surface.

The bridge is nearly a mile long, and I think I hold my breath for most of it. My lungs are burning for air and my palms are slick with sweat when we finally leave the bridge behind us.

"That was crazy!" Evelynn yells, a wide grin on her face.

"I prefer to be in a vehicle the next time I have to cross one of those." Hanna shudders.

"Sorry, Evie, but I'm with Hanna on this one," I wholeheartedly agree.

We're laughing and not paying attention to the boys until Garrett's serious voice booms back to us. "Ladies."

My front tire wobbles as I turn to see what's got him sounding so grave. Cars have been strategically pushed to make the road into a small path. We'll only fit one at a time through the funnel, but there doesn't seem to be any alternative. The cars stretch over the sides of the road, making it almost impossible to get our bikes through there any other way.

"What should we do?" Liam asks, undoing his helmet and stashing it on his handlebars. We all remove our helmets and look around for any signs of trouble. There are sounds from the water, the river rapids crashing over rocks at the side. Birds are chirping happily; nothing seems out of the ordinary. Garrett shrugs. "I guess we go slow and keep our eyes peeled. It seems weird here."

We nod in agreement and start to follow him. At the very back, my skin prickled with goosebumps, I keep checking behind us to make sure we are not being followed. A little while later, the car funnel ends and the road reopens. That was strange—why would someone go to all that trouble?

Garrett calls for a break once we're past the obstacle, and we drop our bikes and backpacks. It's nice to stretch and have some water. The bright, sunny day has turned cloudy, and a weird fog hovers over the road. I leave my sleeping bag attached to my handlebars and throw my helmet down next to them. Hanna says something about a bathroom break, and she and Evelynn start walking toward the tree line.

I hear a duck call, and then suddenly a group of people descend on us from the woods to our left. The river still rages on our right, and we're trapped. The only way back is the narrow funnel we've just come from.

A tall man stands in front of a small group of people, a long gray beard peeking out from behind his mask. Goggles cover his eyes and make it hard to see his facial expression. "What do we have here? A bunch of kiddies out for a Sunday stroll?" The man chuckles, and his group laughs along with him.

I see Garrett tense; even through his heavy winter coat, I can see how stiff he's gone. He and Liam are within an arm's length of the leader. My eyes search everywhere for Hanna and Evelynn, and then I see them. Two of the men have them, holding them by their shoulders as they stare back at us, their faces white. We're caught, and we have no way to protect ourselves.

"What do you want from us?" Liam asks calmly.

"We want to help you, but we have to be sure you can be trusted." A second man nods toward the bearded man and steps forward. "Do any of you require medical attention?"

Garrett seems to relax slightly. "No, we're fine. We don't have much further to go. We appreciate the help, but I think we'll be on our way."

"Don't be silly," the bearded man says, thrusting out his hand. "I'm Bill, and this here is Cliff." Cliff extends his hand to Liam. I watch the boys exchange a wary look before reaching out to return the handshakes.

Everything happens so quickly then, because the handshake was a ruse. The men pull Garrett and Liam to them and start to beat on them. Evelynn screams as the man punches Liam in the back. The person holding her spins her around and gets a fist full of her hair.

All of my friends are being assaulted. I stare from a few feet back, unsure of what I can do or how to help.

Garrett wrenches out of the man's grasp and turns his head in my direction. "Selena, run!"

His words take too many precious seconds to register, but I eventually sling my backpack over my shoulders and take off down the road on foot. I'm far enough over to the right that no one can reach me in time. I run fast and hard, and as soon as I am clear of the group, I dive into the woods, running deeper into the trees for cover. I take one last look back at my friends, but all I see is Garrett, still yelling for me to run. I push forward, willing myself to keep going even when I jump at the distinct sound of gunshots from behind me.

Please let them be okay.

Chapter Thirteen

I'M RUNNING SO FAST that my backpack is sliding back and forth, threatening to topple me to either side. I don't dare look back in the direction of the chaos again—it won't help my friends, and I know it'll stop me in my tracks. Tears drip silently down my wind-burned cheeks, but I keep running.

My chest burns from the exertion, my legs shake, and I use all of the inner strength I have to keep pushing on. I run for what feels like hours through the wooded paths along the main road, but I stay far enough back to try to stay hidden from anyone traveling on it.

I don't know exactly where I am, but I hope that I'm still running parallel to the highway—at least then I'll be headed in the right direction. I've been running for so long now that I can't be sure.

My eyes are blurry and burning, and I squeeze them shut for a moment, trying to get some relief from the stinging. I run and run, and it feels like I'll never be somewhere safe enough to stop.

I am losing strength, coughing against the lack of air in my lungs.

My feet stumble as I trip over something large on the ground, and the combination of my own forward momentum and the weight of my backpack thrusts me face first into the forest floor. I hit the ground with enough force that the breath is knocked from my lungs, and I can't get my hands out in front of me fast enough. My face slams into the ground, rewarding me with a mouthful of dirt and pine needles.

I spit and sputter, gasping for air and trying to catch my breath. I roll to my side, my pack preventing me from rolling completely over to my back. Then I close my eyes and silently count to ten. My heart is still racing, trying its best to slow down after the marathon I've forced on my body. If I tried to stand now, I have a feeling my legs would be as stable as cooked spaghetti noodles.

I focus on my breathing, knowing that it'll do me no good to keep panicking. I need a clear head before I make any decisions. A sob builds in my chest, but I force it down. Crying won't solve anything, no matter how badly I want to crumble.

Sliding my arms from my pack, I pull myself free, pushing myself up into a sitting position. I inhale deeply, blowing the breath out through my mouth. I am overcome by the smells of dirt and pine and earth that wraps around me like a hug, and I focus on them as my breath starts to even out.

I turn my head back in the direction I've come from, looking for any sign that I've been followed, but I don't see anyone. The late afternoon sun filters down through the canopy of trees and makes dancing patterns across the ground. It's quiet and calm here, the sounds of birds and squirrels skittering around a dull, comforting sound.

Then, out of the corner of my eye, I see something nearby move. I freeze. A large shaking bundle sits underneath the trees, only a few feet away from me.

I jerk back, squeezing my knees against my chest as I stare at it in an attempt to figure out what I'm up against. After only a moment's assessment, I see it's a body, huddled in the fetal position, its back facing me. The body is shaking uncontrollably and making soft gasping noises. Whoever it is, they are not in good shape. I don't think they're part of the group I've been running from, but how can I be sure?

This person is wearing light-colored clothing and not enough of it. And it's starting to get even colder now that the sun has begun to set for the day. If they've been exposed to the elements out here for a long time, they could be suffering from hypothermia or worse.

I scan the area around me for signs of any other people, but I don't see or hear anyone. The faint smell of smoke wafts to me from somewhere in the distance, but I can't tell how far or near it could be.

Part of me, a very large part, is screaming inside my head, *GET UP, LEAVE THIS PERSON AND KEEP RUNNING. DON'T TAKE ANY RISKS.*

But I already know I won't do that. This person is clearly hurt or sick, and they need me. I might not be much help, but I can't leave them here and not try.

"Hello?" I say softly, careful not to frighten them. Obviously, tripping over them wasn't the best first impression, but I can't fix that now.

There's no answer, but the body continues to shake, and I know I have to act quickly.

"I'm going to make us a fire, okay? I think we need to get you warm. I'm not leaving you, I promise—I just have to get us some wood." I don't know if they can even hear me, but I go about the task quickly, digging a small area and filling it with dried out twigs and some paper scraps from my pack. I find some larger pieces of wood that will last a little longer and then dig out my matches. The fire is only a few feet away from the huddled person, but I will need to get them to come closer if I want them to get warm.

Once the fire is set, I dig through my supplies and find my fleece blanket. Slowly, I creep toward the huddled body. My hands shake, and I bite my lip as I get close, realizing the huddle is definitely not a child and definitely not a woman. Large, broad shoulders fill out the light-gray hoodie that is pulled tightly over the person's head.

He's slightly dirty, and his clothes smell like smoke, but he doesn't look like he's been outside for too long. I gently grip the shoulder that's up in the air and roll the body in my direction. I expect resistance, but the body moves easily.

With him on his back now, I can see part of his mud-streaked face. He's a teenage boy, probably close to my own age. His eyes are closed, his long dark lashes standing out against his pale skin. His lips are blue, and his skin is an unnatural bluish-gray shade. I'm no expert on hypothermia, but I know if this boy doesn't get warm soon, he'll probably die.

I don't know if I can trust this stranger, but I don't have a choice. I will not leave him to die. "Can you hear me?" I pull my gloves off and press my hand to his cheek. It's ice cold. His eyelids flutter a little, but he still doesn't respond. So I pull him as close to the fire as I feel is safe then drag my pack over next to him, using it to prop him up. "I'm going to try to get you warm."

I wrap the fleece blanket around us, pulling his body tightly to mine in a side hug. He's rather large, even bigger than Garrett, and it takes effort to hold him up at first. I feel the chill from his body creeping into mine, but I hold tight. When I see his hands are uncovered, I tuck them into his hoodie pockets as best I can, making sure to cover as much of his exposed skin as possible. The icy feel of his skin is alarming—I hope I haven't discovered him too late.

I'm also not wearing my mask or goggles, and if this boy is infected, I will soon follow him, but it's too late to worry about that. I have to keep him alive.

The heat of the fire reaches my legs, and I pray it's enough. My breathing is even, and worrying about this stranger has allowed me to calm my own nerves. If those people are following me, the fire will likely lead them right to us, but without it, I don't know how I'd save the boy. I don't know what's happened to my friends or what my plan will be if I'm really on my own, but I know that I'm too tired to do anything else for now.

I have a mission: Get this boy talking. The rest can wait.

"One problem at a time, right?" I ask the boy. His head lulls and lands on my shoulder. It feels intimate, but I don't try to move him away. This position is much like the one Garrett and I were in a few days ago in the theater room. Geez, has it really only been a few days? It feels like weeks since the world went dark.

I shake myself away from the sting of emotion that wells up inside of me.

I need to get this boy warm and lucid. I lean into him more, willing my body heat to reach him. The exhaustion of the day catching up with me, I feel my own eyelids start to droop. No harm in closing them for a few minutes...

I jerk awake, my eyes trying to adjust to the darkness. I don't know how long I've been out, but the fire has reduced to a small pile of glowing ash. It's likely been only an hour or two; I didn't make a large enough fire to last much longer than that.

My right arm is heavy, and I look over, slowly remembering the events of the day. The boy is still tucked against me, the blanket wrapped tightly around us both. I don't feel as cold now; he seems to have sucked in some heat and has finally stopped shivering so violently. His breathing is soft and slow, and his lips still appear blue tinged, but at least he's breathing.

It's quiet, which is a welcome sound. I'm grateful we weren't discovered while I slept.

I shift a little, careful not to jostle him too much. My stomach grumbles, and I feel the first hunger pangs breaking through my sleepiness. I need to move, to add wood to the fire and find something to eat from my pack, but I'm afraid to, afraid to leave his side too soon and have him get a chill again. I wish I had the tent; we will have to find some real shelter soon.

As I sit there, I think about my friends. The guilt I could have been feeling had I not made up with Hanna nags at me, but I remind myself that we did call a truce and push those thoughts away. I'm thankful for this stranger beside me, that I'm not alone, but I miss Garrett miserably. I wish I could go back, stop him from extending his hand to those grown men, grab him, and run. I wish he were here beside me, too.

I've been away from my friends before, but never like this. Never without knowing what will happen to them. My heart feels shattered into tiny pieces, and I don't know if I'll be able to put them back together if I never see my friends again.

The sun is setting—it'll be much colder and much more uncomfortable soon. If I sit here and do nothing, I'll be too dead to help my friends do anything.

So as not to disturb the boy, I carefully slide out of the blanket. I tuck it around him tightly, trying to keep the cold air from reaching inside. My eyes struggle to see in the dark, and I wonder again how anyone ever lived before flashlights and cell phones.

The zipper on my pack sounds much louder than it should, and I dig around for supplies blindly, letting my sense of touch guide me. I choose one of the packages of jerky that Garrett gave me and a slightly bruised apple. I know it's bruised because its once blemish-free exterior feels squishy and bumpy under my fingertips.

My mouth waters at the thought of biting into the juicy apple. I'm thirsty, and despite my small nap, I still feel exhausted. So I close up my backpack, taking only the snacks in my hands, and head back around to my side of the blanket. I hear a strange animal sound somewhere in the distance, and the hair on my neck stands on end. I crouch quietly, scanning the woods around us for anything threatening.

The shadows of the night make it hard to see much, but everything appears still and quiet. I let out a small breath, still on edge.

A large shadow looms in the distance to my left. I must be deeper into the woods and even further from the road than I thought.

The shadow I'm seeing might be a small cabin. I pray I'm right; a cabin would give us a little more protection from the elements and the animals in the forest. I'm annoyed that I didn't notice it before, when I had some remaining daylight on my side.

I look over at the boy. He's still sleeping, and his body barely moves. I don't know him or owe him anything, but I really don't want him to die. If we want to survive, the two of us will need each other. I can't explain why I know this is true, but without a doubt, I feel it in my soul. I need this boy, and he needs me.

My mind made up, I set the food down on the edge of the blanket. Leaving the food and the boy behind, I make my way over to the cabin as quietly and stealthily as I can. I haven't seen any movement over this way or heard anything but animal sounds, but I want to be sure the place is safe before I announce my presence.

My fingers are stiff and cold, so I curl them into fists and then stretch them back out over and over, trying to get blood flow into them.

The structure isn't far, and it *is* a cabin. It's small, and the tiny porch at the front is crumbling from years of neglect. Only two windows allow a glimpse inside. They flank either side of the door, so I can't sneak a peek into the cabin without climbing up onto the dilapidated porch.

I've come this far. I have to take the risk.

Goosebumps flood my skin, and my hands shake with nerves as I take the first step. The porch's wooden floor is surprisingly solid and quiet under my feet. The windows are unbroken. The door is shut and appears to be in working order. I see no glow of candles, and the small stone chimney doesn't have any smoke coming from it.

From all outside appearances, this cabin is unoccupied. So I take the last two steps quickly, rushing to the window on the left and peering into the darkness.

In the growing moonlight, I can see a small bed with some folded blankets stacked at the foot of it. Two wooden chairs, a table, and a bucket next to a wood-filled fireplace sit silently, unmoving. Stacks of wood line the corner along with what appears to be a small bookcase holding various canned and jarred foods and pots and pans.

I blink back tears of relief. No one is here, but I feel like I've hit the jackpot for supplies and shelter.

I try the door handle and am not surprised to find it's locked. I don't want to have to break a window to get inside, but I will if that's the only choice I have.

My eyes scan the porch and the ground below for something that might help me open it, and a strange-looking rock draws my eye. To anyone else, it would probably look like a broken boulder that someone kicked over. But I recognize it—it looks like the hide-a-rock my grandma has at her house, the one that my grandpa bought for her. It's where they keep the spare key because my grandma is known to lock herself out anytime she heads outside.

My heart speeds up, and I rush back down the stairs and drop to my knees in front of the baseball-sized rock. I flip it over, twisting the two sides in opposite directions the way my grandpa showed me. It lets out a satisfying popping sound. Then a piece of paper slides out with the key, and I hold myself back from shouting with happiness.

Our cabin is yours to use if you find yourself in need. We only ask that you leave it as whole as you found it. Take what you need, leave what you can for others. May God bless you.
- The Wilson Family

I hug the note and the key to my chest, my weary body thankful for the kindness of strangers. If we make it out of this mess and things get back to normal, I'll find the Wilsons and thank them properly.

A frigid breeze blows through the woods and pulls me back to the present. It reminds me that every second I spend here, the boy could be getting colder and weaker.

The note goes back into the rock, but I take the key with me. I unlock the door and take a quick inventory of the dark cabin. I find matches and wood, kindling, even a small amount of lighter fluid. So I start the fire in the fireplace, careful not to make it too large. A plastic jug full of water sits next to the bucket nearby, but I'd rather drink the water than be forced to use it to put out a fire.

Once I'm sure the fire isn't going to go out, I slip back outside. Hopefully, by the time I get the boy inside, it'll be warm enough to really help him. That is, if I can manage to get the boy here at all.

I take a deep breath and head back to where I left him.

Chapter Fourteen

I'M ALMOST BACK TO the spot where I left both my pack and the boy when I hear movement. Have those men found us? Could Garrett have escaped and come to find me? Is a wild animal about to eat me for dinner? A million thoughts fight for attention, and my feet freeze in place as my eyes struggle to find the source of the sound.

"Hello?" It's barely a whisper, but I hear it loud and clear in the near silence. "Are you the one who helped me?"

My feet finally obey my commands, and I move slowly toward the sound. The boy is no longer huddled on the ground but stands, towering above me, with the blanket still tucked around his shoulders. He may not be my friends, but he is a welcome sight all the same.

I stare at him wordlessly, and even in the darkness, I can tell that he's beautiful. Strong jaw, full lips that are still slightly blue, a straight and perfectly symmetrical nose... and his eyes. Maybe the moonlight is playing tricks on me, but they almost seem the same glowing silver as the moonlight itself. I'm so mesmerized by him that I forget to respond to his question.

"Can you speak?" His voice is no longer a whisper, and his deep timbre almost feels like an assault in the quiet of the night.

"Um, yes, sorry. I'm Selena." I think about offering my hand for a handshake, but I still can't seem to control my own movements. Instead, my hand jerks awkwardly at my side. Then I remember how the handshake ended for Garrett, and my stomach roils.

"Selena." He says my name softly, looking at me like he's cataloging the information for a detailed report. I feel my cheeks blush under his unwavering gaze.

"And you are? I mean, your name. Uh... what do I call you?" *Smooth, Selena, you sound like an idiot.* I haven't ever met someone my age outside of the Academy, and even though it's terrifying, I'd be lying if I said I wasn't thrilled beyond measure.

"You can call me Axel." The boy smiles and reaches his hand toward me. I glance down at his long, lean fingers. Even in the dark, I can see how dirty they are—mine probably look the same.

He follows my gaze and seems to realize this himself, quickly pulling his hand back and rubbing it against his pant leg.

"Sorry." His eyes drop to the ground, embarrassment clear on his face.

He wobbles on his feet, and I know he must be weak and unsteady. At least he's not wheezing or coughing or showing any other known virus symptoms. I feel a small sliver of relief wash over me.

"It's okay, really." I shake my head, wanting him to look at me again. "I'd like to talk to you, and I think we should eat. I found a place where we can get warm and clean up, too. It's up ahead a short walk—do you think you're okay to walk there?"

He doesn't respond, his eyebrows pinched together in what I can only guess is hesitation.

I try to persuade him softly. "I don't think it's safe for us out here in the open, and it's only going to get colder."

Axel's eyes flash when I mention the cold. He's still blue tinged and shivering slightly, and I'm sure he's terrified by the idea of it getting any colder out here. So he nods and watches me as I sling my pack over my shoulder before picking up our meager dinner from the ground.

The sight of the apple and the jerky prompts my stomach to growl loudly in protest. I'm hungry and tired, but I'm also filled with questions and purpose.

At least I won't have to spend the night alone and scared in these woods. Plus, I want to know everything there is to know about Axel and how he ended up in the woods. It gives me something else to focus on.

I feel the seeds of hope growing inside me.

"Come on, let's get inside and get something in our bellies." I smile, leading the way, relieved that I don't have to drag his body inside.

The cabin seemed a lot bigger when I was alone. Now, with Axel's large body in here, it feels smaller than the janitor's closet at school. I already locked the door behind us and dropped my pack in front of it, happy to let the load rest.

I watch as Axel looks around. The room is filled with a delicious warmth from the small fire, so I flex my cold fingers over and over, willing them to come back to life.

I break the awkward silence. "Do you like jerky? I have some to share, and I'll see if I can find a knife to cut this apple in two. It's pretty bruised, but it's still edible."

My words come out in an anxious rush of babbling, but Axel has found himself a seat in front of the fire, and he doesn't answer me. His clothes are dirty and torn, and I wonder again where he came from and how long he was out there before I found him.

"Axel?" I ask, but he doesn't seem to hear me. His eyes are trained on the flames in front of him.

The hood of his sweatshirt falls, revealing his head completely. Despite his darker eyebrows and lashes, I'm astonished to see the silvery-white hair on top of his head, messy and falling around his ears. His hands reach out over the flames, turning over and over, and then I watch in horror as he moves them even further into the fire. Alarm bells ring in my head.

I launch myself across the small space, pulling his hands back from the dangerous heat. "Are you crazy? You'll burn yourself!" I cry out. The panic in my voice is loud and wild as I grip his two ice-cold hands in my slightly warmer ones.

His stricken expression gives me pause. Maybe he hit his head?

I lower my voice and ask him more calmly, "What are you thinking, putting them in the fire like that?"

"I'm sorry, it felt so wonderful... I didn't mean to anger you." He shakes his head, his entire body drooping.

"I shouldn't have yelled; I'm sorry. You just scared me." My body is still in fight mode, so I press my palms against my thighs, focusing on my breathing and the sound of the crackling fire.

"It's been a long day—let's keep a safe distance from the fire, okay? It's easy to burn yourself and not know it when you're so numb from the cold."

"Yes, I'll stay back." He nods at me, a small smile touching his lips. "Thank you for saving me."

I wonder if he means now or before, but I suppose it doesn't matter. I nod at him. "Of course."

Taking a wash rag and some soap from my pack, I pour only enough water into the bucket for us to clean our hands and faces. I wash mine first and then rinse the rag in the bucket, wringing it out gently before handing it to Axel. He's watched me closely and now repeats my actions, cleaning quickly before rinsing the rag and handing it back to me. Without the dirt smudges on his skin, he looks even more like a painting—smooth skin with some color finally returning to his lips and cheeks.

I find a knife and slice the apple into two halves, carefully removing the core and seeds before handing it to Axel with a handful of beef jerky. He holds the food in his hand, staring at it like it might bite him. I can't stand a picky eater, and we can't exactly afford to be choosy right now—there are no gourmet meals I can throw together. But we will need to eat to keep our strength. We still have a long way to go before we get to Portland. If he's even willing to follow me there.

We sit in the two wooden chairs in front of the fire, and I take the first bite of my apple. Despite its rough appearance, it's juicy and satisfying. My eyes close as I savor the crisp, tart flavors, my mouth watering with anticipation for more. I take small bites, careful to make the meal last as long as I can. When I finally look back at Axel, he's grinning like a kid on Christmas, taking alternating bites of jerky and apple as slowly as I had. Not a picky eater after all.

"Sorry, I know it isn't much." I look over at the small cache of food the cabin offers, but I'm afraid to waste anything we may need later. My heart squeezes, remembering the food cans we'd managed to find at the drugstore this morning. How quickly everything has changed.

"This was wonderful, thank you," he says, surprising me. His smile seems genuine, and I find myself smiling back at him. He wipes his empty hands on his pants, taking a small sip of the water I poured for us. "How old are you, Selena?"

It seems like such an odd question given the circumstances, but then, he's kind of an odd boy. "I'm seventeen. It's been a weird senior year at school so far. What about you?" I'll be eighteen next month. *If I even make it to my birthday.*

Axel smiles. "I turned eighteen last week. But I didn't go to a traditional school, and I've been finished for a while." He shrugs.

Homeschooled, then? I suppose my school isn't traditional, either, but I don't feel like talking about the Academy. "So how did you end up in the woods all alone?" I ask, my curiosity getting the best of me. I'd meant to give him time and see if he offered the information on his own.

He shifts a little in his chair and sets his cup down on the table before meeting my gaze. "I don't know. The last thing I remember was talking with my sister where we crashed—"

"Oh my goodness, you were in an accident?" I scan his body with my gaze, searching him again for injuries, hoping he's not hurt more than I've realized. "Was she hurt? Your sister?"

He has a sibling, like Liam. I feel a small pang of jealousy. It's such a rare thing to have siblings, and I've often dreamed of what it would be like to have real sisters. How much different would that be than my relationships with Hanna and Evelynn?

He shakes his head. "No. I remember she was okay. I was trying to check over all of us... But then, I think I hit my head? The next thing I remember is waking up alone in the woods next to your things and then seeing you. I don't know where they are now."

Maybe he does have a concussion. Should I be worried about that? Dozens of questions spring to my mind at once. "Do you think your car was close by? Maybe we can find your family? It wouldn't hurt to have a few more people on our side—it's dangerous to be outnumbered out here. Maybe they're looking for you?"

"I wish I could remember, but we fell so fast..." He stares into space as if seeing things in his mind that I can't.

Fell?

"You mean... you were in a plane?" Fear grips me. Did the power situation even extend to planes that were flying? How terrifying that must have been for anyone on board. But then, how many people are still traveling by planes these days with all the quarantine rules? It can't be many.

"Ah... yes. Aircraft." He nods. "It won't be flying again, that I remember. Absolutely destroyed."

"You said all of us; who else was with you?"

The rosy tint to his cheeks seems to fade, and he turns away from me. I wonder if I've pushed too much, made him remember things he's not ready to face. Then I see his shoulders shaking lightly, and I realize he's crying.

"Axel? I'm sorry—you don't have to talk about it." I want to cry when I think of my friends, too, but I'm afraid if I let myself start, I'll never stop. Hanna and I had only begun to mend our fences and now... I fold my hands together, giving Axel time to compose himself.

"What about you? Why are you out here all alone?" he finally asks, his face still turned away from me.

I wring my hands, thinking about how I got here. Wondering if I should have stayed and faced whatever fate had in store for our group. "I was with my friends; we decided to leave our school and try to get home to our parents..." I let my voice trail off, and I sniffle before continuing. "We had bikes, and we were making pretty good time, but then we ran into a group of people on the road. I guess they were hiding, and we didn't see them until we were right on top of them."

I swallow the growing lump in my throat and take a sip of my water before continuing. Axel turns back to face me, watching me carefully.

"I thought they might take our things and let us go. They grabbed my friends, but then they offered to help us. There were so many of them, at least eight that I could see, but more seemed to be hiding from my view..." I shake my head, swallowing back tears. "They didn't mean to help us at all; it was a trick. They attacked my friends, grabbed them, and started beating them up. They were ripping through our things, taunting us. My friend, Garrett, told me to run, so I grabbed my pack and sprinted away."

A tear slides down my cheek, and I brush it off angrily. "I looked back. I didn't want to leave them all behind, but Garrett, he saw me hesitate. He yelled for me to keep running, so I did. I ran forever. I ran until I thought I might collapse... and then I guess I sort of did. I tripped right over you in the woods. I don't know if anyone was even following me, but I knew I couldn't stop until I had put as much distance between them and me as I could. And now... now, I don't even know if my friends are okay."

What if Hanna was right all along? Would we all be okay if we'd stayed back at school? Was this all my fault?

"Violence. Hate. Greed." Axel shakes his head, pulling me from my thoughts. "That's all this species offers, isn't it?"

His wording is odd, but I do sort of agree with his sentiment. "Not everyone is awful. I like to think most people are good. The bad ones simply make the most noise."

He studies me again, always looking at me so intently. "People should care for each other, family or not. They should not seek to hurt or overpower or get ahead at the expense of others."

"I think so, too. I think that's why I feel so bad about leaving my friends. I should have stayed with them..." Shame washes over my skin like a tidal wave, threatening to pull me under.

"No, I think you did what was best. It would not have helped them for you to be captured as well, would it?"

He pats my arm, and I blink back tears. "I hope so. I hope they're still—" *Alive*. I can't make myself say the word out loud.

Axel seems to sense my inner turmoil, and his face softens. "And then you helped me. Why?" He pulls his hand back, his eyes locked on mine. "It would make sense after your experience to not help a stranger."

"I won't lie—I was afraid you might be one of them at first, but you were dying. I couldn't just leave you there. No one deserves that. And if I helped you and you turned out to be bad, at least I could live with myself, knowing that I did everything I could. Especially after leaving my friends behind like that."

His face scrunches up at my response. "You were afraid of me, but you helped me anyway?"

"You needed my help. That was enough for me." Now that I've eaten, I feel even more exhausted than before. My body is begging for rest. I cover a large yawn with my hand, my eyelids getting heavy.

"What do you expect to get out of helping me? Surely you have some motive?"

I make a face at him. "Yes, you're right. I was hoping you'd be helpful in getting us out of this mess. Maybe be some big strong lumberjack with survival skills." I'm joking, but I can see that the joke is lost on him because he nods like that makes all the sense in the world. This boy is so strange, and I'm eager to understand his way of thinking so I can figure him out better.

"We should rest—we can decide what steps to take next in the daylight." Axel looks even more tired than I feel. He nods toward the bed. "You may sleep there. I'll make do here." I stare at the wooden chair he's sitting in and can't imagine anyone getting any rest there. We must get as much rest as we can while we're safe and comfortable—we may not have an opportunity as good as this one again.

If we're forced to fight, we will need our strength.

I swallow hard at the thought of sharing the small bed with a boy, especially a boy I don't know. But the floor is cold and hard, and the wooden chair is far too small to sleep on. He could turn on me. Even as weak as he seems now, he outweighs me and could certainly take advantage of the situation. And yet, somehow, I know in my gut he's not going to do that. *Trust your instincts, Selena.*

Despite the fact that I know next to nothing about this boy, I *do* feel like I can trust him. I saved him from certain death out there, and now we need to be a team if we have any chance of surviving this mess.

I take a steady breath, my mind made up. "Don't be silly. That bed is small, but it's big enough that we can both sleep there. This is not the time to be chivalrous. We need the rest, and we're both mature enough to handle it, don't you think?" I narrow my eyes at him, doing my best to warn him with a look. As if I could do anything to save myself if he tried.

Axel's eyes grow wide, and he shakes his head. "No, I couldn't ask you to share your space that way."

"Well, lucky for you, you're not asking. I'm offering, and anyway, it's only sleep. So let's not worry about any of that silly stuff, okay? This is survival—nothing more."

He still seems apprehensive, but the weariness of the day must steal any remaining fight he has, because he nods slightly. I don't wait for him to change his mind; I get to work getting us ready for bed. Of course, I'm taking a risk trusting this stranger, but he doesn't feel like a stranger to me. And if he'd wanted to overpower me and take my things, he's had plenty of opportunities already.

The small bed has cotton sheets and pillows. I hope we won't find any critters inside them, but I'm much too tired to care. I lay the blankets out on the bed and kick off my muddy shoes. My clothes are dirty, and I'd give anything for a shower, but I see no way to shower in this cabin. Rest is my only concern now.

I add a few pieces of wood to the fire, afraid to ask Axel to help after his weird fire fiasco earlier. It's still cold in the cabin, but with the fire going, it's much more bearable than outside in the wind.

I hope like hell that my friends are somewhere warm and safe. The guilt eats at me—I still don't know if running away was the right thing to do. I want to fix this, to find them, but nothing can be done right now. I'm no good to anyone dead.

I take my coat off and hang it over the back of the chair, leaving my hoodie and thick sweater on. "You can climb in first—you're bigger than I am, and I don't want you to feel like you're going to fall out of the bed." I smile, trying to make light of the situation.

The truth is, I've never shared a bed with a boy before. Sleeping as a group in the tent was the closest I'd ever come to spending a night with a boy. I'm too tired to feel nervous about it, though, so I just watch as Axel removes his boots and climbs into the bed with a grace I don't possess.

He presses himself against the wall almost comically. I bite my cheek to keep from laughing at how hard he's trying to force his large frame into taking up less room. I line our shoes up by the door and take one last look around the small cabin, seeing that everything is tidy and in its place. As long as we don't have any visitors, this is such a beautiful gift. I'd drop to my knees and pray to them right now if I believed in a higher power. Instead, I climb into the bed with Axel and try to get comfortable.

Axel still has his back pressed against the wall, and the cold I feel coming off his body is surprising. I'm not overly warm, but I haven't felt that cold since we came in from outside. "Axel, are you still freezing?"

He's stiff beside me, his breathing irregular and fast. I'm still concerned he may have injuries that I can't see. I turn to my side to face him, searching him for signs of pain or injury. He has such a handsome face, and his skin is smooth, porcelainlike. Not a freckle or blemish can be seen in the firelight. Even without the night sky, his eyes still seem to glow with silvery moonlight.

This close, I can see that his lips remain slightly blue. Maybe he does have hypothermia. I try to remember the signs and symptoms from our camping trip lessons—

"I am easily chilled," he says, his teeth chattering slightly. "It's not helpful on a night like this."

"Is the cabin wall cold? We can switch sides if that helps; I don't feel nearly as cold as you look," I suggest, gesturing to my side of the bed.

He shakes his head, and I try not to roll my eyes at his stubbornness. Instead, I lift my hand to touch his face but then leave it hovering awkwardly at the last second. "May I?"

He nods, and I carefully place my palm against his cheek. It's smooth and cold like the granite countertop in my kitchen at home. I can't help my loud intake of breath on contact. He's still freezing—we have to find a way to get him warm. So I leave my hand against his cheek, my own face warming from our proximity despite the icy feel of his skin.

Axel closes his eyes; his hand comes up to cover mine on his face. It's cold, but I welcome the connection.

"You're so warm," he whispers softly.

I know what I need to do, but I hesitate slightly. How would Garrett feel about this? I shake the thought away. This isn't about potential boyfriends or relationships, this is about keeping someone from death. If Garrett can't understand that...

A violent shudder races through Axel, and my inner thought process is immediately silenced. I pull my hand from his and sit up in bed. "I'm going to get you warm, okay? Do you trust me?"

He sits up, too, his eyes wide in the dim light of the fire. "Y-Yes..." He nods shakily.

"Good." I unzip my hoodie and take it off, dropping it to the floor beside me. Then I pull my heavy sweater and t-shirt off together in one swift tug, leaving me in my pale pink bra and jeans.

"What are you doing?" Axel asks, covering his eyes with his hands. "This is not appropriate."

I hold back a laugh, because I'm usually the most conservative in my group of friends. I can't remember a time I've been called inappropriate before this. "Relax, it's no different than a swimsuit top."

"I don't know what kind of swimwear you're talking about, because the females I know do not own those."

Yeah, right, where has this kid been living? Some kind of convent?

"I'm going to take off my jeans now. Can you get your own shirt and pants off? If we're going to get you warm, we need as much skin-to-skin contact as possible." Despite my confidence, I feel my face blush red at the suggestion of our bodies touching.

Grandpa would remind me that medical nudity is not something to be embarrassed about. This has a purpose, and I shouldn't be self-conscious. Like that time I got stung by a bee in my butt cheek. Grandma had to pull the stinger out, but I refused to show anyone my bare butt for well over an hour, instead choosing to remain in pain that whole time. It had been a hard lesson, learning that some nudity is necessary and not to be ashamed of my own body. Obviously, it's still a work in progress.

Maybe I should be more embarrassed, more hesitant, but I know what needs to be done, and that seems to calm all the other emotions.

"You want me to take off my clothes?" Axel looks like he might pass out, and I try to swallow back my frustration.

"It's the only way I can think of to get you warm enough. I'm really afraid that if we don't do something, I'm going to wake up next to your cold, dead body."

I sigh. I mean the words, but I feel harsh speaking them out loud. I don't want to imagine it, his stiff corpse in the bed next to me. But I don't want to be alone, either, and that possibility scares me more than anything.

"My body heat will get you warm, and I know it might be uncomfortable and that you don't even know me, but it's important. I want to get you warm so we can rest and be ready for whatever comes tomorrow. Do you think you can handle that?"

He doesn't answer, but I see him chewing on his lip and wonder if he's fighting his own inner dialogue like I am. Then he scrubs a hand over his face and finally begins to unzip his hoodie.

Underneath, he's wearing some kind of strange jumpsuit. I hadn't realized that his pants and shirt were all one piece under his hoodie. It looks like something a pilot might wear, which I suppose makes sense if he was on a plane. He unzips the jumpsuit next, pulling his arms from the sleeves and sliding it down his body. I turn away while I remove my own pants. Something about watching him undress feels too intimate. Despite my assurance that this is in no way sexual, I feel my own body reacting to the sight of his bare skin.

I kick my pants off the rest of the way and let them fall out from under the blankets. Axel tosses his jumpsuit and hoodie over the side as well. For a minute, we both lay there in silence on our backs next to each other, staring up at the ceiling. This was my idea, but suddenly I feel nervous and unsure about my plan.

His hand finds mine under the blankets, and he squeezes my fingers gently. "Thank you," he says.

I finally turn my head to look at him.

A tear slides down his cheek, and my heart leaps in my chest. Here I am concerned about modesty, and he's moved to tears by my attempt to save him or perhaps by his own weakness. Either way, this boy needs my help, and I need to get over the rest.

I squeeze his hand in return. "I'd like to think you'd do the same for me."

"What do we do now?" He lets go of my hand and turns on his side to face me. The bed dips and jostles under our weight. "You're going to have to help me out here; I don't quite know how to handle this. I am surprised by your willingness to help me. It is both confusing and overwhelming."

I fight a smile. "Next, we try to get as much of my skin touching yours as we can. I'm going to turn around and back up against you. You can wrap your arms around me like a hug—you know, big spoon, little spoon style? And then we try our best to sleep. If we don't rest, tomorrow will be really difficult."

He nods, but I can see his uncertainty. So I roll over quickly, before he can think too much about it, and feel him meet me in the middle.

He's easily a foot and a half taller than me, and my body feels small against him. I can't help the sharp breath that escapes when I feel his skin touch mine. His entire body feels like ice—everywhere that it touches my own, I feel the chill. I shiver against him as his arms come around me, and I lace his fingers with mine in front of us, pulling them into my chest. He exhales loudly behind me, his breath rustling the loose hair around my ears. Goosebumps scatter across my skin.

"You okay?" I ask, my voice wobbly with emotion. I've underestimated how good it would feel to be held after the day I've had. Tears threaten to break through my resolve, but I don't want Axel to misinterpret them. I don't regret my decision to help him. I snuggle into him, my own body adjusting to the coldness of his. The exhaustion of the day throbs steadily through my limbs.

"Yes, you feel wonderful," he says, and I feel a different kind of warmth crawl through my body at his words.

"Goodnight, Axel," I whisper, feeling the first waves of sleep crashing over me.

"Goodnight, Selena."

Chapter Fifteen

Sunlight pulls me from sleep, but my body feels heavy and warm. I close my eyes tighter against the light and try to let sleep take me back under. But movement behind me makes my eyelids fly open.

The events of the last few days come flooding back, washing away all feelings of comfort and warmth. In that moment, I realize that the heaviness I feel against me is Axel's warm body. I'm relieved he's survived the night and seems to finally have thawed out.

The cabin looks the same as we left it the night before. The smell of woodsmoke is all that remains of the fire I made last night. My face feels cold, but the rest of me is safely tucked under the blankets. I dread the idea of getting out from under the warmth, but I know we need to get moving. I also feel a horribly pressing urge to empty my bladder.

Axel hasn't made any sounds, but I can hear him breathing evenly behind me. I hate to wake him after the ordeal he had yesterday, but the longer the sun is up, the more daylight we waste. I'd like to pack some supplies from the cabin before we head out, and I'm not entirely sure what our plan will even be. I don't know if Axel will want to follow me, but I hope he will. I don't want to be alone.

Reluctantly, I roll over, finding myself face-to-face with the handsome boy I rescued last night. His dark eyelashes are long and stark against his pale cheeks. For the first time, his skin appears more pink than blue.

I study him in the sunlight, calm and peaceful in his sleep. I don't really know much about this boy, but I feel safe with him. It doesn't make much sense, and I almost feel guilty for the thought.

I shake his shoulder softly, trying not to startle him. "Axel, hey, it's morning."

His eyelids flutter softly before he finally opens them. Our eyes meet, and a slow smile tips up at the corners of his mouth. "Thank you. I feel surprisingly warm."

"I'm glad. I was afraid I'd wake up next to a popsicle and have to figure out what to do with your body."

Axel and I both laugh, but I'm only half joking.

"We should probably pack up and head out. Do you want to try to find the place where you crashed?"

Axel closes his eyes before he answers me. "We can try, but I don't remember much before you found me. We could try to find your friends if you'd like. Maybe if we head out, I'll see something that will shake some memories loose. Where would you be heading if you hadn't found me?"

My heart aches at the mention of my friends. The look on Garrett's face when he told me to run had been filled with dread. I'm afraid of what I might find if I go back the way I came.

We'd always planned that if any of us were separated, we'd keep heading in the right direction and meet up in Portland. Liam's house was the first one that we'd hit if we stayed on the right path, so we'd agreed to meet there. That would be my plan.

The option is there—I can head back the way I came, see if there are any signs of my friends or what could have happened to them, but I already know what I might find there. I'd rather not see for myself if they'd been killed. With any luck, we'd run into them on the way to Portland.

"I'm heading home. To Portland."

Once we're dressed and have packed minimal supplies from the cabin, I lock the door behind us and hide the key back inside the rock. I'd taken a few extra minutes to write a thank you note to the owners of the cabin and left my contact information. Someday, when this is all over, I intend to pay them back with interest. Without their kindness, I may not have been able to save Axel.

The air is cool and damp with dew, but it's not uncomfortably cold this morning, and the sunlight breaking through the trees feels warm on my face. The scent of pine and dirt is strong here in the woods, and I find I don't mind the smell at all. I'd like to stay in the cover of the woods for safety, but I know that will make the walk too hard and much too long. We need to find our way back to the road, but I'm terrified of who or what we may find there.

My pack is heavy, the added food and water pressing hard into my already bruised shoulders. If only I had my sleeping bag and hadn't lost it with my bike. The blankets I took from the cabin take up precious space and add a bulk to my pack that makes it even more uncomfortable. We may need them to survive the cold night outdoors, though, especially if we can't find suitable shelter.

Axel doesn't have anything but the clothes on his back, so I don't complain about the weight of my belongings. He's quiet this morning, his eyes scanning the woods for anything that might seem familiar. I feel for him, not knowing what has become of his family. My own parents are likely safe and sound at our house in Portland, but I have no way of knowing that for certain.

We take turns hiding behind a group of bushes to relieve ourselves. The sound of my bladder emptying into the pine needles is loud and makes my cheeks burn with embarrassment, but I don't want to be further from Axel than necessary. I keep expecting him to vanish into thin air, but he doesn't.

It's taking longer than I expected to find the road. Every time I'm sure we're close, we only find more forest. It seems like hours have passed before we see signs that point to a road. Only once I see them, instead of going faster, I feel my pace slow.

Anxiety and fear settle like a thick syrup in my veins, making my limbs stiff and heavy. I can see bits of the road through the trees, and while I don't see any cars or people, that doesn't mean they aren't out there somewhere, waiting.

Axel gets ahead of me—he doesn't seem to notice my hesitation, and his stride remains long and confident as he expertly walks through the tree line. I want to call him back, but I'm afraid to bring any extra attention our way. If someone is out there waiting, I don't want to tip them off.

At the last second, he turns, and upon seeing how far I've dropped back, a frown crosses his face. He stops, waiting for me to catch up. My body feels frozen in fear, but I force my limbs through the motions. I need to be brave if I'm going to survive this journey.

"Are you alright?"

I nod *yes* but then shake my head *no*. Am I alright? I'm not physically injured, but I'm shaking with nerves. What if we find my friends and they're not okay? What if they blame me for getting them into this whole mess? We could have stayed at the Academy—at least then we would have had power in numbers and a roof over our heads.

"What is it, Selena?" Axel reaches out and slides his hand softly down my cheek before dropping it at his side. His fingers are cold already, and I worry about how we will keep him warm today. He needs more layers—the wool hat I found for him in the cabin isn't going to do enough to combat the cold when the sun goes down.

It hits me then, like a jolt to my system. If I'd stayed at the Academy, Axel would probably be dead this morning. While there were definitely risks and consequences for my choices, one good consequence is Axel. Of that, I am sure.

"I'll be okay. I'm just scared." I sigh. It's hard to say those words out loud. I want to be brave and tough, but right now, I feel terrified. At least with Axel, I feel less alone.

I step up beside him, ready to face whatever the day holds. Together.

Hours later, we've still seen zero signs of life. The massive highway I thought we were on is actually a small mountain road. Somehow, I must have run way off course, but I don't know how many miles or in which direction. We've been lucky to avoid running into anyone.

Nothing seems familiar to Axel, and we haven't seen any signs of his family or my friends. I'm too scared to admit that nothing looks familiar to me, either. I had difficulty hiding my relief when we saw a mile sign that indicated we were heading in the right direction.

The sunny clear day we started out with is quickly turning gray and cloudy, and I fear the threat of rain. The last sign we passed said we're still sixty miles from Portland. *Sixty. Miles.* In a car, we would be there in an hour, but on foot, it will likely take us at least two days. And that is under the best conditions.

I don't know how many miles off course I've ended up, but I know this mountain road is somewhere in the Mt. Hood Forest and not anywhere near the freeway that I expected I was close to. I'd been so panicked, I thought I had run parallel to the highway, but the signs on the side of the road advertising Lost Lake Resort tell a different story.

The hysterical laughter that bubbles out of me is unavoidable. "Lost is right." I kick at some rocks on the road as I trail behind Axel. His long, easy stride is faster than mine, and I constantly feel like I'm running to catch up. My shoulders ache from carrying the heavy pack, and I'm tired and hungry.

It's probably time to take a break, but the clouds continue to turn darker in the sky, and I am afraid to stop out here in the open and get caught in the rain.

"Did you say something?" Axel turns around but continues to walk backward. I force myself to pick up the pace until I'm a few feet from him.

"Oh, I was saying 'lost is right.' Thank goodness for that sign back there, or I'd be sure we were heading in the wrong direction." The laughter leaves my voice.

"We're heading west. We'll get there eventually." He shrugs. I'm glad one of us is confident about it.

I wipe moisture from my forehead with my sleeve. Despite the cool air, I'm working up a sweat. "Can we stop for a minute? I don't want to, but I need some water."

"Of course." He smiles and helps me take my pack off. Lifting the pack up and down, he frowns. "Selena, this is quite heavy. Would you let me carry it for a while?"

Relief at his offer rushes through me. He'd asked earlier, but I'd been too stubborn to accept his help. I wouldn't make the same mistake twice. "Are you sure?"

"Yes. I should have insisted earlier. Do your shoulders hurt?" I start to shake my head, but I think better of lying about it.

"A little." I rub them with my hands. They're stiff and bruised, and I suspect I have the beginnings of blisters. I'm thankful that my shoes and socks have remained dry at least, and I don't feel any new blisters forming there. He moves to stand in front of me.

"May I?" he asks, his hands hovering over my shoulders. I nod, swallowing hard at the thought of his hands on my body. Lightly, he places his hands on both of my shoulders and begins to knead them with a gentle but firm touch. It feels so good, I almost groan out loud. I roll my head around in a circle, letting my muscles relax under his touch.

"Please don't be afraid to ask me for help. You saved my life; the least I can do is help out." Axel looks embarrassed by the words. I know the feeling. I hate having to rely on anyone, let alone feel indebted to them in any way.

He steps back from me, and I immediately miss his touch. "Okay, yeah, thank you." I sigh. I drop down and pull out the gallon of water I've been carrying in my bag.

We've only barely sipped it so far, but I know that after all this walking, we will require much more water to keep hydrated. We're lucky that it's not the heat of the summer, but keeping ourselves warm burns a lot of extra energy, too.

I take a few big drinks and then hand the gallon jug over to Axel. He thanks me before chugging his share. We're both tired—I can see it in his posture now. And his skin that was pink and healthy this morning has turned slightly gray again, which means he must be feeling the chill in the air even worse than I am. I wish there had been men's clothes in that small cabin, something he could have used to insulate his thin layers.

"Are you doing okay?" I ask, allowing myself to sit down on the ground. My muscles burn and throb, thankful for the break.

He nods, sitting down beside me and stretching out his long legs. "I'm okay, a little cold."

I lie back, using my pack as a pillow, and stare up at the darkening sky. Losing the full sunlight has cooled the day down considerably. I don't know what time it is, but if I had to guess, I'd say it was early evening, close to dinnertime on a normal day. My stomach growls at the thought of food, and Axel laughs.

"Would you like to share the last of the jerky? I know you're probably starving, too." I don't wait for his answer, though I think I hear him say yes. I pull the package from the pack along with a blanket. I toss the blanket around his shoulders before handing him a large chunk of jerky.

"Thank you." He shudders, nestling into the blanket. I have no idea what we're going to do tonight—we need to find some kind of shelter soon. I think again about how much I wish I had my sleeping bag and the tent right now.

Maybe we should have stayed back at the cabin for a few days, built up some strength while we were warm and dry.

"We shouldn't sit here too long. I'm worried it may rain soon. If you get wet, it'll be even harder to keep you warm." I think about mentioning our dire sleeping situation for tonight but decide not to bring down the mood. We chew our jerky in silence instead, and it's salty and satisfying. I could eat plenty more, but I'm thankful for the few bites.

"The friends you were with—are you very close to them?" The personal question surprises me. Mostly, Axel has avoided talking about anything at all, other than our current situation.

"Um, yeah. We're more like family, I guess. We've all known each other since we started school. We go to a special academy together." I busy myself with packing up the water and the empty jerky package.

"And your parents?"

"They're in Portland. They sent me to the school; they wanted me to get a very special kind of education."

"Special how?" Axel reaches out and slides his hand over the top of mine. I stop what I'm doing to face him. His skin is noticeably cold against my own, just as I suspected.

"The kind where they don't have to be in any part of it?" Sarcasm drips from my voice. "They don't like to be bothered with parental duties; at least, they didn't fight anyone to try to be more involved in my life. Hanna and Evelynn have been more like sisters to me. I don't know Garrett and Liam as well even though I've known them for the same length of time, but I was starting to—we were becoming our own little group."

Axel nods but doesn't move his hand. Instead, he turns it over, lacing his fingers through mine. "You're not like I expected. You care about people *and* you care about strangers—" He shakes his head and smiles. "You confuse me."

I stare at our joined hands. Confused is a good word to describe my own feelings. Sparks run up the length of my arm from his touch. I want him to wrap me in his arms and hold me close to him like he did last night, in the cabin.

I've never met someone my own age who didn't go to the Academy. Maybe it's the newness, the excitement of meeting a complete stranger. But I feel a bond with Axel that I've never felt before. It's quick but solid. Something about him pulls me in and begs me to learn more.

I want to feel his lips on mine. I want him to kiss me more than I've ever wanted anyone to. I shouldn't be thinking about him that way—didn't I just start something new with Garrett? I should be ashamed when, for all I know, Garrett is out there somewhere fighting to get to Portland and find me. But my eyes are drawn to his lips anyway, and I can't make myself pull my hand from his.

"What about your family? Are you guys close?" I ask, distracting myself from thoughts of his lips and wondering if the personal questions will be reciprocated while I have his full attention.

He mulls over the question too long, and I wonder if he's going to answer me at all. His thumb traces a line up and down my own thumb while I wait, and I settle down on the ground next to him, leaning into him and pulling the blanket around me with my free hand. Might as well be warm if we're going to take a longer break.

"My sister and I are close. The rest of my family is slightly unconventional, but we tolerate each other." More questions flood my mind, but I don't want to push him too hard.

I stare at the veins in his hand, following the paths they make up to his wrists before disappearing under his sleeves. "And your parents?"

Pain, unmistakable and dark, flashes through Axel's eyes. "They're dead."

I feel a sharp pain in my chest, as if my heart has been pierced by a blade. My hand squeezes Axel's hard as I cry out, gripping my chest with my free hand. I pull my hand away, expecting to see blood, but nothing's there.

Axel looks stricken and drops my hand from his. "I'm sorry, I didn't know you could..." His voice trails off, and he jumps up quickly, the blanket going with him.

The movement jostles me on the ground, but I'm too stunned to react much. My heart is still thumping and aching in my chest, but I feel it starting to subside.

"We should get moving; those clouds do look ominous," he says.

I watch him reach for the pack, tossing it over his shoulders like it weighs nothing and then draping the blanket over himself. I push myself off the ground and follow behind him, still trying to figure out what the hell happened. *He didn't know that I could... what?* He can't seriously think this conversation is over.

"Axel, wait!" I call after him, trying my best to keep up with his quick pace. I'm lighter on my feet without the heavy bag weighing me down. "What was that?"

He turns, and his eyes have turned cold and hard. I feel a chill clear down to my bones. "Selena, drop it. Please."

I don't want to drop it. If anything, he's made me even more curious, but I know that he's not going to budge, at least not for now. I nod and fall in step beside him.

I scan the road for the next few miles, looking for anything that would work as a shelter for the night. Little side roads break off this one, but I'm afraid to venture down one and find nothing at the end. We're too tired to risk wasted steps.

Axel remains quiet, so I keep myself entertained by counting the furry creatures we pass. Six squirrels, two birds, and one tiny porcupine, all oblivious to the human struggle right in front of them.

I see a few old rotting signs for lodges and motels, but nothing looks promising. If we can keep pushing forward, I feel we'll eventually get to a more populated area. But everything has changed over the last few years, and many of these places no longer exist. I'd prefer a more solid lead.

Axel doesn't comment when he sees the signs, evidently content to defer to me. His jaw is set in a hard line, though, and I wish I could read his thoughts.

I'm getting tired, and my feet hurt, but I'm not complaining to Axel. Especially not when he's carried my backpack since we stopped earlier. It doesn't seem to weigh anything when he's carrying it, but I know firsthand how heavy it actually is.

I'm about to give up and tell him we should look for an abandoned car to sleep in when a sign ahead catches my eye.

According to the more freshly painted metal sign, we're only two miles from the Mount Hood Highway. We're way off my original path, but I have traveled this road before, a highway I've driven with my parents at least a dozen times. A ranger station is coming up, and it'll be the perfect place for us to stop for the night and regroup. Relief and excitement bubbles up inside me like I've suddenly been carbonated.

"Axel! Can you make it another two miles?" I can't help the pep in my step. I bounce on my sore calves as I turn to face him head-on.

"Of course. Do you know where we are?"

"Yes, and we won't be sleeping outside tonight if I have anything to say about it."

Chapter Sixteen

When the ranger station buildings finally come into view, I almost cry. But I force myself to slow down and be cautious. We don't know if someone is staying here. If anyone *is* left, though, hopefully they'll be park rangers and not the same kind of creeps my friends and I ran into.

Axel looks nervous, and I try to keep my breathing even and my face blank so he doesn't sense my own anxiety. I can see a few buildings, and I'm hoping one of the smaller ones with a telling chimney will be easy to get inside.

We spend precious time watching for movement or signs of life, but after what feels like an hour, nothing moves. A few cars are abandoned along the road and in one parking lot, but from the state of them, they seem to have been here for years. The buildings themselves all appear deserted—no smoke rises from the chimneys, and I see no shadows in the windows.

I couldn't blame someone for leaving a cabin in a small town like this and searching for power or supplies in one of the bigger towns nearby. We're getting closer and closer to civilization again, and as much as I'm comforted knowing I'll be home soon, I'm terrified we'll find more evil people first.

Axel follows me silently as I try the handle on a small cabin off to the side of the main buildings. It looks like a residence much larger than the hunting cabin we slept in last night. I'd be happy with another cabin like the last, but this larger place could have even more helpful supplies.

I let out a breath as the handle turns. The door swings open easily. It's musty and dark inside—the quickly fading daylight doesn't quite make it through the thick curtains.

"Hello?" I call out softly. My feet make the old wooden floor creak beneath me. I pause, waiting to see if there's any response. But no one is here—it's as abandoned as it looked from the outside.

A large brown couch sits in the main room next to a handmade wooden log coffee table and the most beautiful rock fireplace. A huge stack of firewood lines the wall next to it, and I feel tears prick my eyes. Sleeping in here, in front of the fire, will be so much better than what I had thought our night was going to look like. I was almost convinced we would be trapped outside at the mercy of the wilderness.

I quickly start a fire and light a few of the candles around the main room. Axel waits with the door open until I've finished, giving me as much light as he can. But when he finally shuts the door, I rush over and lock the two deadbolts. I'm not taking any chances while we sleep.

I'm so tired, I consider not even checking the rest of the house and instead collapsing on the couch. But I know that's not smart.

Reluctantly, I carry one of the candles through the house. I see a mostly bare kitchen and two small bedrooms. The larger of the two has men's clothes hanging in an open closet, and I whirl around to tell Axel the good news—and find he's right behind me. "Maybe these clothes will fit you and we won't have to worry about you losing any fingers or toes for the rest of the way." I smile, playfully poking him in the side.

Axel moves some of the hangers aside, assessing what I've found. I hold the candle close so he can see, and he pulls out a large jacket with a fur-lined hood. It looks thick and warm and large enough to fit him. "How did you know this place was here?" he asks, pulling on the jacket and trying out the zipper.

"My dad and I stopped at the information building once when we were looking into camping spots. They mentioned that some of the little cabins around here can be rented out and some are permanent residences. Honestly, I wanted to find something with a fireplace if we could."

"You spend a lot of time in the wild with your dad?" he asks.

"We used to when I was younger. In the summertime when school was out, anyway. My mom decided that I should spend my summers doing things that would get me outside but safely away from crowds of people. A few years ago, she changed her mind—she told me she didn't feel like making the trek out of town was safe anymore. I think if the world were different, I would have liked to travel and explore the mountains everywhere. But I enjoyed it while it lasted."

Mom always means well, and Dad always wants Mom to be happy, so I hadn't bothered to fight them on it. But the waterfall of sadness washing over me now makes me wish I had.

"Well, I guess you're more prepared for this adventure than I am. It's a little out of my comfort zone out there."

"Yeah, I could tell. Haven't spent much time outdoors?"

Axel shakes his head sadly. "You have no idea."

As if the world hears us, rain batters down outside. It's coming down hard, assaulting the roof and running off the sides of the building. It sounds more like rocks than water.

"It's a good thing we came in when we did." Axel sighs, his movements slow now. The hunger and exhaustion are taking a toll on both of us.

"Come on, I'll figure out something for us to eat. We can pick out your clothes tomorrow." I take his hand and lead him back to the waiting fire. The candles flicker around the room, and a little bit of the chill has already left the air. This cabin is much more insulated than the last one.

I find a can opener and a pot in the small kitchen, and we heat some canned beans over the fire. I set the coffee table, and we eat out of actual bowls with spoons. It feels nice to eat something warm.

When we're finished, I drop the dishes into the empty sink. Rainwater streams down over the kitchen window, the storm raging on. We could be stuck out there, but we're not. We're safe and warm and dry for tonight. I say a little prayer of thanks to cover my bases and then head back to the living room.

Axel is standing near the fire, not as close as he did last night, but still abnormally close. His eyes flutter back and forth as he stares at the dancing flames.

"You're not a pyro or something, are you?" I laugh.

He turns, his eyes glowing in that silvery way I'm becoming accustomed to. "'Pyro'?"

My forehead bunches up as I stare at him. "Pyromaniac? You know, someone who has an obsession with catching things on fire and watching them burn?"

His eyes go wide. "Absolutely not. I... it's beautiful. People do that? Set things on fire for the fun of it?"

He's never heard of arson?

Everything seems new to Axel, and I have so many questions. "Didn't you ever have a campfire with your family?"

Axel shakes his head. His expression turns serious. "I didn't grow up anything like you did."

I wish he'd elaborate, but the way his body hunches in on itself makes me think he's done with this line of questioning. I turn away, lifting the plush cushions on the couch to see what's below them. "Yes! Score!" I call out, finding the frame of a pull-out bed underneath.

"What have you found?" Axel asks, stepping away from the fire and following my gaze to the couch.

"There's a bed inside. We can pull it out and grab some blankets from the other room—it'll be much warmer out here by the fire. We're going to need to get some sleep if we're going to finish this trip." I smile. Finally, things seem to be going our way. But in the back of my mind, questions still swirl and fester. There's something about Axel, something different, maybe even dangerous. Whatever it is, it's clear he's not comfortable telling me... at least not yet.

Once the bed is made up and we've changed into more comfortable sleeping clothes, the mood in the room turns awkward. This time, Axel isn't freezing to death, and the urgency to save him isn't there. This time, we're simply two teenagers in a house, alone, getting ready to climb into bed together.

I spy a pack of cards on the side table, which perks me up. "Want to play a few games of cards before bed?"

"Card games?" Axel frowns. "I don't really know any card games."

Seriously. This kid definitely grew up under some kind of rock, and I thought *I* was sheltered. I shuffle the deck anyway, humming to myself as he watches me handle the cards. They arch in a rainbow together, not a single one flying out. I'm showing off, but it's more to distract us both than anything else.

"I can teach you something simple. Go Fish?"

"Go fishing? I thought you wanted to play cards."

I can't help but laugh. "No, silly, the card game is called Go Fish."

Amusement flashes in his eyes; he's messing with me. "Whatever you say." He shrugs, sitting cross-legged on the bed beside me. I quickly deal two piles and hand Axel his cards.

"Okay, don't show me your cards. If you have any matches, two of any number, set them aside. If you have a lone card, for example, a five, and you need a match, you'll ask me if I have any fives. If I have a five, I'll hand it over, and you'll have a match to set aside. If I don't have one, I'll tell you to 'Go Fish,' and you'll draw a card from the stack in the middle. When you run out of cards, you'll draw seven more. The winner is the person at the end of the game with the most matches. Got it?"

Axel grins at me. "Actually, I think I do."

Four games later, it's clear he was paying attention. He's won every single hand.

I showed him how to shuffle, and he's currently amusing himself with the cards. I watch him closely, admiring the way his fingers move so swiftly on the cards. A crease forms between his eyes on his forehead as he concentrates, his confidence growing by the minute. I feel sorry for him, knowing he's never played cards with his family or his friends, but I'm also enjoying teaching him something new.

"You never played any games with your friends, either?" I can't help the questions; they just keep coming. He's a mystery to me, and as the first non-Academy kid I've had the chance to interact with, he will have to deal with all my nosy questions.

Axel stills. He starts to open his mouth but then seems to change his mind and shakes his head.

"What did you do with your friends, then?" Axel doesn't answer me. When he simply continues to shuffle the cards, I place my hand over his. "Axel?"

"I guess we mostly talk, and I like to run. Sometimes, we'd race around the track or see who could swim underwater the longest before taking a breath. That sort of thing."

"Oh, you're an athlete? That's cool. I ran cross-country for a while, but we weren't allowed to compete with other schools, so I started running alone instead of competitively. It wouldn't matter now, anyway—so few of us are left."

"I never played any team sports. We didn't have that—only exercise. I like to push myself, see how strong and fast I can be." A genuine smile crosses his lips, deepening the dimple in his chin. "And I am usually the fastest and the strongest."

I laugh then. That's the first time he's sounded like the other boys I know. "Ha, I bet you are."

"So you and your friends play cards—what else do you do?" Axel turns the question back on me. He slides the cards back into their box and lays down on his side, waiting for me to answer him.

I wrap a loose thread on the quilt around my index finger while I think about my answer. My heartbeat thumps rapidly in my ears. Apparently, I like to lead my friends to their deaths...

The guilt presses down on my chest like an elephant, and I struggle to keep my breathing even. "Well, we watch a lot of old horror movies. They're so ridiculous and more gross than scary—we like to pick them apart and laugh about it. We're also huge fans of smuggling junk food into the school and having candy-fueled dance parties in our room. We share a room at school, Evelynn, Hanna, and I. We've pretty much been together since we were babies."

I swallow back the emotion. "They're really more like sisters to me than friends. We fight sometimes and get on each other's nerves, but we'd fight to the death for each other, too. They're my family."

Axel takes my hand in his. "Maybe they'll be okay."

I hope he's right, but I have the sinking feeling that they're not okay. That none of us will ever be okay again.

I pull my hand from his and tell him I'm feeling tired, climbing into the blankets and turning away. He's being so sweet to me, but I don't want him to see how weak I feel. I'm finally starting to feel close to him, like I might be able to understand him.

But the mood is ruined by my grief. Tears leak from my eyes, and I can't make them stop. I say a prayer that my friends really are okay and that I'll see them again and then let sleep pull me under.

CHAPTER
SEVENTEEN

WHEN I WAKE UP the next morning, it's still raining. The fire is out again, and Axel is snoring softly beside me on the pull-out couch. I cried myself to sleep, so we hadn't snuggled quite as close last night as we did before, but I still felt safer with him next to me. I don't know if I'd be doing this well alone. I'm thankful I don't have to find out.

I slip out of the bed, careful not to wake him. I dig through my pack and find the soap and toiletries I'd packed from my room and a fresh set of clothes. There's no running water here, but the rain has filled up a half dozen buckets on the back porch, and I intend to clean myself up today. I smell like sweat and dirt, which is not helping my mood.

On the porch, I stare into the woods. I don't see or hear anyone nearby. The sun is starting to peek through the trees despite the rain, and the birds are calling out their morning song. It smells like wet earth, as the rain is still pelting down on the tiny porch roof. I risk a quick run into the nearby trees to pee, getting half drenched in the process.

Once I'm back on the porch, I hide behind the ivy-covered lattice on one side and strip naked. I dump one full bucket over my head—the frigid water sucks the air from my lungs, and I shudder. It feels heavenly, though, to wash off the dirt of the last few days—it's worth the temporary ice bath feeling.

I quickly wet my washrag in another bucket and soap my body, making sure to scrub every dirty smudge from my skin. I wash my hair; the lemon-scented suds make me feel fresh and more human again. A rainbow paints the sky above the trees, and I start to sing softly, a song about rain that my grandmother used to sing to me.

The second bucket is less of a shock, and I revel in the feeling of clean hair and a clean body. It's funny how much a person can take cleanliness for granted. I dry quickly and put on my fresh clothes, washing my dirty clothes in the rainwater before wringing them dry. I'll find a way to hang them up over the fire later.

I'm still on the porch brushing my teeth, my hair wrapped up in the towel on top of my head, when Axel comes outside. "Good morning," he says. I take my eyes off the woods to turn in his direction. He looks rumpled from sleep, his silver hair pressed up on one side, his clothes wrinkled and torn. Somehow, he still looks beautiful.

"Good morning. Did you sleep okay?" I mumble around my toothbrush.

"I did. Did you shower?" He laughs, pointing to the towel on my head. "How did you manage that feat?"

I gesture to the three remaining rain buckets on the porch. Pulling my toothbrush from my mouth, I slide it back into my toiletry bag. "I decided cleanliness was worth the sacrifice of this rainwater. And I do not regret it. You're welcome to use some yourself. We still have plenty of drinking water, more than we can carry, so it seems like a good use of the extra."

"Do I smell that bad?" He turns his head to sniff his pits, and I start to laugh. If he smells bad, I haven't noticed, but I appreciate the comedy act.

"I wasn't trying to insinuate anything, but I know I feel a heck of a lot better now than I did when I woke up this morning. If my mom could see me sleeping on clean sheets in dirty clothes, she'd lose her mind."

He laughs, too, dimples flashing in his cheeks. "I'm teasing—I'm just glad to see you smiling. And a shower does sound good. Are there more towels somewhere?"

"Sure, I'll grab you one. I'll leave the soap and toothpaste here for you, too." I quickly duck inside, his laughter following me through the door. The sound makes me grin wider. The cry last night and the rainbow this morning seems to have improved my mood. I can't completely shake the gravity of our situation, but a permanently sour mood doesn't help either of us.

I hang my wet clothes and the towel from my head over a wooden drying rack in the house before grabbing a fresh fluffy green towel and rushing back to the porch. I slip slightly on the wet wood as I come to a halt.

"I got you a towel—" The words die on my lips. Axel has his back to me, but he's already undressed, water cascading in rivulets over his pale skin. His naked backside is staring at me—he's all angular lines and lean muscles—but before I can close my eyes or turn around, something else catches my eye.

Dozens of red scars mar the porcelain skin on his back. Puckered and angry-looking, they remind me of the scar on my knee where I had to have surgery after a running injury in the eighth grade. They're too straight, too uniform to be from any kind of accident. Even fully healed, they appear deliberate and painful. All my questions about where he's from come crashing down on me. Did his parents do this to him? Is that why he doesn't want to talk about his family?

Axel starts to turn, and I finally squeeze my eyelids together, heat radiating over my face, holding the towel out in front of me as a shield. "Sorry! Your towel!"

I keep my eyes tightly sealed but I feel the weight of the towel leave my fingertips and hear him drying off. I back up slowly toward the kitchen door, my breaths coming fast and ragged.

I can't get the image of those scars on Axel's back out of my mind. I can see them clearly, even with my eyes closed, slashes of pink and red in various stages of healing. I feel the glass door behind me, and I make sure I'm facing away from him before opening my eyes. I rush into the kitchen and double over, pressing my hands into my knees. I think I'm going to be sick.

"Selena?" Axel asks softly behind me, his bare feet making faint slapping noises on the kitchen floor. Tears leak out from the corners of my eyes as I try to get a hold of myself. I take a deep breath through my mouth and wipe the tears from my face before standing. I don't turn to face him, afraid he'll see too much in my face.

"I'm sorry, I'm okay. I just need a second." Even after the small cry I allowed myself last night, I've been holding in all my emotions for days now, and they've reached a fever pitch. I feel them threaten to level me with their force. I thought I was doing okay, but thinking about how Axel might have gotten those scars was clearly my tipping point. I want to smooth them out with my fingertips, touch each one as if I can remove the hurt there somehow.

Axel doesn't respond, he just comes around to face me, tipping my chin up so I am forced to meet his gaze. He holds me there, my chin in his large hand, searching my eyes for something. He's dressed now, but his hair is wet like mine, drops of water catching the sunlight from the open door like glittery gemstones. We finally get a break in the rain, and the quiet overwhelms me.

"Tell me what you're thinking right now," he says. His voice is so quiet I almost miss it.

I think about lying, but I don't want to. I blink back fresh tears. Someone hurt this boy, this boy who has been so courteous to me, this boy I feel is already my friend. "Your back... what happened to you, Axel?"

A light flashes in his eyes, and he grips my shoulder with his free hand, the other still firmly grasping my chin. And suddenly, I'm not in the kitchen anymore.

I'm lying face down on some kind of medical table. I can taste metal and hear a symphony of voices around me. My own back is on fire. I feel the cut of knives, the pricking of needles, an influx of searing pain... I feel strong hands pressing me down, the bite of restraints on my wrists and ankles. My body is simultaneously ice cold and burning from the outside in. Fear overwhelms me, and I cry out, but no sound comes. It's as if my tongue is paralyzed and I have no way to tell these people that they're hurting me.

I fight with everything I have as they continue to cut into my skin. My body refuses to move on my command, my heart is racing, and I'm screaming silently inside my head... Someone help. Please. Please. Please.

And then Axel lets go. His hands fall away from my body, and everything stops. I'm back in the kitchen next to him, our hair still wet from our porch showers.

I struggle to breathe, the fear slowly draining from my body. The pain is gone, but the memory of it is seared into my brain. "What the heck was that?" I cry out.

Axel shakes his head, his eyes wide as if he's seen a ghost. "It's impossible... it's never worked before. They said it could never work."

"Who are 'they'? Who did that to you?" I don't know how he shared that with me, but I know without a doubt that's what happened to him. Bile climbs up my throat, and I swallow the acid back, willing myself not to vomit. That was the memory of the scars on his back. Somehow, he answered my question without speaking a single word.

"Humans." He sighs. I watch him run his fingers through his wet hair, his neck turning red in his anger.

"Humans?" It's a strange answer, but I'm afraid to say anything more. I cross my arms over my chest, hugging them to me. The cold air from the open door gives me a chill. Goosebumps cover my skin, but I can't seem to move my feet to close it. Axel looks tortured, at war in his own mind. I wait as patiently as I can for him to speak again.

"They call us *HATS*. H-A-T-S." He turns back to face me, taking my hands. I involuntarily flinch at the contact. "I won't show you again without telling you first. I think I can hold it back. I'm sorry if I scared you before. I didn't think it would work." He frowns, his face pinched with regret.

I nod, but I'm too confused to fully trust his words. I just want him to keep talking. "Who calls you that?"

"Are you sure you want to know all of this?" he asks. I'm surprised that my answer is yes, despite the fear growing inside of me. I'm not scared of Axel, but I *am* scared of what he has to say. I want to understand him. For better or worse, I need to know everything there is to know about this boy and what he's been through.

"Yes. Please." I shiver again, and this time Axel closes the door and leads me over to the sofa bed. We sit, and he wraps a blanket around me before he takes both of my hands in his again.

"The humans call us *HATS*. It stands for Human Ardorian Test Subjects. We're not from your planet. Not originally, at least. I mean, our ancestors weren't." His thoughts are disjointed, and he squeezes my hands as he tries to find the right words.

If he's not from our planet, does he mean aliens? He expects me to believe he's some kind of alien. Do I even believe in aliens?

And yet, somehow, I do believe the words. I believe *him*. I feel absolutely certain that he's telling me the truth. But I have so many questions—this is so much bigger than abusive parents or the sheltered upbringing that I'd speculated before. He isn't some child from a strange family... he was tortured, used for science?

I tread lightly with my questions. "You said *Human* Ardorian... what does that mean exactly?"

"Half of my DNA is human; the other half is Ardorian. We are a failed experiment, one where they were breeding us with humans, hoping to come up with some kind of superhuman. When it didn't go as they planned, the project was set to be terminated." His shoulders slump as he remembers.

"I don't understand; why don't we know about this? I've never heard of any Ardorians... Where were they keeping you? How long has this been going on?" The questions spill out of me, bubbling up and pouring over the edge like a pot forgotten on the stove. *So much for treading lightly, Selena.*

"They kept us at a base on your moon—there's an outpost there. It's where our original ancestors grouped and reached out to your people for help, a mistake they lived to regret. The humans pretended to want to help them but then took them prisoner.

"They kept the original crew for decades on that base, allowing them to reproduce so they could continue to experiment. And then they got this bright idea to start crossbreeding them with humans, but it didn't end how they wanted. We have issues—temperature control, for one. And while we do look like humans and have most of the same body chemistry, we also have different abilities. Ways of communicating without words."

"Like you showed me before. And like when I asked about your parents for the first time?" I rub my chest, remembering the pain I'd felt there.

I'm angry for him, for his people... for the poor souls who were subjected to unspeakable things. My seething anger drowns out the shock of his words.

"I didn't mean to share my feelings with you that first time." He shakes his head. "I told myself it was a coincidence that you felt my pain—I was convinced you didn't feel it physically but more like empathy, perhaps. But the second time, I knew for sure. We call them projections. It's what the scientists were trying to improve on, to see how they could use it as a weapon. That was part of the failed experiment. On the moon base, I could never share anything with anyone who wasn't Ardorian."

Until me.

"If you're an Ardorian, where does that make you from?"

"There's no real translation for our planet's name in your language. The closest they could come up with was Ardor. That's why we are called Ardorians."

My head spins. So much information at once, and yet, I'm eager to hear more. Anything that Axel is willing to tell me. "But you're half Ardorian and half human?"

"Yes, one of my parents was *human*." The way he spits out the word *human*, as if it leaves a sour taste in his mouth, gives me pause. I could understand why he'd be upset with the scientists who did this to him, but does he hate the rest of us, too?

"Did you know them... your parents, I mean?" I ask instead, trying not to push too hard. My head is spinning with questions. None of this seems possible.

Axel closes his eyes and takes a deep breath, pulling his hands from mine. I immediately miss the physical connection, but I don't reach for him. I let him have his space.

"Not in the way you knew your parents. My mother was human, a volunteer from the space program. Once I was born, she handed me over to the scientists. I was never allowed to know which of the Ardorians was my father. There were more than a dozen possibilities. They raised us together, all the HATS. The full Ardorians, men and women, cared for us. They were only allowed to speak Earth languages with us, and they weren't supposed to pass on any information about Ardor or our abilities to us. But the humans were never aware when they were sharing their memories with us. That's the thing—we could easily use our abilities with the Ardorians and with each other but never with someone who was fully human."

My heart hurts, but this time, I know it's my own feelings, because Axel isn't touching me anymore. "I'm so sorry, Axel—that's horrifying. I don't know how anyone can treat another living being that way, especially their own son."

I think of my mother, who, despite her quirks and less-than-motherly instincts, has always loved me. Yes, she sent me away to school, but only because she agreed before I was even born to do what was best for me. She was trying to keep me alive. It would do me good to remember that.

I pull my knees up into my chest and rest my chin on them. Axel has gone quiet, and he's watching me closely, his eyes heavy with emotion. He still looks the same to me—he's still Axel, the same silver-haired, moonlight-eyed, slightly blue-lipped boy he was the first time I saw him. And while I have no reason to trust his outlandish story, I do. I feel the truth of it in my bones. Like the first moment I laid eyes on him, I knew I was meant to find him somehow. I've never believed anything more.

"Why did you tell me this?" I stare into the ash pile in the cold fireplace, unsure why I suddenly feel so self-conscious.

"Are you sorry that I did?" he asks, running his hands back and forth over his pant legs.

"No, not at all. It just seems like a lot. Especially to trust a stranger with." I finally let my eyes find his gaze again. The glowing moonlight there pulls me in. His eyes are like nothing I've ever seen before, and I can't seem to escape their pull. He moves slowly, turning so that we're inches apart. I let my hands fall from my knees and turn to meet him. My heart is racing with anticipation. It pounds away in my ears.

Thump, thump. Thump, thump.

"Are you scared?" he asks.

"No. Despite everything you've told me, I trust you somehow." The words are a whisper as they slip past my lips. I *should* be scared. I should feel more shock, more confusion, but somehow, I only feel drawn to him. He's been kind and honest, and I'd be lying if I said I wasn't completely enamored of him.

"I trust you, Selena. I can feel you. I can feel what you're feeling, and I know I'm safe with you." His lips tremble slightly when he says this. His gaze falls to my lips. I know his intention before he even takes his next breath. And I'm sure I want him to kiss me as much as I'm sure he's about to.

I bite my lip slightly, releasing it before closing my eyes and leaning toward his mouth. I feel his lips touch mine, barely, a whisper of a touch. And then his hands are cradling my head as he pulls me in further. When his lips finally press deliciously against mine, overwhelming emotion washes over me, making me sigh into the kiss. Surrendering to the moment.

I sense what he's feeling, warmth and safety and desire all wrapped up and tingling through my mind. He must be projecting again. He said he wouldn't, but I'm glad that he is. Maybe he doesn't even know he's doing it.

The feelings coil around my limbs, and I buzz with electricity. It's intoxicating and frenzied, and it feels almost magical. I let my own hands fall to his chest, not to push him away but because I want to feel him under my fingertips.

He's solid and real, and this is truly happening.

His tongue slides against mine—it's warm and slow and feels like silk as it caresses my own. I'm wrapped in the scent of lemon soap and something entirely Axel. I never want this moment to end.

This. *This* is what Evelynn was telling me about. This is how it's supposed to feel.

This is living.

Chapter Eighteen

THE RAIN CONTINUES ITS torrent against the cabin for most of the morning and into the afternoon. Axel and I decide it would be best to wait a day and see if the storm lets up. To be honest, I'm relieved to hear him say it. After days of constant movement, rest sounds like something foreign and impossible to find. But my muscles are aching from overuse, and I have bruises and blisters all over my body.

I'm still reeling from the kiss we shared—the emotions inside me are swept up in a swirl of excitement and newness. We haven't talked about it, but I don't regret the moment at all. I keep hoping that it will happen again. I wish I could tell Evelynn that first kisses really can be amazing.

The grief is waiting there, right below the surface. I try my hardest not to think of my friends or what has happened. I need to rest my mind and my body. Everything at once is just too heavy.

Axel isn't from Earth. That should weigh more heavily on my mind than it does, but I've accepted it. It doesn't change his character or make the heart that beats in his chest any different from my own. It's simply another interesting thing about the boy who has captured my attention.

Knowing he's different, and that his place of origin couldn't be any more different than my own, doesn't bother me. My biggest concern right now is just keeping him warm. Earlier, I searched through the bedrooms, finding hats, gloves, and plenty of warm jackets to get us through the rest of our journey. Even though we will be heading away from the mountain, the weather could quickly become a problem, especially for Axel. I can't seem to find a way to keep him warm without having him sit directly in front of the fire.

Axel added some wood to it, and I showed him how to keep it going before leaving him to warm up so I could scavenge the house for anything useful. Despite our mostly hidden location, every time I pass a window, I can't help but stare out, making sure no one is coming for us. Part of me is also watching for my friends. Though they would've had no reason to even know to come this way, a part of me holds on to the hope that they survived.

Piling up the good clothes and a few helpful things like a pocketknife and a good-sized canteen, I head back to the main room. Axel is lying on the bed facing the fire, his back to me, and I pause, watching him breathe. He looks peaceful, having a moment to catch his breath. He's had an even crazier journey than I have, and he's lost so much. He can never go home.

My lips tingle as I think about our kiss. I touch them with my fingertips like I can recreate the feeling. I'm drawn to Axel in a way I've never felt before. I can't explain it, but I know it's right. I like Garrett, and he's important to me, but I never felt anything like this with him in all the years I've known him.

Guilt washes over me, knowing Garrett might be hurt out there somewhere, wishing for my company. And I'm here, warm and safe, and I've kissed another boy.

Axel turns on the bed and smiles at me. "Find anything?"

I push away my guilty feelings and smile back at him. I have to take comfort where it's given. The world is in turmoil, and this is my one gift. Axel and I were meant to find each other; I choose to believe in that. "Some good clothes for you. Hopefully, they'll do a better job at keeping you warm than the ones you have now."

"You can come help keep me warm if you want." He winks, and I can't help but laugh. I join him on the couch, wrapping the blanket around us both. He tucks my head under his chin and holds me close. We lay that way for a while, staring into the flames and letting our bodies rest. I try not to think about the next few days and what we might find in Portland as I slowly drift off to sleep.

I'm greeted by the sun early the next morning. It bleeds in through the gap between the curtains, and I feel it dance across my eyelids before I even open them. The morning brings with it the sound of birds chirping and the *drip, drip, drip* of water somewhere. Sometime in the night, it finally stopped raining, and today, we will need to continue our journey west to Portland.

Axel's arm is wrapped securely across my waist, his fingers gripping the blanket. I trace his fingers one at a time with my own. I'm comforted by the warmth I find there.

He's been warm for a full day now; I wish I knew it would last.

I turn in his embrace, my face only inches from his. "Good morning, sleepyhead."

His eyelids flutter softly, and a slow smile slides across his face. "Good morning." He looks me over, raising his hand to tuck my hair behind my ear. "Can we stay here forever?"

The question makes my stomach flutter. I wish we could pretend our little bubble here was all there was. That we didn't have friends and family out there we needed to get to. That the world wasn't collapsing in on itself, falling into chaos and heartache. I'd gladly stay here with him, asking him all the questions I could come up with. I still have so many, but I don't want to make him uncomfortable.

"I'll start packing things up; you should go change into those warm clothes we found." I press myself into his chest, wrapping my arms tightly around him as if hugging him can somehow keep me from falling apart. "I wish we could stay here, but we have important things to do."

Axel groans but pushes himself up to a sitting position on the bed, taking me with him. "Fine, we will get dressed and eat something and head out. But first..." He takes my hand in his, drawing patterns on my palm with his thumb. "What happens when we get to Portland?"

"My friends and I have always planned to meet at Liam's house. If his brother is there, he could have more information about what is happening right now." I pause and take a shuddering breath. "And if any of them made it out of that situation and kept walking, that's where I think they would go."

Axel looks up from gathering his shoes. "And if we don't find anyone there?"

"Then we will see if we can find my family."

"Okay." He nods. I wonder if he's thinking about his own family. I still don't exactly understand how they got separated, but it's clear that Axel doesn't remember much of what happened before I tripped over him in the woods.

"Once we've tried those things, we will come up with a plan to see your family, too. Maybe by then, the power will be back on, and this will all be a distant memory."

Axel doesn't look convinced, and to be honest, the further we get, the worse it seems. If his people were all together when they crashed, why weren't they still with him in the woods? What kind of ship did they even have? How had he ended up all alone and dying in those woods?

I pull myself up off the bed and get to work. If I don't make myself move now, I know that I won't. I'll allow myself to get pulled back into Axel's arms and worry about useless, meaningless crap when I should be getting on with my life.

I think about my friends, Garrett and Hanna, Liam and Evelynn, and how pampered our lives were before this. We weren't prepared for the violence and the consequences of the real world. Our fancy school had grilled us on physical fitness and personal hygiene standards, on algebra and social etiquette. But nowhere in our studies did they teach us how to survive a massive power failure or how to navigate scary emotional situations. They'd wrapped us too tightly with bubble wrap in an attempt to keep us pure, and we'd suffocated instead.

I'd give anything to be back at the Academy on any normal day, hustling to get to class on time, where my biggest worry would be something trivial like whether I'd remembered my favorite lip gloss or not. Why did we think we could head out on our own and make it? Hanna had been right to be mad at me. I'd listened to Garrett's ideas about safety and blindly agreed to follow him anywhere. We could have talked to Mr. Mason—maybe he would have taken us all together or at least helped us make a better plan.

I'd let Garrett talk me into leaving, but the truth is, he didn't have to ask me twice.

I stuff supplies into my backpack, fighting back tears for my friends. The memory of gunshots echo in my ears. Had those awful men shot my friends? Had they tortured them? Did any of them try to follow me, to make sure I didn't get away?

I ran like a coward. I ran and never looked back. And I hadn't even tried to retrace my steps and see if they were okay. If by some miracle they make it to Portland, will any of them forgive me for that? I won't blame them if they don't. And if they are dead, part of me knows that it is my fault.

Axel needed me in the woods, and that had taken over all of my concentration. I'd replaced my friends in a matter of hours. What kind of a person does that make me? My stomach pitches, and I try not to think of the answer to that.

"You ready?" Axel reappears in the living room. He's wearing the big winter coat with a fur-lined hood that I found that first night, and he looks ridiculous but also warm. He's chosen thick black work pants, the kind I've seen some of the groundskeepers wear at school. I nod my response, standing on my tiptoes to pull a wool hat over his messy hair.

We'd found a second backpack, which is perfect because now we can share the load. I hand Axel his bag and adjust my own on my back, my shoulders crying out in protest.

I take one last look around the peaceful living space and log the memory somewhere safe in my mind. I don't know how the next few days will go, but I do know I'm thankful for the brief shred of peace we found here.

My friends might not be the only worry on my mind, but I do care about them. I will make it to Portland for all of us. I can't let this all be for nothing. I close my eyes and pray they'll forgive me.

I'm sorry.

Then I open my eyes and take a steadying breath. If we are going to make it, I cannot keep looking back. The only way to go is forward. "Let's do this."

Chapter Nineteen

The rain has stopped, but the ground is damp, and the air has cooled considerably. Our breaths come in little white puffs as we set out on the highway toward Portland. I'm relieved to know we're going in the right direction this time.

It's still early, and the birds are chirping in the trees. It's always quiet out here in the mountains, but without the occasional car going by, it's a thicker quiet than before.

Axel asks questions about the trees and the squirrels, and I answer as many of them as I can. It's weird to think he's never seen most things in real life before. I suppose there was a limit to what he could experience growing up on a space station. He's used to the dark and the cold and the inside of a sterile environment, but everything here is new and different.

According to the map at the ranger station, we have forty-five miles left until Portland. If we walk nonstop at an average pace of three miles per hour, we can make it there in the next fifteen hours, give or take. It will be a feat, but I'd rather not sleep outside if we can help it. We've been lucky enough to avoid it so far. We're more rested and fed than we have been since the beginning, and I can only hope we can pull this off.

The closer we get to Portland, the more likely we are to run into other people. After my experience in the town outside school and then the ambush with my friends, that part makes my palms itch with fear. Axel and I will have to be careful and on full alert. I hate to reiterate Axel's hatred toward the human species, but I can't avoid warning him about what could happen.

I find the smell of the wet soil and trees calming. It's fresh and earthy and much better than the stale air from the cabin. Even Axel seems to come alive in the fresh air. He has a bounce in his step today, his lips upturned at the corners as if he's permanently smiling.

We walk side by side, keeping a steady pace. Axel has been quiet for what feels like an hour, and the silence allows all of my questions to come seeping back in. I finally break the silence myself.

"You never told me how you escaped the base on the moon. I can't imagine they let you go without a fight. Will you tell me about it?" I reach out and take his gloved hand in mine. He's quite a bit taller than me, so I have to bend my arm slightly to keep hold of his hand. I give him a reassuring squeeze.

"There were a few humans who helped us out from time to time. Sympathizers. They had to be careful—a few times, a sympathizer was found out, and we'd never see them again. If one of us got sick or needed something, they'd come through with medicine or whatever we needed. Sometimes we were separated, and they'd get messages back and forth between us, let us know that everyone was safe and alive." Axel's voice is thick as he talks, like he's got something stuck in his throat.

"There was one in particular—we called him Father. I don't know what his real name was, but we had to be so secretive, it was better to talk about Father, needing to speak with Father. The humans thought it was some kind of religious thing for us. Much like the Father in Heaven some humans speak of."

"And Father helped you?" I ask, imagining the human man who risked everything to help Axel and the Ardorians.

"For a time. A few years ago, he stopped coming. He was getting older, and it was no longer safe for him to keep coming and going from the moon. Many of the scientists were traded out after a few years of working with us." Axel kicks a rock off the road, watching it bounce into the trees. He stops walking and pulls me closer to him.

"Did you miss him when he stopped coming?" I stare into his moonlit eyes and see the pain there.

"He was always kind. There were rumors that he'd been helping since the beginning. That he was a true friend to the Ardorians. But no, it wasn't him who saved us in the end. It was another scientist, a woman. She found out that the project was going to be scrubbed. With all the new viruses here on Earth and the failed experiments with crossbreeding, they were ready to cut ties and head back home permanently."

"So they were going to let you go?" I know how naïve I sound the second the words leave my mouth.

A bird calls out, and I look for it in the trees, using the sound as an excuse to pry my gaze away from the despair reflected in Axel's eyes.

"No, Selena, they were going to terminate all of us."

Tears well in my eyes. "How could they do that? You are children, and even if they hated the Ardorians... you're still half-human. What about your mother?" Anger flashes through me, hot and red, drying my tears.

"The scientist may have been one of our mothers, but we'll never know now. She warned us. The oldest of the true Ardorians had already been planning their attack for years, so they executed it, knowing they didn't have any longer to wait. They attacked the humans on the base, got the children onto an original ship, and launched us to Earth. The ship was small, so it could not hold many of us. They sacrificed themselves for the young. They blew up the whole moon base, killing everyone so we could have a chance to live."

I shake my head. It's too much, too horribly sad and sadistic. How could my people have pushed them to take such a risk? They gave up everything so that their children, a mixture of human and alien, could live. They could have chosen to sacrifice the half-human children and be free to continue their own race, but they didn't.

"Can you show me?" The words shake as they leave my lips. I want to see it, feel it like Axel did. Share this pain with him so that he doesn't have to carry that burden alone.

Axel smiles through the tears sliding down his reddened cheeks. "It's kind of you to offer, Selena, but I don't think—"

"Please, Axel, let me share this with you. I want to see them. I want to know your people."

Axel wraps his arms around me, crushing me to his chest. I feel his chin press into the top of my head. It's the kind of hug that's almost too tight to bear, but I'd rather stop breathing forever than end the contact. I have so much empathy for this boy... and something more. I feel something sparkling and distant that I can't quite put my finger on.

"If you're sure, I'll show you," he whispers in my ear, kissing my cheek softly before standing tall.

"I'm sure," I say. I spy a log up ahead that looks like a good place to rest, and I move toward it. "Let's sit and drop these bags for a minute while you show me."

Axel removes his gloves, wiping his hands on his pants before following me over to the fallen log. The log is wet. I pull a towel from my backpack to protect our pants at least a little before playing with the braid on my shoulder nervously. As much as I want this, I'm apprehensive after feeling his memories of the experiments in the lab. My back still burns at the memory of the knives sliding through my skin.

"You don't have to do this." Axel chews his bottom lip. He looks even more handsome today. The cool air seems to have pinkened his cheeks rather than turned his lips blue. It's a nice change—I like the contrast of his pale hair and eyes against the healthy pink flush to his cheeks.

"I want to." I smirk at him, taking his hand in mine. "Do it quickly, before I work myself up too much."

Axel leans forward, cupping my chin with his free hand again, staring into my eyes with his silver ones. "Remember, it's not really happening to you—you're only seeing it through my eyes."

"Okay." I bite the inside of my cheek and nod to let him know I'm ready. He takes both of my hands in his, then I'm thrust right in.

The room is completely cloaked in darkness, but I can hear shouting in the distance. I'm lying on a metal bunk. I reach up, fumbling around for a light switch. When my fingers hit a round button on the wall, the room is suddenly flooded with light. I blink rapidly, trying to see through the haze of sleep that still clings to my eyes. The room, all shades of white and metal, is stark and sterile. I see a built-in desk and chair with some personal items on it and a few books on a shelf, but nothing else is in sight.

"Dax?" I call out, struggling to my feet. I pull the hoodie off the back of the desk chair and slide my arms in, struggling into a pair of shoes by the door. The shouting outside the room grows louder, and an alarm begins to blare.

"Emergency. Report to your duty stations. Emergency. Full report," a robotic voice repeats on a loop.

No one else is in the room with me, so I stumble through the door and out into a dimly lit hallway.

It's chaos. People are everywhere, running, screaming. Lights flash, and that alarm continues to blare in my ears. An older woman runs by, grabbing me roughly by the arm. "We must go now. Follow me."

"Go where? What's happening?" Fear stabs at my chest, and I struggle to keep up with the woman, my legs refusing to cooperate. "Where's Lyra?"

"She's already on the ship. Come, we must hurry. There's no time!"

We rush down the hallway and through a garage, then down, down, down, three flights of metal stairs that clang and groan under the barrage of boots as people rush by. There isn't enough light, and everyone is tripping and struggling to stay on their feet as we descend. Finally, we reach a large door, and the woman shoves me through. "Godspeed, my son. I am so sorry."

I take one last look at her face before she turns to run back up the stairs. The same tilt of her eyes, the same dimple in her chin as I see in the mirror greets me. The resemblance is too uncanny to ignore.

Mother.

Pain and recognition slice through me like a knife.

"*Axel!*" *someone shouts behind me. A loud explosion sounds somewhere nearby, and I cover my head with my hands, dropping to my knees on the floor.* "*Axel, get up! We have to go now!*"

A girl comes into my view. She's tall and lean, and her eyes are an almost transparent light blue. Her hair is a massive swath of short silver curls. "*Lyra? What's happening?*"

"*We're leaving. They're about to blow up this entire station. They thought they could kill us all and no one would fight back... they thought wrong.*" *She takes my hand and pulls me to my feet.* "*We have to hurry. We only get one shot at this.*"

Behind her is the ship that the ancestors took from Ardor so many years ago. It's small but imposing, triangular in shape and coated in varying shades of black and gray material. We've never been allowed this close to it. I'm surprised to find that the entrance is a ramp, much like the human jets we've studied in class. Lyra pushes me ahead of her into the ship, and I try to wrap my head around what's happening.

Inside are all of my classmates: Dax, Nova, Elara, and Leon. Each one is strapped into a smaller pod-shaped device, an oblong compartment with a glass window. Nova waves at me, her fear clear on her face.

Once Lyra and I are on board, all of the HATS are accounted for. I see a small command center at the front of the ship, so similar to a jet that I almost question if we're in the right one.

"*You need to get in a pod, Axel. Marc will be driving this thing, getting us out of here.*"

"*Marc? But what about everyone else? Is there another ship? How will they get out?*" *My voice is loud and accusatory. I can't help the panic I feel creeping into my throat.*

Lyra shakes her head. *"They're sacrificing themselves so we have a chance. But if you don't hurry up, it'll all be for nothing. You have a chance right now to help save us, so what will it be, Axel? This place is going to blow either way. At least this way, we get to take some of those human devils with us."*

My stomach lurches, and I feel like I might lose the contents, but I swallow back the feeling. "Where is Marc?" I ask the question as I move toward the last two open pods. "And does he not need a pod as well?"

"He doesn't expect to survive the trip—there's barely enough room for us as it is. There were only six original members on this ship, and we don't even know if it's been repaired enough to make the short journey to Earth. We have to try, though; we're the last of Ardor. We have to try."

As I'm about to protest, Marc comes running up the ramp. He's bleeding from somewhere center mass; blood has saturated his white jumpsuit. I watch him take inventory of us, counting out loud and sighing with relief. "Okay kids, here goes nothing."

I strap myself in, and the door on the pod closes over me. I can only see Marc at the helm now, pressing buttons and pushing levers and yelling something. Inside my pod, I feel oxygen start to flow, and I'm engulfed in absolute silence. I take deep breaths, trying not to think about everyone I've ever known being blown to bits. Trying not to think about the human woman who gave me up and sacrificed herself to give me a chance to live.

My Ardorian family, gone in one single blast.

The ship moves, and it feels like my body is being shaken up like soil samples in the tumbler. I can only see blackness out the window—I hope Marc knows what he's doing. The nausea rears its ugly head again, but I hold it in. I can't puke in here; that would make a miserable situation even more unbearable. I close my eyes, and then, moments later, the world lights up. It's so bright that even through my closed eyelids, I can see it.

White light. Turbulence. We're being tossed around by the shock of the blast. My head swings wildly from side to side, and then there's nothing but darkness.

I jerk back to reality, choking on air and tears. I didn't even know I'd been crying. Axel is staring at me, a mixture of fear and concern on his face. "Are you okay?" he asks.

"That was a lot." I force myself to take deep breaths, slowing my heart rate down.

"I didn't remember some of that until I showed you—" He rubs his hands on my shoulders, his eyes not meeting mine. "I think I wanted to forget."

I have to work to shake off the feeling of being tossed around in the pod, my stomach still rolling at the memory. "That must be why you don't remember anything from the crash—you must have blacked out. I'd put money on a concussion."

"It still doesn't explain why I was alone in the woods, though. One answer at a time, I guess." His face falls, and I can feel the frustration radiating off of him. "If I'm the only one who survived... all of those people... they're all dead—"

"Your mom, she—" Seems neither of us is willing to finish our thoughts out loud. That woman sacrificed her own life to save her son. Maybe she hadn't always been worthy, but I would hug her now if I could, thank her for saving this boy sitting next to me.

Axel shakes his head. "No, what she did was the right thing to do, but she still abandoned me. She still handed me over to those monsters. She stood by while they did all those things to us... She never tried to reach out to me before then. I can't forgive her now, not because of one moment when she finally did what a mother is supposed to do."

"Maybe she was doing everything she thought she could do? Maybe if she had done more, they would have sent her away and she wanted to stay close to you? We will never know what obstacles she was facing. I'm not excusing her behavior, but I *am* glad she got you out in time."

"We should start walking again. We have a lot of ground to cover today." Axel jumps to his feet and puts his pack back on without looking at me again. I've hit a nerve, and I know it. I press my lips together to keep from digging the hole any deeper and grab my backpack. He's right; we have a lot of walking to do. Maybe things will look a little brighter when we get to Portland.

Chapter Twenty

WE ARE EXHAUSTED, SOAKING wet, and chilled to the bone when we finally cross into the city. It's eerily dark without the sea of glowing lights that normally accompanies Portland. Part of me had held on to the hope that they'd have power here, that it was far enough from school to have been spared whatever happened. Seeing the complete darkness makes me wonder if the whole world has gone dark.

Welcome to Portland.

I used to love the sight of the city lights. Sometimes, I could convince my grandpa to break curfew and drive to the bridge so we could look out at the city, the lights reflecting and swirling on the river like colorful fish. I'd listen to his stories about life before the viruses desolated everything. About how people would party together on boats, walk together on busy sidewalks, make friends out of complete strangers standing in lines for things. I long to know a world that afforded such freedoms. To meet people who aren't in my family or part of the Academy. I've never even been on a boat.

They stopped making new movies and producing music and entertainment before I was born. All that remained were relics of a reality long gone, movies and lyrics that seemed like they came from some other world. I can't even imagine what it would be like to share a room with thousands of people to hear someone play music on a stage. I wish I could experience that, but my mind can hardly even conjure up the image of that many people all together at once.

My grandpa mourned the loss the most. He'd seen how it could be, watched everything he loved about society disappear before his eyes. I think sharing his stories with me pained him greatly, and as much as he wanted me to know about them, at some point, it always proved to be too much, and he'd grow quiet.

In those quiet moments, my imagination would try to create pictures from the stories he told me. I loved to imagine my grandma and grandpa at a concert, dancing and singing together.

I hope that somewhere my grandpa is safe, untouched by the viruses and destruction, so that he can one day wrap me up in his arms and tell me his stories again. As off-kilter as my world is now, it would be unrecognizable without my grandpa in it.

We continue to walk toward our destination. Unfamiliar sounds permeate the silent city. I try not to think too hard about the noises, what could be animals or people scurrying about in the darkness. I'm too scared to investigate them, instead focusing on moving my feet, one in front of the other. My shoes scratch across loose rocks on the road, sweat drips down the back of my neck despite the cold air around us, and I feel a weariness deep inside that I can't shake.

Axel has been quiet, but I'm too tired to keep up a conversation anyway. He drops behind me sometimes, still following but with some distance between us. I wish he'd stay right next to me—I feel safer when he's within arm's reach.

Liam's family lives in a gated community a few blocks from my grandparents' neighborhood. I'm relying heavily on muscle memory to find his house. Everything looks different in the dark with only the moonlight glinting off the wet pavement to guide our steps. I'm on high alert, my eyes scanning every direction for movement or danger.

When I can see the open gate for Liam's neighborhood, my heart catches in my throat. Despite all the setbacks, despite losing my friends along the way, my destination is finally within my grasp. An exhausted sob slips past my lips. The tiredness washes over me, vibrating in my bones. While my heart beats double-time, my feet pick up the pace on their own.

"We're almost there," I say more to myself than to Axel, who senses my urgency and jogs beside me.

As I turn onto Liam's street, the two-story brick house seems to call to me. I've never been past the wraparound porch. The few times I'd been allowed to meet Academy friends anywhere but the Academy, the rules had been outside playing only. They were always limiting our exposure to each other but also, I know now, limiting our exposure to the world around us. If only our families had known it would prove to be a disadvantage, always being hidden from the world and its struggles.

The windows are dark. Not a single house on the street appears occupied, but I have to try. I take the wooden steps up to the front door, my pace slowing so I can catch my breath. Axel's hand on my shoulder makes me stop short of the door. "Whatever we find here, Selena, you're not alone."

His words bring me back to reality. It's been days since the power went out and months since any of us have talked to our families. Something could have happened to them. What if all we find here is more disappointment or, worse, the bodies of the ones we love?

I press the fear down. Getting worked up with what-ifs won't do anyone any good. With one last look at Axel, I raise my hand and knock.

A swarm of bees gathers in my chest, anxiety so great I'm not sure I'll be able to speak if anyone comes. A muted noise comes from the other side of the door, and I hold my breath, straining my ears around my own buzzing to hear.

"Hello?" I call out, my voice shaky but loud enough to reach the other side. "My name is Selena Santos; I'm friends with Liam. I'm looking for his brother, Chase."

The distinct sound of metal on metal as the deadbolt slides out of its hold makes my whole body tremble. Someone is here. I reach for Axel's hand and squeeze hard, our gloved hands interlocking with a shared hope that not all is lost.

The door opens barely a crack, the flickering light of a candle casting shadows over the face of a man who appears to be in his mid-twenties, far younger than anyone I've seen outside of school. "Is it only the two of you?" the deep voice asks, his tone dripping with authority.

I have no way of knowing if this is Liam's brother, Chase, or if this is even someone related to Liam's family at all, but I'm quickly running out of options. If this is how I die, trying to reunite with my friends and find answers, then so be it. It beats hiding away in fear for the rest of my life. This trek we made cannot be for nothing.

"Yes. I'm Selena, and this is Axel." I raise our joined hands. "We're hoping you can help us." I don't tell the man in the shadows that Axel isn't from the Academy. It'll raise too many questions that I'm not sure how to answer yet. Besides, until I know for sure who he is and if he can help us, it seems smarter not to give away too much information.

"And Liam?" he asks.

"We got separated. I was hoping he was already here." Tears gather in my eyes; my friends haven't beaten me here. *Where are they?*

The man nods and pulls the door open, and with his face fully illuminated by candlelight, I can see his resemblance to Liam immediately. Blond hair, not curly like Liam's but cut into a military style, and the same wide mouth. "Come inside before someone sees you. But don't try anything stupid—I don't want to have to shoot you."

We follow Chase into the house. It's dark except for the glow of his one candle. The windows are all covered in thick curtains, and I'm not surprised the house looked unoccupied from the outside. Then I smell chicken soup, and my stomach growls in protest. My feet are aching, and if I sit down, I might fall asleep without even trying.

Axel holds tightly to my hand, my fingers going numb inside my glove from the pressure and the drastic temperature change. The house is much warmer than it was outside.

Chase motions for us to sit on an old leather couch in a spacious living room. I can see pictures of Liam and his family on the mantle above a dark fireplace. He lights a few more candles on the coffee table before taking a seat across from us in a reclining chair. I remove my gloves and backpack and sit as well.

"You say you're from the Academy, but how are you here?" He sits motionless in the chair, his full attention on me and Axel. His dark clothes blend in with the black leather of the chair he's sitting in, and he looks every bit like the soldier Liam said he was.

I shrug my shoulders. "We walked."

Chase doesn't react. He just continues to watch me. I try not to fidget under his gaze. "Liam told us that we should come here and see if you had any information on the power situation or any idea what we should do next. We could do nothing from school, and with only two teachers around, we didn't feel safe waiting there."

Chase nods, clasping his hands together over his lap. "And where is Liam now?"

I take a deep breath before I answer. "We were about halfway here when we ran into a group of people on the road. They attacked my friends... I was the only one able to get away. I had hoped that they would make it here somehow—"

"You were the only one who got away?" he asks, his face still impassive, but I notice a flicker of something in his eyes.

My body shudders as I realize the mistake I've made. In retracing my steps for Chase, I've forgotten to lie about Axel coming with us from the beginning. My mind races, trying to come up with some believable explanation, but Chase's eyes are narrowed on me now. He's reading me, and I've never been good at keeping a poker face. I'm not afraid of him, though I probably should be. This is another necessary risk, trusting him.

"Well, Axel..." I feel the boy in question stiffen beside me. He's been silent so far, but I can feel fear radiating off him in waves.

A loud commotion at the front door saves me from having to respond. Chase stands from his chair and presses a finger to his lips, motioning for us to remain silent. "Did someone follow you?" he whispers.

I hadn't seen anyone else, but those noises in the darkness could have been anything. "I don't think so," I whisper back.

Someone begins beating on the door. The vibration it sends through the house is too loud to be a knock—it has to be fists banging, maybe even feet kicking at the door. Chase pulls a gun from behind him, silently sliding the chamber back, loading it with practiced ease. "Wait here, and stay quiet." I suspected he was armed all along, but seeing his gun solidifies it.

Though we both stand, ready to move if we need to, Axel stays back near the couch. I can't stop my feet from inching closer and closer to the door. Chase sets his candle down on an entryway table and peers through the peephole.

"I thought I told you to wait in the other room," Chase chastises me in the darkness. He takes a small step back from the door. The banging stops, and the silence makes my anticipation even greater. "I think I recognize this person. Might be one of your friends, but we should be sure before you open that door."

I won't wait. Hanna or Evelynn could be on the other side of that door, and Chase is taking too long to respond. It's too quiet now—someone had to have been banging frantically for a reason. I gently shove him out of my way and stand on my tiptoes to look through the peephole for myself. Even in the shadows of the night, the recognition is instant. My breath wheezes out of me as I fumble with the deadbolt and chain, my hands shaking in my urgency.

The door bangs hard against the metal door stopper, hitting the wall from the sheer force of my panic. Leaning against the porch rail looking bloodied, exhausted, and filthy is Garrett James. Bathed in the moonlight, Garrett gives me a weak smile. I rush across the creaking wood to reach him, relief charging through me like a live wire. Our chests collide together as I press into him.

He's alive.

"Selena..." He breathes my name and then goes slack in my arms.

CHAPTER
TWENTY-ONE

As CAREFULLY AS POSSIBLE, I guide Garrett's limp body down to the ground. He's too heavy for me to hold up for long, and I don't want to accidentally drop him. Even as I look him over, trying to assess the damage, I find myself searching the dark street for any sign of the rest of my friends.

The wind whips against my cheeks, the slashing cold biting into my skin and making my eyes water. I scan every direction, finding nothing but the wet, black surface of the road glittering back at me. Closing my eyes against the sting, I fight to hold myself together.

Chase is suddenly beside me, setting his candle down on the wooden porch beside Garrett's body as he checks him over for wounds. He holds up his wet hand for me to see. "He's bleeding from somewhere—there's a lot of blood. But his pulse is good, and he's still breathing."

Garrett's face is pale—the parts that aren't caked in dirt stand in stark contrast to his ghostly white skin. His clothes are torn, and a red stain has seeped into his puffy yellow winter coat, making the fabric turn a sickly shade of orange. I pull at the zipper, spreading the coat wide so we can see his body easily underneath.

"Here, the injury is here." Chase points out a spot on Garrett's left side. The stain on his shirt is deepest there, a rip clear in the fabric.

"We should get him inside," Axel says from behind me. I'd almost forgotten he was here. The shock of seeing Garrett is pulling my mind in so many directions. Part of me believed he was dead. The other part was afraid to think anything at all for fear of drowning in the helplessness of the situation with my friends.

They might be dead. Some of this blood could belong to them. We won't know until we get him inside and wake him up.

It takes all three of us to get him inside the house. Axel and Chase take most of his weight, and I hold his head in my hands to keep it from banging on anything as we maneuver him through the house. Chase leads us to a spare bedroom around the corner from the front door. It's mostly void of furniture and small, and when Axel retrieves the candle, it lights the room fairly well on its own.

We lay Garrett down right on top of an old patchwork comforter, and he doesn't move at all. Even as his weight makes the old mattress dip slightly below him, he is still. Chase leaves to get the lanterns and first aid supplies, and I remove Garrett's soiled jacket and muddy boots for him, tossing them out of the open door so I won't have to stare at the bloodstains a second longer.

His jeans are splattered with red stains, too, and the large spot on his left side glares at me through what used to be a white t-shirt.

Axel hands me a wet rag. I don't know where he got it, but I get to work cleaning away the dirt and blood from his face, trying to see if more injuries are hidden under the filth there. So many questions are flashing through Axel's eyes—I can feel them radiating off him in waves—but he stays silent. He simply gives me the time and space to clean up my friend.

Is that what Garrett is to me? My friend? Is that what he thinks he is? How am I going to explain Axel to him? He's been out there fighting to stay alive, and I've been warm and safe with Axel.

Guilt, black and thick, fills my lungs. I clear my throat, trying to breathe around it. I'd run, and he'd fought a bloody battle without me.

I stare down into Garrett's dirty face, questions swirling in my head, too many to keep track of. I lean down close to his ear, choking on the knot in my throat. "What happened to you, Garrett? Don't you dare die on me now."

Chase returns with lanterns and his medical bag. I take Garrett's hand and sit off to the side, out of his way. Chase works quickly and quietly; Axel assists him as best he can. I can't stop staring into Garrett's face, hoping he will wake up and everything will be okay.

I don't know how long I sit there, waiting for the boys to finish, but my mind wanders back to Hanna, Evelynn, and Liam. Did they stop somewhere? Are they waiting for us to come back to them? Was Garrett coming here to tell us they are alive?

What if Hanna had been right the whole time? What if we would have been safer waiting it out at school? If something terrible happened to them, if they—

"Hey." Axel's hand slides down the side of my face before cupping my jaw. When my eyes meet his, the silvery depths are flooded with concern. "Chase thinks he's going to be fine. Looks like a bullet grazed him—nothing vital was hit. He probably passed out from shock and blood loss, but he's stitched up, and he's resting peacefully. Now, Chase is going to make us something to eat, and then I think you should rest."

My eyes shift back to Garrett, my heart making a strange flop inside my chest. If I had stayed and tried to help my friends, Axel would likely be dead. At least Garrett is here and breathing. I stand, pulling a blanket over Garrett before turning to face Axel.

"Garrett, he... If things had continued to head in the direction they were going, I think he'd be my boyfriend. At least, that's how it felt before this whole thing started." I hold Axel's gaze as I speak the words. "I know that something is happening between us, and it's been so fast and unexpected—"

Axel takes a step, reaching his arms out for me. "I don't expect you to have the answers, Selena. I don't have any, either."

I lean into his strong arms, letting them wrap around me. He feels surprisingly warm, as if he's finally shaken the permafrost that used to cling to him. I press my ear against his chest, listening to his steady heartbeat. This doesn't seem like the right time to be worried about relationship statuses, not when we are all in the fight for our lives, for answers, for a future.

"Thank you." My words sound muffled against the soft gray sweater he wears, the perfect shade to bring out the moonlight color of his eyes. No matter what happens with Garrett or with Axel, I feel content simply knowing they are both alive and here with me.

Axel picks up one of the lanterns, and I follow him back out into the living room.

Chase is back in his chair; he's started a fire in the fireplace and set three bowls of steaming soup on the coffee table. Exhaustion pulls at my mind and my limbs. I stare longingly at the leather couch, but I know I need to eat before I can rest.

"I have a lot of questions for you, Ms. Santos, but they can wait until morning. I think we've had enough excitement for one night." The kind smile he gives me is a familiar one. I've seen it from Liam many times before. They favor each other, both brothers naturally charming and effortlessly beautiful.

I nod my relief. "Thank you, Chase. I appreciate everything you've done for Garrett, for us."

"Sit, eat. I'll show you where you can sleep when you've finished." Chase kneels before the coffee table and takes a bite of the soup. Axel quickly joins him.

I notice how much younger Chase looks now, despite the authority he wears so well. Where he's been trained by the military, the rest of us are a bunch of kids, trying to survive a world we don't even know how to navigate properly. We need him—of that, I am sure.

The soup warms me as it quenches the hunger I've ignored for too long. None of us speak as we eat, content to sit in silence and enjoy the warm meal. Silence feels safer than words, because as much as I know we all want answers, part of me is afraid to hear what Garrett has to say when he wakes up.

"Selena?" The sound of my name pulls me from a deep sleep. My eyes flutter as they try to adjust to the light.

Chase had given me my own room, the one next door to the guest room where Garrett was sleeping. After washing up and putting on clean clothes, the comfortable bed sucked me in, its warm arms cradling me and soothing my sore body to sleep. Axel had been given a bedroom upstairs, and it felt strange to be in my room without him. But I was so tired that I fell asleep quickly, with no tossing and turning—I slept so well and so deeply, I don't think I even dreamed.

"Selena..."

I sit up quickly, the blankets bunching around my feet. Sunlight filters in through the open curtains and bathes the room in warm light. Garrett stands in the doorway, watching me. His face has more color this morning, but he still looks weary and tired, his clothes ruined. My heart aches at the sight of him, the thought of where my friends might be clawing at my mind.

I choke back the questions I really want to ask. We can take this slow—no need to rush bad news. "Hey," I say softly. "How are you feeling?"

Garrett rubs his eyes with the palms of his hands before meeting my eyes again. "You're really here?"

I stand, careful not to get caught in the tangle of blankets, and cross the room. The wood floor feels cool beneath my bare feet. Garrett's dark hair is matted, and I suspect some of what's caked there is his own blood. He will need a shower today and some fresh clothes. As I look him over, leaning there against the doorframe, I notice that the same dark-brown eyes I looked into on movie night—it feels like a lifetime has passed since then—are watching my every move.

He may be bruised and bloodied, but he is still Garrett.

"I'm really here. You're really here. And most importantly, you're going to be okay." My lips turn up in a half smile as I speak only the facts. "I want to ask you so many things, but I think it's only fair we feed you and let you get cleaned up before any of that."

Garrett doesn't seem to hear my words. Instead, he pulls away from the door jam and takes my face in both hands before gently kissing my forehead. I can feel his warm breath, his body trembling as he takes in deep gulps of air. Then he lets go of my face and crushes me to his chest, his head still dipped to press against mine. I'm careful not to touch his side where I know he's bandaged. The last thing I want to do is cause him more pain.

"You don't know how good it is to see you," he murmurs against my hair.

"I'm glad you're okay," I reply, closing my eyes against the sweetness of the moment. I know I will have to tell him about Axel. I need to ask him what happened to him and our friends. We still need to speak with Chase about what happens now and how he might be able to help us. But I don't move away from his embrace. I let Garrett have this one peaceful moment.

Chase calls out from down the hallway. "Breakfast is ready."

Reluctantly, I break Garrett's hold on me and step back. "Let's get you something to eat. I'm sure you're starving."

Chase is just as surprised as I was to see Garrett up and moving. He's taken the time to heat the last of the soup from last night over the coals in the fireplace for Garrett. Breakfast for the rest of us is fruit, some kind of dried meat, and a couple of energy bars. I'm thankful for anything at this point, and I tell Chase as much.

I notice Axel has yet to come down for breakfast and hope he's finally getting the rest he desperately needs. Besides, it gives me a moment with Garrett before I have to start explaining myself.

Garrett's spoon clatters into his empty bowl, and he folds his hands together on the scarred wooden table. The bloodstain on his tattered shirt glares at me while my leg bounces under the table as I wait for him to break the silence that's fallen over the kitchen.

"How did you get away?" His voice shakes, and I reach across the table to put my hands over his folded ones.

"When you told me to run, I did. I didn't stop. I ran so far and so fast and for so long that I didn't realize how far off the main road I'd gone. I heard gunshots, and I wanted to turn around and help you, to come back and face whatever it was together, but I knew I couldn't. I kept running until I physically couldn't run anymore."

Garrett nods at me. His face is still emotionless, and I wish I could read his mind. "I was afraid you wouldn't run. I saw that look you gave me, the hesitation in your eyes. I prayed like hell you'd go anyway." Some of his hair falls lopsided over his forehead, and as I reach up to smooth it back, he catches my wrist in his hand.

"I thought you were dead," he says, his Adam's apple bobbing with the emotion breaking through. "I thought you were dead, and it filled me with so much rage."

I stare down at the table between us, the swirls in the wood grain blurring from the tears forming in my eyes. "And our friends?" I finally allow myself to ask the question that has been eating me alive. Inky black fear tightens in my chest as I wait for him to answer me.

He lets go of my wrist then, and I hear him take a deep breath. I continue to stare at the table, afraid to see what his eyes will tell.

"The gunshots weren't from the people holding us up—they came from the woods behind us."

I snap upright in my chair. "Wait, what?"

"A group of people came out of the woods and started shooting. They hit some of the men holding us... I dove in front of Liam, and that's when I felt the burning in my side. I fell backward, slammed my head on something, and I think I must have blacked out." He stands, pacing back and forth behind his chair. Chase is frozen at the sink, watching Garrett, waiting for news of his brother. My leg resumes its impatient shaking.

My lips tremble as I speak. "It's my fault. I should have stayed at school and waited for someone to come... or left without my friends and let them make their own choices—"

Garrett stops pacing and turns to look at me. "What happened is not our fault."

I shake my head. He's wrong. This is my fault. Our fault, his and mine. It was our idea to leave, and we'd been too selfish to leave our friends behind.

I slump against the table, unable to keep myself upright any longer. Silent tears, hot and fat, drip down my face and over my lips. I can taste the salt of them as they slip into my mouth. "It *is* my fault, Garrett. I talked them into coming with us. *Me.* I did that. Not you. And if I hadn't, they'd still be alive..." My voice cuts off, drowned by the ocean of tears in my throat.

"No." Garrett's voice gets louder. "No, I don't think they're dead. At least they weren't among the bodies when I woke up."

Chase pushes off from the counter and grabs Garrett by the front of his shirt. "I understand you've been through an ordeal, but I'm going to need you to tell me exactly what happened. Don't leave anything out."

He nods quickly, swallowing before pushing back from Chase's grip. "I woke up on the ground, in my blood, alone. It was dark, so I don't know how long I was out. They must have thought I was dead—there was so much blood. The small group of shooters were gone, but so were Liam, Evelynn, and Hanna. They must have taken all of our bikes, too. Bodies were everywhere but none that belonged to us. So I looked around the area as best I could, and when I didn't see anyone, I grabbed what was left of my gear and started walking. I had to stop a lot to rest, and I used broken cars to hide away from the weather, but I kept bleeding. I didn't know if I would make it."

"And you didn't see any signs of Liam and the girls or the people who shot at you along the way?" Chase asks. He crosses his hands over his chest, his body rigid in his impatience.

Garrett sighs loudly, throwing his hands into the air. "Look, I could barely walk. It's possible I missed something, but I swear I didn't see anyone or anything that made me think they came this way. I was hoping they'd be here when I got here."

"What did the shooters look like?" Chase asks, rubbing a hand over his face.

I hear a sound behind me, and I sense Axel has finally entered the kitchen. Garrett's whole body goes still, his face draining of color. "Like him. At least one of them looked like him."

Chapter
Twenty-Two

For a moment, time seems to stand still. My mind struggles to catch up with the accusation that sits heavy in the air. Garrett moves lightning fast for someone recovering from a bullet graze and a head injury—one of the kitchen chairs clatters to the floor as he rushes past me to get to Axel.

I fumble in my chair, trying to stand. Chase is faster than me—he pushes off the counter, heading in the same direction that Garrett went. In the hazy morning light, everything looks like a dream, but I know I'm no longer sleeping.

"Who the hell are you?" Angry, accusatory words spit from Garrett's lips. I turn in time to see him and Axel both circling each other like angry bulls. I think Chase is going to break it up, but he comes to my side, holding me back from the unfolding scene at a safe distance.

I try to think of the right words to diffuse the situation, but I'm still trying to work out what's happening myself. This is all too much for one morning, and I feel my breakfast threatening to come back up. Fighting and arguing are the last things we need right now; we need to figure everything out, use our words before we choose the right actions to take.

I squeeze onto the arm Chase is using to hold me back. The shooters looked like Axel. Could they have been his shipmates? The people I'd seen in the visions he shared with me?

"Please, don't fight." The simple plea is all I can manage.

"Who is this guy?" Garrett yells, but he doesn't turn back to face me. His body stays squared off with Axel. "How do you even know him, Selena?"

Axel won't meet my eyes, either, as his gaze is trained on Garrett. A true standoff.

"When I was running, trying to get away, I found him in the woods. If we can all be calm and sit down and talk, I'm sure we can figure this out." I look to Chase for help, but he's studying the boys and not paying attention to me.

"What do you mean 'you found him'?" Garrett's voice is harsh as he takes a step closer to Axel. "He probably broke off from his group and followed you."

"He didn't follow me. He was on the ground, unconscious, freezing to death." I continue to talk, hoping he will hear me through his fear and anger. "We traveled the rest of the trip together. He couldn't have been with that group; he was too far away at the time—"

"But he looks like them, has that same bizarre silver hair. I remember thinking maybe they were some kind of haloed angels—you know, until they started shooting at us."

Not angels. *Aliens.*

Axel holds his hands up in surrender. "I can assure you, I have never held a gun in my life."

Garrett shoves Axel in the shoulders, pushing him backward, his socks sliding easily across the polished floors. "And what? You expect me to take your word for it?"

"Do you think it was your sister?" I ask Axel. The question momentarily distracts them both. I know it's a risk asking him in front of Chase and Garrett, but I need answers, too. "Do you think your sister and the others would hurt my friends?"

Axel frowns, and I can see that my question has hurt him. He's been kind to me—I have no reason to believe his family would be any different. Except I know how the humans on the moon treated him. That would be more than enough motive for his sister to want revenge on our species. If she saw what she thought was more senseless violence happening—

"Axel isn't from the Academy?" Chase's voice is steady, as if he already knew that from the beginning. I'd felt him catch my mistake the night before, and now he is confirming it.

I stare at Chase, pleading with him wordlessly. *Help me diffuse this situation, don't just stand there and let these two fight each other.*

"No, I'm not," Axel says, answering for me. He runs a hand through his silver hair. "I'm not from anywhere near the Academy."

A chill runs through my body as I realize that Axel may feel forced to out himself. I understand Garrett's fear—I should have taken a moment to tell him we had another occupant in the house, explained before it came to this. But it's too late now. The mood in the room is electric, the tension volatile. We are going to hash all of this out one way or another, and I hope we can do it peacefully before someone ends up hurt.

"Can we please sit down, talk this through?" Goosebumps break out on my arms, and I bite my lip as I wait for a response.

Chase gives me a reassuring squeeze, stepping away from me and toward the two adrenaline-charged boys. "She's right; let's take a step back, have a seat, and talk this through. We all want answers, so let's get to it." He pats Garrett softly on his back. "You good with that, buddy?"

It takes Garrett another few seconds to drop his gaze from Axel's, his shoulders slumping slightly in defeat. He seems unsteady on his feet now as the adrenaline leaves his body. I close my eyes for a moment, letting the relief of the diffused situation wash over me. This fight may be far from over, but they seem content to let it go for now. Garrett needs rest, not more stress on his body.

Chase guides Garrett back to his side of the table, righting the toppled chair and taking a seat next to him. I sit back into mine, pressing my body against the back of the hardwood with force. I need all the support I can get to stay upright.

Axel is slower to move but takes the seat next to me, his hand trembling slightly as it finds mine under the table. I worry if he shares too much, these boys may not understand him as easily as I did.

"Now, Axel," Chase says calmly, "why don't we start with you telling us about your sister and where you're from."

"For at least the last sixty years, scientists have been experimenting with humans, trying to find a way to fortify their immune systems against the hundreds of viruses attacking Earth. Since this is not something the human population would likely have approved, it was done at a location that has no laws or regulations. They didn't need permission to work outside of the law, and there was no limit to the lengths they were willing to go."

Garrett rolls his eyes. "He sounds like he's reading from a textbook. What kind of history lessons are you giving us? What does this have to do with your sister or whoever was shooting at my friends?"

"Let him get his story out, then you can ask your questions, kid," Chase says, nodding at Axel to continue.

Axel squeezes my hand under the table. "I was never allowed to know much about the experiments myself—I was a test subject. It wasn't exactly a voluntary job. I call Lyra my sister, but I have no way of knowing if she's biologically my sibling. We just look so similar that we suspect we have the same donor—"

"Wait." Chase holds up a hand. "You're saying you were part of human trials in a government operation?"

"Yes. We were created to be test subjects. We grew inside a womb, but we had... Well, our DNA is not the standard human DNA."

"Like the Academy kids?" Chase looks at me when he asks the question, and my mind starts to race.

"Do you know what makes us different?" I ask Chase. My parents always told me that as long as I could survive the viruses, they didn't need to know. But the girls and I had spent many nights in our younger years trying to speculate what changes they'd made to our DNA to make us different. Everything from vampire blood to radioactive spider venom had been thrown out. But theories from old movies and comic books aside, we had no real evidence to back those claims. In the end, we figured it was some experimental vaccine administered before we were born, and they didn't want to tell us that. Especially when some of the kids at school still got sick and possibly died.

"I know more than I should," Chase says. "Before they decided to expand the Academy programs and do large groups of test babies, they did smaller test groups. I was part of that first round. While the contract for Liam required him to go to the Academy, mine stipulated that if I was healthy enough, I'd join the military for a minimum contract of ten years. With more and more of the population dying off, they needed assurances that they could keep some control over the people. They needed bodies on the ground. Immune bodies."

"Academy programs? As in, more than one academy?" I pull my hand from Axel's, desperate to move my body. How could there be more than one academy? We were told we were the only ones. Our parents paid so much money to be considered. "Is everything we know a lie?"

Chase gives me a sympathetic look. "By the end of last year, on average, seventy-five percent of the Academy student population had succumbed to the viruses. As each academy had one hundred students to begin with, this means only twenty-five of the experimental children per academy are truly immune."

"Why so few?" Garrett asks.

"Because from the beginning, only twenty-five percent of the students were part of the same program they used in the original smaller group."

Axel drums his fingers on the table. "Your group?"

Chase nods. "The other students were under one of three other trials, all of which proved to be unsuccessful. This last year was the worst for infection across the globe. Very few people have survived, and those who are still around are unlikely to make it through the winter. In my own military unit, only a dozen remain, only those of us who were part of that original test group."

I stand, my body shaking. "What about our families? Our parents, our grandparents..."

He doesn't answer me. Instead, he turns his attention back to Axel. "Where did you say this experiment was taking place?"

As annoyed as I am that Chase is ignoring my questions, I wait to see how Axel will respond. He hasn't said where, and I know why. Chase knows more than he's telling us now, too—I can see it in the way his normally rigid body has relaxed. He's still every bit the soldier, but something's different in the way he's holding himself now. I see an easy confidence, as if talking with us has unlocked a piece of the puzzle for him. I want to know what that is.

Garrett is abnormally silent. His earlier rage must have drained all the fight out of him. He stares at his own folded hands, his face impassive. Maybe he's completely checked out.

My heart and mind are at war with one another. I want everyone to be honest and spill all their secrets, but I know that means putting Axel at risk, too. I'm frustrated and getting more and more impatient by the second. And I feel betrayed by my own family—did they know about all of this?

"Are you familiar with the space program?" Axel asks.

Chase's lips twitch. "You're from the moon program, aren't you?"

I've reached my breaking point. My hands press into fists at my side. "Alright, Chase. I think you need to start talking. If you know so much, why aren't you sharing it with the group?"

"Ms. Santos, with the magnitude of how much you don't know, I'm not even sure where to start." Chase motions to my chair, urging me to sit back down. I glare at him but sit like he wants me to. "Liam told you to come to me, correct?"

Garrett shakes his head. "He told us you might have some information, but he didn't say much more than that."

"And your grandfather never told you anything like this?" He stares at me hard. "I would have thought Mr. Santos would have shared more with you."

Why would Chase know anything about my grandpa? I want to pull my hair out. "I'm confused. You know my grandpa?"

"I do. And if I'm correct, I'm not the only one who knows him. You're sure he never told you anything in confidence about a space program?"

Chase is smiling, but his eyes continue to search my face. He's always trying to read me. Does he think I'm lying?

"My grandpa told me many stories about his life before the viruses, but never once did he say anything about a space program." Anger bubbles up like carbonation in my blood. Did Grandpa know things about a secret space program, about what was happening to Axel and his friends, and he never told me about it? Why would he know something like that?

Chase claps his hands together, his eyes never leaving mine. "Well, then. It's time we pay him a visit."

CHAPTER
TWENTY-THREE

CHASE PULLS AXEL OUT into the living room to speak with him privately, and I stare after them, immobilized by everything I've heard.

"Selena?" Garrett says my name, his hand reaching for me across the table. "What the hell is going on?"

I shrug. If he thinks I have all the answers, he's wrong. Apparently, the people closest to me have been keeping things from me my whole life. My grandpa has always been the most important person in my world, and now...

Now, I feel like he was a stranger the whole time. How does he know Chase? What does he have to do with the moon program and Axel? All those stories he told me about the world before everything fell apart that I thought were so important... and he had information about the Academy, about our future, that he didn't share with me that whole time. Information of real value.

"Your guess is as good as mine." I let my head fall into my hands and try not to cry. I'm sick of feeling weak and confused, which is starting to make me angry. I hold onto that anger, my fury burning hot and white. I let it rage inside me, because I cannot let the grief in, not now.

Garrett comes around the table and pulls a chair out, sitting in the one next to mine. I lift my head from my hands and look at him. I can't help but think about the day in the cafeteria when he sat next to me last. When our friends were safe and nearby. When everything still made sense in my world. Our lives had never been ordinary or ideal, but they were a lot better before all of this started happening—of that, I am certain. I finally understand that old saying, *Ignorance is bliss.*

"Who is this Axel guy?" he asks me again.

"I told you, I found him when I was—"

"No, Selena. Who is he to *you*? Because I get the distinct feeling he thinks you're his girl." I can hear the hurt in his voice, and I wince a little when he tucks my hair behind my ear. It's so familiar, and yet, it no longer feels as comforting as it once did.

Garrett's brown eyes are so dark I can hardly see his pupils, the deep brown blending in with the black. He looks tired, but I can tell now that he is on the mend.

I don't know how to find the right words to describe everything that's happened between me and Axel. I don't know how to rationally explain the pull I feel to him, the connection like a tether I almost feel I could reach out and grasp with my hands. It doesn't seem possible to feel the way I do after knowing him for only a few days. How quickly his presence filled the space that I thought would someday be filled by Garrett.

"Garrett, I... What I feel for Axel, I didn't expect it. I didn't see it coming..." I reach out to touch him, to comfort him in some way as I try to tell him that I've fallen for a boy I hardly know, but he sits back out of my reach.

"Don't." He turns away from me, wiping his eyes. He's crying, and I feel horrible for hurting him this way. "Let's go talk to your grandpa like Chase wants to and get all the information we can. Then I think I'm going to head back toward the school and see if I can find any trace of Liam and our friends."

"Okay." My words are too quiet, yet I can tell he hears me anyway. He stands but doesn't walk away. I dig deep to find my voice. "For what it's worth, Garrett, I'm really glad you're still alive."

He shifts on his feet, showing a vulnerability I haven't seen in him before. "If our friends are gone, do you really think it was our fault?"

His question makes my stomach pitch, and I press a hand over my mouth to keep from gagging on the bile in my throat. "I think it's something I'll always blame myself for."

Garrett nods, and I feel like he understands what I mean. He'll carry the guilt, too; I can see it in his eyes. "Would you do it again?"

"What? Ask them to leave with us?" I've asked myself this a million times over, and despite how everything turned out, I know in my heart I would have always brought them with me. "Yes. I'd do it over again, even though it didn't work out how we expected."

"Selena, will you promise me something?" he asks. He reaches a hand toward me but then pulls it back as if remembering he doesn't want my comfort.

"What's that?"

"Be careful. I don't trust that kid, and I don't think you should, either. I don't even know if I trust Liam's brother." He does walk away then, and I hug my arms around myself. Perhaps I've mistaken Garrett's fear and distrust for bravery this whole time. He might not trust

Axel or Chase, but right now, I'm not sure I even trust myself.

When the sun starts to set, Chase tells us it's time to head to my grandpa's house. We're only a few blocks away, but he feels safer moving in the dusk than being exposed in the full daylight. While there aren't many people left anywhere, meeting only one hostile person is enough to lose your life. I can appreciate the extra precaution, even if I feel more than impatient waiting to hear what my grandpa has to say.

Garrett hasn't spoken to me since he told me not to trust Axel, and Chase and Axel have been discussing the best plan of action for getting to my grandpa's house. I've spent the last few hours drowning in my own thoughts. I told everyone I needed a nap, but I haven't slept. I've only laid on the bed, eyes closed, heart breaking.

Are my parents okay? Nothing in the house made me think that Liam's parents had been here for a long time. When was the last time he'd spoken to them? I'd talked to my mother last—months ago now—and she'd told me my father was unavailable, and I hadn't questioned it. Did that mean he'd been sick or worse?

What about Hanna's and Evelynn's families? Was anyone we loved still alive? Chase seemed to think my grandpa was still alive at least; otherwise, he would never have suggested we risk traveling to see him.

"Okay, stay close, and stay quiet." Chase's authoritative voice cuts through my thoughts, shaking me out of my own head. I have to be smart; I need to be alive if I'm going to learn the truth.

We slip out the back door. The trees are thick here, and we're less likely to be noticed leaving the house this way. The air is much cooler outside than it was in the house, and I pull my jacket tighter around me. It smells like rain, but the ground is dry tonight, and I don't see any impending clouds in the twilight sky.

Garrett follows right behind Chase, and Axel falls in behind me. Our feet are quiet on the grass, and we stay close to the bushes as we round the house to the street.

Everything I know feels like it's shifted or changed. I don't know what is up from what is down, what is truth and what is fiction. So I try to focus on the things that remain solidified in fact. The trees are tall and green, the sky is filled with stars, and the moon shines brightly overhead. The air still smells like pine and dirt, and these are still the streets of my childhood.

Chase stops, scanning the road and listening for movement before motioning for us to follow him. My feet are sore from days of walking, and they protest at each step, but I keep moving anyway.

We continue this way for the three blocks it takes to get to my grandpa's street. It takes ages to move the short distance, but I stay quiet and hope no more surprises are in store for us.

When the small blue house comes into view, I breathe a sigh of relief. My grandma's flower bushes call out to me like beacons of light in the darkness. Unlike Chase's house, I can see the flickering of candlelight through my grandma's handmade curtains. Someone is inside, and I can only hope it's them. Why would anyone choose to squat in their little old house when there are so many larger, fancier houses left unoccupied? It has to be my grandparents.

At the front door, Chase pauses, listening. "Okay," he whispers to us as he scans our surroundings. "I'm going to check around the house and make sure it's safe, and then we can—"

I don't let him finish. I'm sick of taking orders from all three of these boys, no matter how well-intentioned they may be. I'm tired of waiting around, too, paralyzed by fear. So I raise my hand and knock loudly, three times, like I've always done when I've come to see them.

Chase sucks in a harsh breath and glares at me in the hazy darkness. "Or I guess we do it your way." He steps back, gun in hand, ready for anything.

The door slides open, and warm light filters out from the hallway. My grandpa stands there in a white shirt, black pants, and those silly red suspenders he's always worn. The light behind him is reflecting slightly off his shiny bald head. The familiar smells of sage and rose greet me in the breeze. It's more like coming home than I'd imagined it could be.

"Selena? My blue-eyed girl," he says, opening his arms to me. "What a wonderful surprise."

I had planned to hold my ground, to be angry and demand that he answer for the things he's kept from me, but one look at the man I adore most in the world, and my resolve crumbles faster than an Oreo in milk. I rush into his waiting arms and hold on for dear life.

"Ahh, sweet girl," he coos, holding me tightly and rubbing my back. "Tell your friends to come inside; we have a lot to talk about."

I don't have to say a word—everyone follows us into the house. Grandpa has oil lanterns lit on many surfaces, and it's almost like having the lights back on. He holds me to his side as he walks us to his small living room where the same two recliners and an old sagging couch greet me. The same yellow-tinged carpet that my mother swore was once a shade of cream, the same paintings of wildflowers my grandma had lovingly painted over the years. The only thing missing from view is my grandmother herself. Her chair is empty, her favorite crochet blanket folded neatly over the back. I've never seen the blanket not bunched up in the chair with a book resting on top, waiting for her to return from the kitchen chores or whatever had pulled her away.

"Where's Grandma?" I ask, unable to walk another step.

Grandpa pats my head. "Oh, Jean, my lovely bride. She's resting now."

"In her room?" My voice shakes. I know what he's saying, but I don't want it to be true. I can see it in his eyes, in the downturned corners of his wrinkled mouth, the heavy slump in his shoulders. He's lost her, the love of his life.

"She's resting with her maker," Grandpa says softly. "She went fast but gently."

I shake my head against his words, tears burning my eyes and grief shredding my insides like barbed wire in my chest. I don't want to know any more, but I can't stop the question from leaving my lips. "And my parents?"

Grandpa crushes me tightly into him. I can hear his heartbeat, soft but still beating. "It's been a hard year for us. I'm so sorry, my sweet, sweet girl—it's only you and me now."

His big hands, disfigured from years of arthritis, fight to hold onto me as I push away. I'm unwilling to take comfort when I've been denied so many other emotions, so many other truths. "Why didn't anyone tell me? Why didn't someone tell the school to let me know?" The words rush out of me, each one more painful than the last. I feel overwhelmed with betrayal. All this time, they've been gone, and I've been living my life at school in absolute darkness.

"Grandma left not long after you were home last. Your father died a few months later, and your mother—" Grandpa's breathing changes. "Your mother was two weeks ago. She held on as long as she could, worried you wouldn't take it well."

Grief chokes me, and anger, hot and loud, roars in my ears. "She worried how I would take it? But not enough to let me know she was sick? Not enough to give me a chance to say goodbye?"

Grandma. Dad. Mom. Hanna. Evelynn. My friends at school. My teachers.

So much has been taken from me. It is too much to bear.

I'd missed seeing my mother again by mere weeks. If only she'd told me she was sick, that our family was all but disappearing... but then what? It's not like the school would have let me come home to see her. We had rules to protect everyone, no matter what the emotional cost.

I let out a frustrated scream, hugging my arms tightly around myself, desperate to hold the pieces together. I cannot take the weight of all I've lost; I want to lie on the floor, tuck my knees into my chest, and let all the grief and fear and devastation consume me. I will not be going back to the girl I was before; I have to let her go entirely. In her place, I will become a harder, angrier version. If I have any hope of finding my friends, of coming out of all this alive, I cannot allow these emotions to take me down, no matter how much I want to surrender to them. I must keep moving. I must shut myself off from the pain.

Grandpa lifts his hands in surrender. "I didn't say I agreed with her, but it was her choice to make. I promised her I wouldn't tell you." He coughs, his chest rising and falling rapidly. His hands move to cover his mouth. I can hear the wetness in his lungs.

He's dying, too.

The one family member I have left. The virus will take everyone I love. It's already taken too much.

"You're infected?" Chase asks the question before I can. "How long?"

Grandpa waves us off. "I'm old, my life has served its purpose. And if the Lord sees fit to take me today, I'll gladly take that trip home."

"You should have told us before we came inside." Garrett backs slowly toward the hallway. "You've exposed us all—"

"You're all immune." Grandpa looks annoyed at the suggestion. "It's the only thing that gives me peace these days, knowing your lives will go on."

Chase and I share a look. "How do you know we're immune?" I ask. "I know we were all part of the Academy, and Chase was part of the experiments before that, but can you be sure? The students that didn't make it, how were they different?"

Grandpa sits down in his chair, staring at his own feet while he speaks. His hands tremble in his lap as he fights to catch his breath. "I was part of the first research team, the one that promised a future of immune children. I signed up without knowing what would be asked of me. The horrors I would witness and the pain I would be asked to inflict on innocent lives."

He pauses, finally raising his head to look us over. His gaze seems to fixate on Axel. "You there, what's your name?"

Axel steps forward, his eyes filled with tears. "I'm Axel. Do you remember me?"

Grandpa leans forward to get a better look at Axel and then smiles. "Yes, son, I remember you well. I suppose if you're here, the plan finally worked."

Axel shakes his head, the tears falling down his cheeks. "No, Father, only a few of us escaped. The rest were lost. They didn't get what they wanted from my people. Instead of continuing, they chose to terminate the program."

Grandpa nods, his face deep in thought. "Our plan to get you out was always meant to be that way. Your elders only wanted the children saved. The new generation."

"Why is he calling you 'Father'?" Garrett angrily jabs a finger at my grandpa. "How do you know him?"

Grandpa isn't fazed by Garrett's anger, almost like he expects us to be angry. He stares off into the distance, remembering. "I spent many years traveling back and forth between the moon base and home. The ISS resupply missions I told my family I was helping with, they were far more than that. I am not his father, but that is the name his people gave me. His people are the reason I know that each one of you is immune to the viruses here."

Chase takes a seat on the couch. The light from the oil lantern flickers across his face as he leans forward and presses his palms against his knees. "Who are his people?"

"Ardorians," Axel says. "We're not from your planet. At least, my ancestors were not from your planet. I was born decades after they were taken as prisoners of the moon program."

"Aliens? The immunity was made from aliens?" Garrett is still backing away from the room slowly. Even after his shower and changing into clean clothes, he still looks battle-worn and tired. I imagine we all do. I've known that Axel is an alien—this isn't news to me—and it doesn't appear to be shocking to Chase, either. But Garrett had no idea, and his fear seems to be draining all the color from his face.

"We can't make a vaccine from them. If that were the case, we could have mass-produced it and saved everyone." Grandpa takes a labored breath.

The room is silent. Only the light moves as we wait for Grandpa to continue. I take a seat next to Chase on the couch, and Axel follows, sitting on my opposite side. Garrett remains at the edge of the room; he's backed himself up against the wall.

"We tried to use their blood. We tried stem cells. Bone marrow. Organ transplants. Every vaccine we could make from their samples. We tried everything we could think of. We caused immense pain and suffering to those poor souls, and they just wanted to live peacefully on our planet. They'd only asked us for refuge when their own planet was no longer hospitable... and after all of that, after all the testing and sacrifice and death..."

"How are we immune?" I ask. I can feel the hairs on the back of my neck standing at attention, my whole body vibrating with anticipation.

Grandpa looks me straight in the eye. "The only way to be immune is to be Ardorian."

Chapter
Twenty-Four

The only way to be immune is to be Ardorian.

"How?" It's the only word I can get to pass through my lips. What does he mean by that? I've always known the Academy kids were special, but not all of us had been immune.

The only way to be immune is to be Ardorian.

"Each of you has one human parent and one Ardorian parent. The Ardorian people have a far superior immune system, a scientific marvel that we were unable to replicate or enhance using their biology. As a final test, we wanted to see if you could crossbreed humans with Ardorians and have a hybrid with the same immunity to the viruses. Chase was one of the first successful births here on Earth, but there were several successful attempts on the moon before we brought the project here. It was the only way to ensure that the human race would continue in some way."

"But Mom and Dad... My parents weren't my parents?" I chew on my thumbnail, unsure I want to hear the answers Grandpa has for me. Is he even my grandpa?

"As far as your parents knew, you were their biological child." Grandpa sighs. "And you are. By half."

"Which half?" The accusatory tone of my voice just comes out. I feel utterly betrayed by everyone I love.

"Only a handful of lab technicians would know that. Whether it was your mother or your father who were Ardorian wasn't important, because your human mother carried you believing that it was the same as any other IVF pregnancy. Your parents loved you as their own, as nature intended. We had no way of knowing if parents would reject their child if they knew the truth. We didn't have the time to risk that outcome."

I look like my father. My tan skin, my shorter stature, the curl in my hair. Grandpa must have known that I was truly his grandchild. Except for my blue eyes—we've always joked that they must have come from some distant relative on my mother's side. And the whole time we were laughing and joking, my grandpa had known the truth.

They had come from my mother.

Only Michelle Santos was not my mother. My heart was already broken, but I can feel fresh cracks splintering across the surface—any more pain, and it might fail altogether. My parents loved me, did the best they could for me. At least they hadn't lied to me. They had been as lost in the dark as I was. Had my real mother even known about me?

"We both know which parent I look like," I say.

"Yes, I have my suspicions, too. But you must understand, Selena, that none of that matters. We loved you, and we raised you—you're ours."

I can't help but shake my head. "But it doesn't make any sense. If we're all half Ardorian, why did all those Academy kids get sick? Chase told us that seventy-five percent of Academy students have died across all academies. Only twenty-five percent are immune—how is that possible?"

"Because only twenty-five percent of each academy is half Ardorian. One-quarter of the children were used as a control group. Despite what their parents were told, they were untouched. One quarter were given high doses of immunity-boosting injections and a carefully curated diet. One-quarter were given experimental vaccines as quickly as they could be developed. And those of you who remain, I suspect, were all part of the true experiment, the one that started with Chase."

I press my fingers to my forehead, feeling a migraine starting. If I hadn't met Axel, if he hadn't shown me those memories in his special way, I might not have believed a word my grandpa was saying.

Chase squeezes my knee. "This is a lot to take in. I've been suspicious for years, but even now, hearing everything confirmed, it's a trip."

"Why should we believe anything you say?" Garrett says. "It all sounds like a bunch of made-up garbage. Maybe you're sick and delusional." He spins around and stalks toward the front of the house. A blast of cool air hits us as he thrusts the door open, and then he's gone just as fast as he slams it loudly behind him.

"I'll talk to him," Chase says, patting my knee before heading out to find him. I stare at the empty hallway in silence.

I don't blame Garrett for feeling this way. I don't want to believe any of it is real myself. I prefer radioactive spider bites and vampire blood to this alternative. I'll even take a zombie apocalypse as long as it meant an equal chance of survival for everyone from the beginning. They experimented on Axel's people, they experimented with us, and in the end, all our families died anyway.

Grandpa coughs again, wheezing for breath. As angry and betrayed as I feel, it hurts to see him suffering, knowing he will not survive this sickness. He hasn't said how long he's been ill, but judging by the look of him, he is close to the end. Has the stress of seeing us, of explaining everything, pushed him closer to his grave?

Another question comes flying out before I can stop it. "But if Chase is older than Axel, how are there no older kids in Axel's group?"

I search Grandpa's eyes as he hesitates. "The first few groups of half children on the moon were studied more frequently. The scientists were desperate to find a cure for humans. Those children never lived for very long."

Nausea courses through me, a cold sweat breaking out over my skin as I think of the barbaric experiments those poor children were subjected to, experiments that were ultimately fruitless and didn't produce a cure for anyone. All those people on the moon base, turning a blind eye to their suffering... perhaps they deserved what they got in the end.

"Why didn't you tell me any of this, Grandpa?"

"I didn't enjoy keeping this from you or your parents. I did what I thought was safest for everyone. I wanted you to live." Tears fell down my grandpa's weathered cheeks. "Can you forgive me, my blue-eyed girl?"

I don't answer him. Exhaustion pulls at me from every direction. Fear, heartache, betrayal, confusion, and pain all fight to be acknowledged inside of me. I push all of them back, refusing to give in to any of them. I don't know if I can forgive the deception and the betrayal, and knowing that he was complicit in the torture that Axel and his family endured makes that feel impossible. But he is my grandpa. He is still Raymond Santos, the most amazing man I've ever known.

"Why didn't you try to stop them? Why did you let them do those horrible things to Axel's people?" My lip trembles with the words.

Axel turns toward me; he seems so far away on the other end of the couch. He doesn't reach for my hand, but I feel the pull between us all the same. "He *did* help us—that's why we called him Father. He fought for us many times. Because of him, we were not allowed to be test subjects more than once per cycle. It seemed like whenever he was around, they would subject us to the painful tests less and less. Sometimes, he would sneak supplies to us. I'd heard some rumors about an escape plan, rumors that he'd been the one to set the rebellion in motion. We could have called him Raymond, but if anyone overheard, he would be at risk. Instead, we called him Father, and even when he stopped coming, we remembered him."

I wonder if Axel has memories of my grandpa he can share with me. I don't know how to ask for something like that, but maybe it's better not to see those memories for myself.

Grandpa nods at Axel. "They suspected me of many things; that's why they grounded me, forced me into retirement. Nothing I could say could convince them otherwise."

"We always knew you wouldn't be able to help us forever," Axel says softly. "We didn't blame you."

"But you should have." Grandpa fights through another round of coughing before he continues. I can't help but notice it's taking him longer to recover each time. "After all, I was the one who pushed for more academies. I wanted humanity to continue like the rest of them, but more than that, I wanted Selena. I wanted our family to live on through a new generation. I would do it again, but I am sorry that it was at such a cost to your people, Axel. I don't expect you to understand."

"We all want to live; I can understand that much." Axel gives him a half-hearted smile. "I've always hated the violence and pain that your kind inflicted on us. You trying to help us was something we held on to, a spark of hope in the darkness. Although I'm half human myself, I didn't live a human life. I didn't know how alike we truly are, until Selena."

Axel scoots closer to me on the couch, finally reaching for one of my hands. I let his long fingers tangle with mine, his skin soft and familiar against my own. "She saved me when she didn't have to, and even when she thought we were different, she never stopped trying to help me."

I stare into Axel's silver eyes. I think about that day on the trail when he shared his memories with me but didn't understand how it was possible. It was possible because we are the same. We share the same lineage.

"If we don't know who our parents are, how will we know which of us are related?" I ask.

Grandpa laughs as he looks at the two of us, clearly understanding my meaning. "Ah, well, *that* I can help with."

What if we are related? Axel's eyes widen, his thoughts likely following my own.

"When Ardor was dying, the Ardorians took all matters of samples from their people. They had thousands of bloodlines cataloged and stored on their ships. We never reused a sample, only for the human families who were in the program twice. Chase's family used the program a second time, therefore both Chase and his sibling are true blood siblings. We thought it would help keep suspicions down if multiples were truly siblings. Siblings are rare on their own now, so it was a simple task."

I let out a breath, relieved to know that I haven't fallen for my own sibling. Stranger things have happened. I wonder if Chase even knows that he and Liam are true siblings.

He and Garrett have yet to return, and I wonder if he'll be able to calm Garrett down. Garrett has been through so much.

I don't know if any of this information would have helped me growing up. Maybe it would have been more painful to know before now. I'd had seventeen years believing I was exactly like my parents—maybe that had been a gift.

"Do you know all the families with half children?"

Grandpa shakes his head. "I only know a few of the families from your Academy. I wasn't meant to know any of them, but some of the reports I came across in my time on the moon were telling, and I took an interest in those who were close to you. I knew the headmaster's son, Garrett, was chosen; it was part of the deal for him to lead the school. I also knew of Chase, of course, and subsequently Liam."

"And my roommates?"

"Yes, Hanna Grant, Evelynn Pierce, and the Anderson girl were all chosen."

"Kelly? Kelly Anderson?" I ask, a fresh wave of confusion rushing over my skin.

"Yes." Grandpa snaps his fingers. "Kelly. Her grandfather was one of the founders of the moon project."

I try to remember the exact symptoms Kelly had presented with. She'd been complaining of stomach cramps, she'd been hot and nauseated, but we'd shrugged it off. Getting a stomach bug at school wasn't unheard of, but then, one day, she'd been gone. If she'd been immune—

"But that can't be right. Kelly got sick; she's been gone almost a year."

My grandpa doesn't answer me, and when I look up, I realize he's closed his eyes. "Grandpa?"

Axel pushes to his feet, tugging our joined hands so I will follow. He crosses the room and presses his fingers to my grandpa's neck.

"His pulse is weak; I don't think he has much longer."

I still have a plethora of questions. And I want more time with my grandpa—I've just gotten him back. Why does everything have to end so badly? Why can't the universe see that I need a win?

Axel brushes his fingers over my cheek. "I'm going to go check on the others. Would you like a moment alone with him?"

I nod. As much as it hurts, and as much as I want to pretend it isn't happening, this might be my one chance to say goodbye. My parents are gone—I'd missed my chance to tell them I loved them one last time. And as angry as I feel right now, no amount of anger can erase the love I have for my grandpa.

Axel leans down, his lips pressing against mine like a whisper. "Come find me when you're done."

CHAPTER
TWENTY-FIVE

I TUCK MY GRANDMA'S favorite blanket around my grandpa, and his eyes flutter open as he smiles at me. I have always loved the way his eyes crinkle at the corners, how he's always looked at me with such adoration, unlike anyone else. His eyes are always the ones I look to for comfort, for approval, for a reminder that I am not alone. I've loved him more than anyone else, and I've always felt those feelings returned tenfold.

"Thank you for coming to see me, my blue-eyed girl." His breath wheezes out of him, and I swallow past the lump in my throat. "Your grandma would be so proud of you. You're brave and strong, like her. Like your mother and father, too. I think they're waiting for me now on the other side."

"I love you." Tears burn in my throat, and I cough to clear them. I want to tell him I'm not nearly as brave as he thinks, but I don't. "Thank you for trying to make things right, for telling me about the moon project. For telling me who I am."

Grandpa's smile falters. "Humanity was dying long before the viruses, Selena. We turned on each other; we were greedy and selfish. People didn't look out for each other like they should—they climbed on each other's backs to get ahead—"

A coughing fit interrupts him, and I climb into the chair with him, laying my head on his chest. It rises and falls rapidly, and I can hear a whistling from his chest that I hadn't noticed before. He smells like cedar and sage and safety and *home*. My life is tipping like a seesaw, and on the edge of the shift, I cling to the comfort he offers for dear life.

"I hope that you can find each other, those of you who will be the future, and that you can accomplish what we could not." He rubs a hand over my hair, pressing me to him.

"What do you mean by that? What do you want us to accomplish?" I let the tears fall silently. I won't let myself break down, but some of the pressure begs to be released. If only for this moment, I'll let them fall.

"Know each other, learn from our mistakes. Live a life with hope and meaning. Love each other."

I nod against him. All of those things sound wonderful, peaceful, even. I only hope we can live up to his dreams for us. Evelynn, Hanna, and Liam, Axel's sister, Lyra, and the others—maybe we can find them, too. Start a new life together, build our version of a family. Chase and Axel can find their home with us, we can all lean on each other while we figure out our way forward. It's a dream I desperately want to become a reality.

"Find the other academies. There are hundreds of you. If you work together, you can start something wonderful. And maybe, someday, you can forgive an old fool for being selfish and making the wrong choices." He pats my back the same way he did when I needed soothing as a child. I've never needed it more than I do now.

I lean back so I can see his face clearly; tears are streaming down his face. I kiss each papery cheek softly. "I do forgive you; you were only doing what you thought was best for our family. I love you, and I always will. I only wish we had more time—there is so much I want to say, so much I want to ask you."

Grandpa hugs me tightly while more coughing fits shake his body, jostling us both in the chair. His breathing grows more labored by the second. Between breaths, he tells me to be strong, to trust my own heart. That even if my DNA is not what I've always thought, it doesn't change the person I've always been on the inside. He apologizes for leaving me behind because even he knows the end is near. There will never be enough time, he says, and time waits for no man.

His death will make me an orphan without any aunts or uncles, cousins, or siblings. I will remain the last standing member of the Santos family.

"I love you, kiddo." Grandpa smiles weakly, and then he closes his eyes, and I hold him while he takes his final breath.

I hold my grandpa for a while longer, letting my silent tears soak through the crochet blanket. I trace my fingers over the worn gray yarn. I let the memories of my childhood play through my mind, all the beautiful days we spent staring out at the city lights while he told me about the world before the viruses. The songs he'd sing to me over his guitar or banjo. The camping trips I'd taken with my father. The days my mother would read to me for hours. My grandma's voice singing to me as she taught me how to garden or attempted to teach me to cook and crochet. The silly nights watching scary movies with my friends. All the moments that made me into the girl I am today.

I'd do it all over again, even if it destroyed me.

Kissing my grandpa's cheek one last time, I pull myself out of the chair and wipe the tears from my face. We have no undertaker to call, no emergency services to come take care of his body. I'll have to ask my friends here to help me bury him in the backyard, maybe under the cherry tree where my grandparents often sat together. I cannot leave him here unburied.

The living room already feels different without my grandparents' lively spirits. Life will never be the same without my family around to share it with—of that, I am certain. Yet Grandpa's words rush through my mind on a loop, and I feel the smallest flicker of hope for our future twinkling there. Maybe we can make things better than they were before. Like it or not, we'd been chosen to survive, and we can't let that go to waste. We have to make sure the sacrifices our families made were not in vain.

A picture on the mantle catches my eye, all of us together at the table, enjoying a meal as a family. It was taken a few years ago—Grandma had set her timer and then rushed back to join us. She'd stumbled and cursed, and it was so out of character for her that we were all laughing uncontrollably by the time the picture was snapped. It captured a pure and truly happy moment, one I'd never like to forget. I dismantle the frame and tuck the picture into my back pocket.

If only I would have known how short my time would be with my family, maybe I would have appreciated the little moments better. I should have written to them more often, been more present when I was home from school. I'd been far more distant than I needed to be, and I pray that, despite my physical absence, they'd felt my love in their hearts in the end.

An old song my grandpa had loved came to mind then, something about life being a dance and being thankful we don't know when it will end, because we might not dance at all if we knew it couldn't last forever. I vow to hold on extra hard to the memories of joy and try to let the more painful ones go.

A light knocking comes at the front door. As it creaks open, Chase pops his head around the corner. "Selena, do you need us?"

I do need them. More than ever.

I swallow back the fresh batch of tears that threaten to choke me. "You can come in."

All three boys come back into the room, their faces solemn and eyes downcast. Axel must have told them he feared my grandpa had passed on. One glance at his body in the chair, and it's clear he's no longer with us.

"I'm so sorry, Selena," Garrett says, his voice low and gentle. "I know you two were close."

I know Garrett is still upset with me, and his kindness, despite his anger, touches me deeply.

"Do you think you could help me bury him?" I ask no one in particular. It will likely take all of us to move him outside.

"We'd be honored. Where would you like us to take him?" Chase asks.

I lead them to the backyard, through the thick grass long overdue for a mow. Winter will be here soon, but for now, the garden remains green and thriving, oblivious to the struggles of man. Grandma's toad lilies and plumbago flowers continue blooming in beautiful shades of purple and blue. The cherry tree leaves have turned orange and red, and the effect is stunning. The backyard has always been a refuge for my grandparents, and more than ever before, I understand why.

Next to the bench where I'd planned to bury my grandpa, the dirt sat disturbed, and a bouquet of pink snapdragons lay on top of a slightly rounded shape. My grandma is already here. Nothing else would have made me more certain of where my grandpa wanted to be laid to rest.

"Here, next to my grandma."

Chase motions to a nearby shovel. "This shouldn't take too long. If we can do anything else to ease your pain, say the word."

I press a hand over my heart, massaging the hurt there. Time will help, but for now, everything is fresh and raw. In some ways, it feels like I'll never heal from all this heartache.

I miss my friends terribly. Hanna and Evelynn, wherever they are, have no idea that we've finally solved the mystery of our special DNA. Hadn't Garrett told me that he wanted to head back toward the school and try to find them? As scary as that sounds, I want to go, too.

With Chase's help, we won't be unarmed or as vulnerable as we've been. And maybe some of his soldier friends will come with us. My muscles still ache, and my blisters and bruises haven't had nearly enough time to heal, but it will be worth all the pain if we can be reunited in the end.

If Garrett is right about the strangers looking like Axel, finding my friends might mean finding Axel's family, too. There's nothing left for me here in Portland, anyway—the only home I have now is with the boys in front of me and hopefully the rest of my friends.

Garrett and Axel find more shovels and begin to help Chase dig. They don't owe me or my grandpa anything, and yet they jump in without complaint.

These boys will never know how much this small act means to me. I've only known Chase for a day, and yet, I feel like we were always meant to connect. He is part of Liam's family, and that makes him part of mine. In fact, we've all been tethered to each other since before we were even born. Destined for a future none of us could have ever predicted.

I take a deep breath and blow it out slowly, wrapping my arms around myself. "Chase, when we're done here, I think it's time to talk about heading back to the Academy. Your brother, my friends, and Axel's family... they could all be out there waiting for us to find them. It's time for us to head home."

Chase stops digging and looks up at me, determination flashing in his eyes. "I was hoping you'd say that."

Carrying my grandpa to his final resting spot takes all of us. He's tucked lovingly in his blanket beside my grandmother in the flowerbed. I say a prayer over his grave because I know that's what he would have wanted me to do. I hope that he and my grandma have already found each other in the afterlife, whatever that looks like.

I turn my face up toward the star-filled sky, each one twinkling against the velvety blackness of the night, and the moon catches my eye. It is the same moon I've lived under my entire life, only now, it feels like even that was a lie.

Grandpa had always known. He'd told me countless stories about Selene, the Titan goddess of the moon. He'd been fascinated by her story and had been the one to suggest my name to my parents. In the end, my mother chose Selena. Had he been leaving me breadcrumbs my whole life and I'd never connected the dots? I let out a laugh, hugging myself against the wave of hysteria that beckons to me.

The boys say their condolences to me and pat me gently as if I am a fragile piece of glass they are afraid will shatter at any moment. In so many ways, I feel that to be true. Only a thin barrier exists between me and utter devastation, at some point, I will have to allow the feeling and the tears to come.

Now is not the time, though—we have another journey to prepare for. I don't know when I'll ever have the luxury of time again.

The boys give me a few minutes to myself out in the garden, and when I rejoin them in the house, Chase takes charge like I need him to.

We pack up some helpful food items and other supplies we will need in the coming days. Grandpa would have wanted us to take anything of use—nothing should go to waste. No one here will need them now.

Chase asks me if I want to spend a night here, but it feels cold now, empty without the two souls that made this house a home. When I shake my head, he doesn't press me. He just accepts it and tells us we'll head back to his house for at least tonight. We are all tired, and it has been an emotional few hours. It will be better to get a good night's rest and regroup in the morning.

We travel back to Chase's house in silence. We are learning each other's movements, and it makes the trip back feel twice as fast as before. The house is dark and empty, just as we'd left it. Knowing that soon hybrids like us will be the only people left on the planet, if we aren't already, is a strange feeling. If only we'd have had more time to ask questions, to get used to the idea that everything we thought we knew about ourselves had changed with the information my grandpa shared with us.

I walk past everyone and into the bedroom I stayed in the night before, shutting the door behind me. Chase will want to talk about our next steps. I'd seen the look of betrayal on Garrett's face, and I know he feels like the last to know everything... and then there's Axel. I wonder how he will feel in the morning, when he's had the night to process everything he heard. When he realized that my family was at least partially responsible for the unjust treatment of his people.

Our people.

There is so much to untangle.

Right now, though, I am too tired, too weary to process anything. My heart is broken, and the foundation of my entire existence has been obliterated. But I just strip down to my t-shirt and underwear and climb into the bed like any other night. I roll myself up in the soft cotton sheets, squeeze my eyes shut, and beg sleep to come for me once more.

Chapter
Twenty-Six

I'm standing before all the people I love. My friends, people I know from school, my parents, my grandparents, even Axel—they are all here. It's a warm sunny day, and we are in a large clearing in the woods. Everyone is staring at me, waiting for me to speak. I open my mouth to tell them that I love them, but no sound comes out.

One by one, they start to disappear. First my teachers, then some of the kids from school, my parents, Evelynn, Liam, and Hanna, and then my grandparents, Garrett...

I try to scream, to beg them to stay, but each time I open my mouth, I hear only silence.

Everyone is gone—only Axel and I are left. I reach for him, and he puts his hand out as if to take mine. But right before our fingers make contact, he disappears into the wind.

A guttural scream bursts from my silent lips. Devastated, I beg for those I love to be returned to me. My fingers claw at my own eyes, trying to unsee the loss of all those I love.

But I receive no response. No one returns. I stand here alone.

The last man standing.

A dull roar sounds in the distance as a huge black tidal wave crashes through the trees, annihilating everything in its wake. I stand frozen, unable—and perhaps unwilling—to run for my life, and as the murky wall finally hits me, I feel every emotion I've held back for weeks cascading through me.

My body thrashes through the waters, hitting trees and rocks as the water drags me across the forest floor. My bones snap, my skin tears, and all my feelings bleed out of me.

I gasp for air, the water filling my lungs. I am going to drown.

And then I am falling, and with one hard thwack, I feel the air rush back into my burning lungs, and I open my eyes.

I'm tangled in the bed sheets, lying on the cold hard floor next to my bed. Sunlight edges into the room from the window.

I slept through the rest of the night, but I must have fallen out of bed during my nightmare, and that's what jolted me awake. My t-shirt is soaked with sweat, and I feel hot tears staining my cheeks. I've been crying in my sleep.

The tidal wave of grief I felt in my dream lingers, and my body jerks against a fresh sob.

Time is up.

I can no longer escape the feelings I've been tamping down for days. Even in my sleep, my body begs for a release from the pain.

I curl into myself and let the pain come.

Tears come endlessly, and I wonder if it is possible to cry for an eternity and never run out of them. I cry for the man who raised me, for the friends who have become my family, and for myself. For the impossible future that I felt looming before me. I cry so long the light behind the curtains fades into darkness and then slowly grows light again. My body aches, my eyes and face feel swollen, and I am impossibly tired, but still, I cry.

Someone finally comes to check on me—I hear their footsteps but can't see through my blurry eyes who they belong to. I'm not sure it matters. I haven't bothered to pick myself up off the floor and get back into bed, my limbs still tangled in the bedsheets on the hard wood. I can't find the energy to physically move my body.

"Do you need some help?" Garrett's voice is the last one I expect to hear. "Or are you content to stay down there?"

I hear the bed creak under his weight, and I brush at my eyes, trying to clear them. My throat feels raw from sobbing, so I don't try to answer him.

"Alright, then," he says, a loud sigh escaping him. "You stay there, and I'll do the talking."

I pull the sheet tighter around me and attempt to sit up. My bones feel like gelatin, so I settle for propping myself against the side of the bed instead, a foot away from Garrett's legs. I can't see his face this way, only hear his voice. My head throbs painfully.

"I know you pretty well, Selena, and I think you're down there beating yourself up because you let yourself break down. Which is crap because you're one of the strongest people I know."

He's not wrong. I absolutely feel like I'm wasting precious time wallowing in self-pity. We have far too much to do—we need to get moving.

Garrett ignores my silence and continues. "I'm sorry about your grandpa; I know you two were close. For you to be grieving right now is more than acceptable—I don't know how you can't see that. We thought you might want your space, so no one bothered you before, but I thought you might need a friend."

I press the sheet against my eyes. "I thought you were mad at me."

"I was unfair to you before. I don't have any right to be mad at you. You were right about me and Kelly; she was important to me."

I nod, even though I don't know if Garrett is watching me. I sniffle, fighting back my emotions. I want to hear this. I need this distraction, and it's comforting to hear Garrett's voice devoid of the anger it held before.

"You asked me about Kelly, and I never gave you a straight answer. Maybe because I didn't want to face the truth. Selfishly, I hoped if we got something started, it would hurt a little less."

"You don't have to—"

"No." Garrett scoots closer. Then he presses a warm hand to my shoulder, silencing me. "I want to. I should have been upfront with you from the beginning. When the power went out and everything hit the fan, you looked at me like I mattered. You needed my help, and for the first time in a long time, I felt something more than my grief. But even then, Kelly was there between us, wasn't she?"

Kelly and Garrett are a package deal; they always have been. I'm not sure if he is actually asking me the question to hear an answer, but I respond anyway. "Yes. She was always there, and even if we didn't say it, we both felt it. I know it."

"I loved her, you know? And even though she's gone, I still love her. Maybe I always will..." Garrett's voice wavers with emotion, and I shut my eyes.

My own voice is gravelly and ragged, but I need to comfort him. "She loved you, too—we all knew that. I think that's why I was struggling with trying to be more than friends, Garrett. To me, you have always belonged to Kelly."

"I do like you, Selena. It's just..."

Taking the sheet with me, I struggle back onto the bed, leaning my head on Garrett's shoulder. "We're better as friends, Gare. You need to heal, and then, who knows? Maybe you'll find it again. This connection I feel with Axel, it's new, and I don't know where it will go, but it's not something I can deny, either. What if he's my Kelly?"

Garrett wraps his arm around my back. "Then you're right—you can't risk never feeling that. It's worth the pain. I'd love Kelly all over again, even knowing how it ended for us."

"I'm sorry that she's not with us."

"I just wish I could have said goodbye. I knew she wasn't feeling well, but she never came to say goodbye." Garrett gives me a squeeze. "Promise me you'll say goodbye."

I shake my head. "We'll always be friends; you know that, right? I'm not going anywhere. No more goodbyes—you're stuck with me. I can't stand the idea of losing anyone else."

Garrett laughs, his body shaking mine. I feel my own smile and realize I've finally stopped crying.

"You think I should risk falling for him even though you don't like him?" I tease.

"I don't have to like him, that's your job, but be careful, Selena. Our entire lives are a lie, and we don't even know ourselves. So I think you have to ask yourself: What do you really know about him?"

I think about telling Garrett that I've seen the world through Axel's eyes myself. That I felt something when he showed me his memories. I think about telling him that I am more scared of what Axel thinks of me now, knowing about my grandpa and what my family cost him.

Thinking of my grandpa reminds me of what he said about Kelly, how she should have been immune. But what if he'd been mistaken? Either way, Kelly is gone. Garrett might hurt more if I bring it up. As much as I want to unload everything on him, I simply nod instead.

"Good." He laughs. "I'd hate to have to beat him up."

"What's everyone else doing?" I ask, hugging the sheet around me. When he doesn't answer right away, I turn my head to look at him.

"I don't know if you're going to like the answer to that." He sucks his bottom lip between his teeth.

I roll my eyes. "You'd better start talking."

Reluctantly, he tells me they left. While I'd been unraveling in that dark bedroom, Chase had come up with his own plan of action. He wanted to give me time and space to grieve and get my head right, but he hadn't been willing to sit idly by while I did that.

Chase has taken Axel with him back to the military base to meet up with his soldier friends. We'd need their help and their supplies to get back to the Academy.

Garrett stayed behind to keep an eye on me. I wonder why he'd been the one to volunteer and not Axel. Maybe I was right—maybe Axel needs some time and space himself.

He told Garrett to be ready in two days, which means I only have one more day to get myself together.

I spend too much time boiling water over the fire to make myself a bath. It's a terrible waste of drinkable water, but I want to feel human again.

Human.

That word will never hit me quite the same again. While I *am* half human, I have another half to learn. Does it even make a difference? What makes a human *human*, anyway? Some arbitrary letters and numbers on a screen? Some

DNA sequence? The girl I've always been will always be inside of me.

I dunk my head under, letting the hot water silence the sounds of the house and the thoughts that jumble together in my mind. If I'm being honest with myself, I am not the same girl I'd been that day in the cafeteria sharing pizza with my friends. I am stronger now, surer of myself. I had walked my way home, despite the dangers, despite the odds of finding what we hoped for being stacked against us. I had saved a stranger in the woods. I had found my way home despite the heartache and obstacles at every turn.

I did what I came to do. I'd tracked down what was left of my family, and I have answers that I wouldn't have found otherwise. I am an orphan now, and yet, I have breath in my lungs and a fight in my spirit. And with Chase and his friends, we have a real chance to make it back to the Academy—and hopefully, to our friends.

I have found my own bravery.

Coming up for air, I feel a new sense of resolve wash over me. I can do this. *We* can do this.

After my bath, Garrett and I pack what supplies we think would be helpful and get as much rest as we can. I help him change out his bandages, and we take turns reading to each other. I feel both energized and terrified for the trip ahead.

I hope that Chase and his friends will have bikes for us. The idea of taking that long walk all over again and so soon makes my legs shake in protest. Garrett told me he'd shown Chase where the Academy was on the map and the route we'd planned to take from the beginning. Garrett had mostly stuck to the original route, where I'd gone off course into the woods. It all looks so much easier as lines on a map.

Once he's sure I'm going to be okay, Garrett takes a quick trip to his own house despite Chase warning him it isn't safe. I can't blame him for wanting to try. I offered to go with him, but he said he needed to go alone—that it was only a few miles, that we hadn't seen any signs of survivors in the neighborhood—so I don't protest.

It doesn't take him very long to go and come back, a handful of hours at most. I've barely finished drying some of our laundry over the fire when he returns. He's come back sullen, and I know without asking that his trip didn't go how he'd hoped. I don't pry, I just make him a cup of warm broth and let him sit with his thoughts.

When he is finally ready to talk, he simply says he didn't find any sign of his family there, which is better than finding their bodies but not by much. His voice is steady, but I can feel the ache from across the room.

All those months, we'd been waiting for calls from home. We'd all been robbed of the chance to say goodbye to our families, and now they are gone forever. At least I saw my grandpa one last time. But I still hold out hope that we'll have a chance to see our friends again. That hope is the beacon I will follow, for better or worse.

Chapter Twenty-Seven

Two days later, in the early morning, Garrett is telling me a story about his mom when I hear something outside. We are perched on the couch, anxiously waiting for our friends to return—Chase and Axel are due back any time. I can't stop myself from rushing over to the window, peeking through the small slit between the curtains to see what is making the low rumbling noise.

Garrett follows close behind me, staring out the window above my head. "Are those trucks?" he asks.

Four military vehicles of various sizes amble down the empty street, heading straight for us. The green metal glints in the morning sunlight. Garrett is tense beside me, his jaw and fists clenching as if readying for a fight.

I hold my breath, and when I'm sure I'm going to pass out from fear and lack of oxygen, the trucks stop. Chase pops his head out of the driver's side window of the first truck, waving his hands at the other drivers who line up behind him.

I sigh, relieved. "Have you ever seen anything more beautiful?"

Garrett doesn't answer me; he just hurries to the front door to meet Chase. The morning breeze rushes in as he swings the door open. Chase is waiting there, a grin wide on his face. "I thought maybe you two might like a ride this time."

"How did you get them running?" I ask, slipping my backpack over one shoulder. I can't begin to tell him how grateful I feel about not walking back to school. This pack will hurt a lot less if the truck is the one carrying it.

"We have a special armory on base. I don't know what you know about EMP attacks, but we keep the vehicles in a special Faraday facility. We keep quite a few important things safe there, actually: spare parts, generators, weapons. And since our superiors are all gone and we're likely the last people on Earth, we took the liberty of commandeering them for the greater good."

"Please tell me you have parts that can repair solar panels and generators for the Academy." I press my hands over my mouth in my excitement.

Chase's responding smirk tells me everything, and I launch myself at him, hugging him tightly.

"Hey, hey." He laughs. "Just doing what I was trained for."

Garrett joins in. "You've been holding out on us this whole time."

"A guy has to keep some cards close to his vest, and a soldier has to keep even more things classified. I needed to be sure my team was willing to help. I filled them in on everything Mr. Santos told us." Chase pats my back when he says my grandpa's name. "They're in. What do we have to lose at this point?"

"Where's Axel?" I ask, peering around the open door but not seeing him on the porch.

Chase points back at the truck he'd come from. "He's pretty popular with the guys right now. He's in the back of my rig telling them stories about growing up on the moon. He's pretty funny when he warms up."

As happy as I am that Axel is making friends, I missed his company.

The idea of making the trip back to the Academy has always come with fear, but at least for this trip, we will have power in numbers. It doesn't hurt that they are all trained to fight and use weapons, either. "How many guys exactly?" I ask.

"Fifteen if you count me. There were more, but not everyone stayed behind. We're all hybrids or whatever it is we're calling ourselves now. Guess you'd say we're the last men standing."

Immune. We are all immune to the virus, but none of us are immune to loss, to this emotional aftermath. As much as we need the soldiers to help us on our mission, that they would so willingly join us after all the losses they'd suffered is a miracle.

Fifteen soldiers, two Academy kids, and one boy from the moon. Eighteen people will be around to see the beginning of a new world. Despite everything, hope soars inside of me.

"Dude, I'm just happy they came, and you brought tanks!" Garrett's eyes shine as he looks over the vehicles, reminding me of the way little boys look at their toy cars and GI Joes.

Chase shakes his head. "Those aren't tanks, buddy. The one in the front with the .50 cal, that's an MTVR, the big one behind it is an LMTV, and the other two are Humvees."

"Semantics. I don't need your acronyms. You can call them potatoes, for all I care. They look like luxury limousines to me." Garrett laughs. "Limousines with guns."

"They'll come in handy, that's for sure." My sore legs have never felt more relieved.

"Are we ready, then?" Garrett asks, swinging his own backpack onto his shoulder.

Chase nods, rushing toward the hallway. "Grab your coats, and head out. I need to grab a few things from my room, and then we'll be Oscar-Mike."

Garrett looks at me. "What the heck does Oscar-Mike mean?"

"I think that's soldier for *it's time to go home.*"

Chase joins us shortly after, barking orders to his men. They nod at us, throwing our bags into the back of the largest vehicle before taking their own assigned seats among the vehicles. They move with such practiced grace, like the dance of a well-oiled machine. It's mesmerizing to watch.

Garrett helps me up into the back of Chase's truck. The seats are placed vertically in two rows that face each other. Axel's alone on the left side, and three other soldiers sit on the seats to the right. Garrett and I quickly fall into the two empty seats beside Axel. Chase takes the driver's seat, a female soldier on his right.

It isn't a tight fit back here, but it feels small with so many bodies inside and very little daylight filtering in through the thick windows. The soldiers in their uniforms look professional and intimidating but smile at us warmly. Being surrounded by soldiers is going to take some getting used to, but I'd much prefer that over being outnumbered or alone. I try to think of them the same way I had the security guards around the Academy, but they had purposely stayed out of sight for our comfort.

"How are you?" I nudge Axel with my shoulder. "Seems like you got to have all the fun the last few days."

Someone had given him his own military uniform. It fits him better than the clothes we'd managed to scrounge up from the cabin. He looks handsome, his silver eyes are shining bright again, and his cheeks are a healthy pink. I stare down at the fresh combat boots on his feet. My own shoes look like they've been through a war—the once light-gray laces are stained with mud while his are a fresh clean tan color.

I'd washed my clothes, but I don't feel as refreshed as Axel looks. Not on the outside or the inside. I have so many questions to ask him, so many things I want to say to him, but we are so far from alone that now doesn't feel like the right time.

Axel looks from me to Garrett. "I was in the best health; the smart choice was for me to go, allow the two of you more time to heal."

It's an answer but not the one I was hoping for. He doesn't meet my eyes, and I try to ignore the sting of rejection I feel. If he needs time, I can give him that.

"I'm Quinn, and this is Riley and Marx." The soldier across from Axel points to the other two men beside him. "I'm sure Callahan didn't mean to skip the introductions." He rolls his eyes.

"Watch it, soldier," Chase calls from the driver's seat. "There's plenty of time for all that later."

"I'm Tess," the female soldier says, turning around in her seat to face us. "These jerks call me Olson, but I'd prefer you call me Tess."

"Hi, Tess. I'm Selena Santos." I nod back at her. "You already met Axel, but this is my friend, Garrett James."

"Nice to meet y'all." Quinn winks.

"We really appreciate you helping us get back to the Academy. We're hoping our friends headed back that way and we can all be reunited... but either way, when we left, other students were still there."

"Other hybrids?" Tess asks.

"Yes, others who are immune to the viruses." I sigh. I don't care for the term "hybrid," but it's the easiest term for now. I'm still having trouble wrapping my head around the fact that all of us here are part Ardorian.

Axel is quiet. Despite Chase claiming he's been animated and funny with the soldiers before they came to get us, I sense Axel is not as happy-go-lucky as he wants everyone to believe. I want to take his hand in mine, to feel our connection as strong and alive as it had been when the two of us were alone, but too many eyes are on us, and we have nowhere to go.

Or maybe I am the thief of his joy.

I sit back against my seat and try to concentrate on the vibrations of the truck as it moves along the roads. It will only be a few hours to the Academy as long as we don't have any surprises along the way. Working vehicles make a huge difference in travel time. The things we had always taken for granted now feel like immeasurable miracles.

Tess switches seats with Garrett once we are out of the city and onto the freeway. Even though he's already shown Chase how to get to the Academy on a map, Chase says he'll feel better having Garrett confirm he's going in the right direction. Without GPS or a very specific spot on the map, finding the right location is not as simple as it would have been pre-blackout.

I twist the tracker around my wrist. Though it hasn't worked since before we started our journey, I haven't taken it off. It represents a tiny piece of a life that feels years in the past. I was never attached to it before, but taking it off feels like giving up on something I'm not ready to part with yet.

When we pass the spot near the bridge where we were ambushed, I hold my breath. Chase and his men are on high alert, but it appears the area has been abandoned. No one comes out of the woods, no one shoots at us, and the trucks simply amble between the cars and head across the bridge. I don't look too closely; I don't need to see any bodies on the ground to know what happened here.

Even though I don't see the carnage myself, my heart races with anticipation for what we might find back at school.

The soldiers chat quietly with each other, and Garrett and Chase talk about military vehicles and some of the different training operations that Chase had been on. The soldiers check in with each other over hand radios every so often, the sound of the electronic devices is foreign after all our time in silence.

Axel responds to questions from Marx and Riley, but he doesn't attempt to speak with me. So I close my eyes and pretend to sleep next to him. It's easier than staring awkwardly around the truck cabin. I could have tried harder to get him to talk to me, but part of me is relieved to sit in silence. Whatever we find at school today has the potential to make or break any remaining hope for our future.

We find the town where Garrett and I had investigated the blackout, Hidden Maples. Evidence of the events from that day still remain. The windows of the buildings are broken, with furniture and trash left behind by the looting townspeople strewn across the sidewalks and roadway. Everything looks dark and deserted. I see no signs of the people we'd seen at the church that day, and as relieved as I feel not to have anyone around to cause trouble for us, the reality that they are likely sick or dead still burns in my chest.

When we make the final turn before our school, Chase pulls the truck to a stop. "Listen, we don't know what we're going to find here, and I want us to be prepared for anything. Maybe the three of you should stay back, let us professionals assess the situation."

My heart hammers in my chest, blood rushing loudly in my ears. "Absolutely not."

Chase's eyebrow quirks. "Excuse me?"

"While I understand that you are a soldier and this is what you are trained to do... this is my home. The kids that live here are my family, and they don't know you. What if they think you're a threat?"

Tess puts her hand up to silence Chase. "What are you suggesting, Selena?"

"I think Chase and I should walk up together. The rest of you can hang back and come when we know it's safe. And if it's not, then at least the rest of you can get away safely."

Chase laughs, rubbing a hand over his face. "You're a brave girl, Selena. I can see why Liam would be friends with you. But if you think any of these men are going to walk away if this goes south, you obviously don't understand how we do things."

Garrett shifts in his seat. "I'll go, you can stay behind. They know me, too."

I shake my head, already tugging my coat back on. No way am I letting Garrett do this. "You've already been shot once. I have this."

Garrett grits his teeth. "We're a team. If you go, I go. No more goodbyes, remember?"

I sigh in defeat. I promised him that much.

"Fine, but you'd better not get shot this time."

"Chase won't let that happen," Tess says beside me. "You two will be in good hands. The rest of us will be right behind you."

Tess smiles at me, and I hope that we'll get a chance to be friends. She seems like the kind of badass girl who can teach me a thing or two.

"Alright, kids. We will head out on foot, but Tess is right, the team will be right behind us. If things get wild, they know how to handle themselves."

"Fine," I say, "but let me do the talking."

CHAPTER
TWENTY-EIGHT

WE WALK SIDE BY side down the road, the gate to the school within view. From this distance, nothing looks out of the ordinary. The guard station is still unoccupied, but it had been that way the day we left school, too. The air is cool. We'd taken a few hours to get here, but we have plenty of daylight left. The air smells like it wants to snow, and I shiver inside my coat.

The doors to the school are closed with no one mingling outside the building. I hadn't expected a welcoming party, but I feel nervous with how quiet everything seems. The way the sunlight reflects off the school windows, it's impossible to see through them.

Chase takes in our surroundings, scanning every entrance and window. I wonder what the Academy looks like to him; the fancy brick building seems smaller now that my world has changed.

At the double doors, Chase puts a hand on my arm. "Whatever happens, if I tell either of you to run, do not hesitate."

I nod. The adrenaline in my blood is making smooth movements hard. I feel clumsy and like I'm coming out of my own skin. Garrett is breathing heavily beside me, his hand on the door handle.

"Hey, just breathe," Chase says, giving me one last smile before pushing on the handle and swinging the door open.

The school foyer is not empty. A young woman with silver hair holds a gun aimed right at me. Behind her, a handful of young people stand frozen, eyes wide and fixed on us. None of them are my friends.

"Who the hell are you?" Her words come fast and harsh, mirroring my own feelings. Chase and Garrett tense on either side of me, all of us frozen inside the doorway. I know without turning that Chase has also drawn his weapon. I can see the tip of the barrel out of the corner of my eye. I need to diffuse this situation quickly.

"That's the freak who shot me!" Garrett cries out.

I stare at the girl, her face suddenly familiar to me. I saw her in Axel's vision. This is Lyra. She is even more attractive than I remember from the vision. Like Axel, she is tall and lean, but her silver hair is a shade darker than his, her eyes a nearly translucent blue. She has strong cheekbones and a thin nose and is strikingly beautiful—and currently looking incredibly dangerous.

Her arm shifts as she aims her gun at Garrett. "Don't give me an excuse to shoot you again, because this time, I won't miss."

"Please," I beg her. "We're not here to fight. We're looking for our friends."

Lyra returns her gaze to me, suspicion clear on her face. "There's no one here for you; we're claiming this place for ourselves. If your friends are the people who brought us here, we no longer have any use for any of them—or you, for that matter."

"They're still alive?" Garrett's sigh of relief vibrates through me.

"Yeah, no thanks to you." Lyra snorts. "I was the one who shot those animals who attacked you."

"You shot me and then left me for dead. Why should we believe you haven't done the same thing to our friends?" Garrett asks her, his hands clenching.

"I'm not an animal," Lyra says. "But if you give me no choice, I will shoot you. On purpose this time."

We are getting nowhere. I take one step forward, my hands out in front of me. "Listen, we're more alike than you realize."

Lyra laughs, shaking her head. "You have no idea what you're talking about."

"I know your brother. I know Axel," I say, still holding my hands out. "I believe your name is Lyra."

Lyra's gun swings back to me, the barrel aimed straight at my chest. I can hear Chase swear under his breath, but I ignore him, keeping my eyes on Lyra.

"My brother is dead," she says coldly.

"He's not. I can bring him here to you, but I need to know my friends are okay first. Can I see them?"

Lyra's blue eyes narrow on me. She wants to believe me; I can see it. I'd seen her hand tremble slightly at the sound of Axel's name. "If I did believe you, which I'm not saying that I do," she says, "what assurance do I have that you won't take your friends and run?"

I put my hands down and take a deep, steadying breath. "I don't want to run; this is my home. You're the one holding the gun—I'm only asking to see my friends. My friend Chase here, he can put his gun down if you promise to keep your word."

"Like hell," Chase barks behind me.

I know Chase is trying to keep us alive, but I bite my lip to keep from crying out in my frustration. We've come so far—I need to see for myself that my friends are here and that they are okay. "Fine. You can keep your gun on me, but let me see my friends."

Lyra shakes her head. "Bring me my brother. Then you can have your friends."

A flash of movement catches my eye at the back of the cafeteria, and I hold my breath as I watch the soldiers fall into position. Chase's men are surrounding us, moving without a sound. They must have entered from the other side of the school. Lyra and her friends haven't seen them yet, so I try one last time to change her mind.

"Please, Lyra. Axel and I are friends. He's fine, and I promise I'll bring him to you. I only want to see my—"

"Lyra." I hear Axel's voice behind me at the same time I feel a gush of cold air from outside—he'd come in after us. I watch recognition flash across Lyra's face; Axel's sudden appearance is the perfect distraction from the soldiers quietly taking their places around us.

"Axel." Her voice is cold, nothing like the warm sisterly tone I expected. "What is the meaning of this? You're working with these *people?*" She spits the word as if she's tasted something nasty.

"It's not what you think." He steps forward, coming to my side before stopping. Lyra's gun remains pointed at us.

"Well, it looks like you're a race traitor to me," she says.

"How can he be a race traitor when we're all half of each race? If you would give us a minute to talk to you, I think you will understand that we're on the same side." I don't know why, but I continue to try to reason with her.

Lyra practically growls in response, taking a step closer to us.

Axel takes my hand in his, and I suck in a breath. I've wanted to feel his touch for days. The connection between us feels electrified and fills me with quiet confidence.

"She's telling the truth, Lyra. The students here, and my friends who came with me, are the same as us. They have Ardorian parents; it's how they have survived the viruses here."

Lyra laughs hysterically, her arm shaking with the movement. "You can't be serious, Axel. I'm sure these humans have been filling your head with lies. They are not your friends. Do you not remember the things their kind put us through? They'll do anything to survive."

The soldiers are moving in, and with all eyes locked on Axel and Lyra, even her friends are unaware of the danger they are in. I don't want this. I don't want anyone to get hurt. Why won't Lyra relax and talk to us about this?

But I know why. Those scars on Axel's body are all the evidence needed to understand why Lyra, and even Axel, might be unwilling to trust any of us. My grandpa had been a witness to the torture they'd endured so that humans might have a chance at survival.

"Come stand with us, brother—you don't need this girl or her friends."

Axel squeezes my fingers tightly. "She saved my life, Lyra."

Lyra frowns. Her gun shifts toward me once more, and I feel the weight of her gaze on me. "That's unfortunate, because I'm about to end hers."

"Now." Chase's voice booms loud from behind me, and then the wind is knocked out of my body as something slams hard into my back. My hand slips free from Axel's, sending me flying across the tile floor. Gunshots split the air, and I cry out, scrambling to get to cover.

The previously quiet common area of the school erupts into chaos. People are yelling and screaming as I slide under one of the tables. I look back to where I'd been standing with Axel moments ago and breathe a sigh of relief.

"Are you okay?" Chase calls out to me. He'd managed to tackle Lyra to the ground. Tess is clearing the gun she'd been holding. It appears she'd misfired, and no one had been hit.

Axel watches wide-eyed as his sister thrashes around on the ground under Chase's hold. Chase slips handcuffs over her wrists before pulling them both to their feet.

"Alright, Rambo. Maybe we can get you to calm down and talk now?" he asks.

Lyra says some choice words back to him, and he grins at her.

"Well, I do like your spirit." He chuckles.

"Just cooperate, Lyra." Axel sighs. "These people are not the enemy."

Garrett claps him on the shoulder. "Your sister is crazy, but Chase is right, she's also kind of a baddy."

Tess rolls her eyes. "Of course, if it's a chick with a gun, you think she's a badass, but if it were a man pointing a gun at us, he'd just be stupid, right?"

With the immediate danger gone, Chase looks amused. "Come on, let's find somewhere we can keep her and her buddies contained while she cools down. Garrett, is there a place like that nearby?"

"Sure. A nice room we used for detention is around the corner. I'll take you there."

I watch as Garrett and the soldiers lead Axel's family toward our detention hall. Lyra and the four other kids I'd seen on the ship in Axel's memory are all accounted for. At least they are all alive.

Tess is talking with Axel, trying to make sure he is alright. Garrett is busy with Chase, and everything in my body is screaming to find my friends *right now*.

The time for patience has passed. I turn and run, my feet slapping hard against the floor as I make my way through the school to our room. My winter coat feels too hot against my clammy skin, but I don't want to waste even the few seconds it will take to remove it. I pound my fists on our door, my hands clammy with anticipation.

"Go away!" Hanna's voice bellows through the door.

Hanna. My chest squeezes; they really are here.

"Not on your life!" I cry out. "Open this door before I get someone to kick it down."

In less than a second, the door is swinging in. Hanna's wide brown eyes scan me from head to toe. Her red hair is wild around her face, but she's wearing her favorite pajamas and appears uninjured. "Holy crap. How are you here? I thought it was that evil b—"

"Selena?" Evelynn's voice is like music to my ears. She joins Hanna in the doorway, tears already falling down her cheeks.

"It's a long story; I promise I'll fill you both in." I sigh, reaching for my friends.

A small cry sounds from somewhere in the room, and I freeze. "Who else is in there with you?"

Evelynn and Hanna share a look before pulling me into a group hug. My body feels weak as the excitement of the day washes over me. I let them hold me up, reveling in the familiar smell of our room. All of us are crying. We are a collective mass of tears and sniffles, and I don't care. We are finally back together.

When they pull away, Hanna takes my hand, leading me inside. "It's a long story, too... better you see for yourself."

Stepping to the side, Hanna gives me a full view of our room. Everything looks exactly how we'd left it—even my bed looks untouched. But my eyes lock on the back corner that had remained unoccupied for the last year, a jolt rushing through me as Kelly stares back at me from her bed.

Grandpa wasn't mistaken about her immunity status—Kelly is alive. She is alive!

Before I can ask any of the millions of questions that flash through my mind, I hear the same small cry from before. Kelly lifts the bundle of blankets on her lap and holds them to her chest. "I think there's someone you should meet."

I'm frozen in place, my tongue glued to the roof of my mouth as I try to understand what I'm seeing. She stands and carries the bundle with her, stopping in front of me. She looks tired but as beautiful as ever.

Her blonde hair is braided neatly to one side, her signature pink sweater giving a healthy flushed hue to her skin. There is no sign of any lingering sickness about her. Words fail me as she pulls the blanket to the side to reveal the sweetest little round head to me.

A curious face looks up at me from her arms. Deep-brown eyes, much darker than Kelly's, study me as I study them back. He is mostly bald, with a dusting of brown hair on the top of his head, and I have absolutely no doubt in my mind that this is Garrett's child.

The baby's little chubby hand reaches out for me, and I swallow back the lump in my throat.

"His name is Hank, after his grandpa," Evelynn chimes in. "Isn't that the sweetest? He's six months old. I'm sad we've missed so much already."

"Here, you can hold him," Kelly says, gently passing him to me. He is precious and much lighter than he looks—he's the first baby I've ever held in my arms. That distinct baby smell that my mother told me about is real, and I press him close to my chest to take it all in. Kelly has a baby.

"He's perfect," I say. "This is the reason you were so sick? This is why you left?"

Kelly nods. "Headmaster James—you know, Garrett's dad—he found out because I went to the nurse with my symptoms. He helped me hide my pregnancy from everyone. We couldn't tell anyone; it was too much of a risk. They would have wanted to study him, and neither of us was willing to let that happen. I only wish I'd told Garrett before—"

A broken sob slips past her lips, and I suck in a breath. I've been so taken by surprise seeing Kelly, it hasn't occurred to me that everyone in this room thinks Garrett is dead. With all the grief Garrett has been battling for the last year without Kelly, he is going to lose his mind when he sees her. He doesn't even know he's a dad.

"Wait, Kelly, Garrett is here. He's here. He came with me!"

Evelynn rubs Kelly's back as she struggles to get her grief under control. Hanna shakes her head at me in her confusion. "What do you mean, he's here? He's dead; we saw his body."

"He wasn't dead. He thinks that when he was shot, he hit his head, which knocked him out. So with all that blood, and then being unconscious, he probably did *look* dead. But when he came to, you were gone, and he chose to keep going. He made it to Liam's house not long after I did. He's helping some of the other people here with me, but he's going to be thrilled to see you, Kelly."

Hanna steps away from Evelynn and Kelly, pulling me in to whisper in my ear. "But you and Garrett, is that still a thing?"

I laugh a little at the absurdity of our situation. We've been fighting for our lives, crossing miles of the unknown while death and new life and everything in between surround us, and yet, we are still teenage girls, worried about wayward hearts and the boys who hold the power to break them. Maybe not everything good has changed. Maybe we've managed to hold on to some of our innocence in all of this.

"No." I smile. "He's always been Kelly's. This is the best news, I promise."

Hanna purses her lips but lets it go. "Well, I guess that's a relief."

"Where's Liam?" I ask, thinking of Garrett and Chase a few hallways away.

"He's in the theater with everyone else. That jerk, Lyra, only let us in here because of the baby. Apparently, she's not completely heartless, but I still don't like her."

"We have her under control for now." I sigh. I hope that, between Axel and the rest of us, we can convince Lyra that we can all live peacefully together. If that's even what Axel wants—I still can't get a read on how he is feeling after my grandpa's house. We really need to have a private talk about everything once any of us gets a chance to catch our breath.

Kelly wipes frantically at her eyes, her hands reaching for Hank. "I can't—you're sure, he's really here?"

I nod at her, pressing a kiss to the top of Hank's sweet bald head before passing him back to her. "He's really here.

He's never going to believe this, Kelly—he's really missed you."

Evelynn gives me a sad smile. "We didn't know you were alive, either, Selena. I'm sorry we didn't come after you."

"I was so angry with you..." Hanna's lip wobbles. "And then when we thought we'd never see you again, all I felt was regret for how I treated you."

"Hey, now, no more apologies. We're all alive, and now we can all be together again, and that's what matters." For the first time in weeks, I finally don't feel like crying—at least, not the sad kind of crying. This is my home, and as devastating as it was to lose my parents and grandparents, it's comforting to have my found family safe and sound. I can focus on that, and we will survive the rest together.

Hanna wipes at her own tears. "I know we have so much to talk about, and I have more questions than I can even make sense of in my brain right now, but what do you say we go make this band reunion complete?"

Evelynn rushes for the door. "That's not even a question; let's freaking go!"

In all the days we've been without power, this is the first time I truly wish I had a camera to capture the moment before me.

Chase and Garrett are letting everyone out of the theater as we round the corner. Chase is trapped in the embrace of his little brother, and Liam is barely containing himself. Shouts of happiness ring out across the hall. Garrett's eyes meet mine, and I feel goosebumps across my arms as I step aside to let Kelly and Hank steal the show.

They don't speak. In fact, the entire hallway goes quiet as Kelly walks toward Garrett, little Hank tucked on her hip, his little happy coos the only sound breaking the silence. I watch Garrett's face as recognition sparks and a shudder vibrates through his body, and then he's bridging the distance between them like a man possessed. He cradles Hank's little head in his hand, tears falling from his eyes as reality hits him. He presses a kiss to Kelly's forehead then another to her lips. "It's really you. You're really here."

She nods through her own emotion, running her free hand over his face before squeezing his shoulder as if testing the image before her to ensure this is real. "We're really here."

His arms wrap around the two of them, and as they cry together, there's not a dry eye around the room. This is what life is all about. This is hope. This is our future.

I turn away, wanting to let them have their private moment as they become a true family for the first time. This has to be better than any outcome Garrett has ever dreamed up. He has his heart back, and if I know him like I think I do, he will never let them slip away again.

"Wow." Evelynn sniffles. "Best day ever."

I hug my friend again, in whole-hearted agreement.

Hanna pokes me in the side. "You're sure you're good with that?" she asks, her eyes searching my face for any cracks in my bravado.

I don't turn back to look at Garrett and Kelly. I don't need to see them together to know that it is right. My heart is not broken—it's full of love and happiness for both of them. Garrett will always be special to me, but that doesn't have to change because he has his family back.

"Yes, I'm sure. Like I said, I have a lot to tell you."

Someone grabs me from behind, and a vise-grip of a hug pulls me off my feet, crushing my lungs and making me cry out in surprise. "Holy crap, where were you hiding?" Liam's voice makes me relax a little, but I shove against his hold until he relents and lets me back down on my feet. He laughs as I straighten out my coat and try to catch my breath.

"I was looking for your brother. You know, like we planned."

Liam nods to where Chase is talking with the other kids. "Does that mean I have him to thank for getting everyone back here?"

"You do," I say. "He's a pretty cool brother. Maybe someday you'll be as cool as he is."

Liam grabs his chest. "Ouch! I think you permanently broke something with that comment."

Hanna pokes him in the side. "Oh, be quiet. You don't have anything in there to break."

My friends are safe. Things have turned out even better than I dared to dream they could. Chase and his friends are here, and we have a real chance to fix things around here and not only survive but have a fresh start. We have things to hope for now, things to be excited about. A future to build together. Everything is falling into place, but there is still something left for me to do.

Behind my friends, I catch a glimpse of Axel. He is standing off to the side watching all of us, his hands in his pockets. Wearing the army uniform, he blends in with Chase and his team, but no one can mistake his physical resemblance to Lyra.

Evelynn follows my gaze. "Uh, please tell me that is not Queen B's super-hot evil twin."

I shake my head. "If one of them is evil, it's not Axel."

"His name is Axel? We know this boy?" she asks, her hand tightening around my arm. "I have so many questions."

"And I promise, I'll answer them," I say, giving her a reassuring squeeze back. "I just need a minute alone with him right now."

Chapter
Twenty-Nine

AXEL DOESN'T SAY A word as he follows me down the hall and into an empty classroom. My chest feels tight, and my cheeks are too warm. I slip out of my winter coat, laying it on a desk before taking a seat on Mrs. Dempsey's couch. The green suede still looks new, but the cushions are lumpy from years of use. Like so many things, looks can be deceiving.

Haven't I looked at my own reflection my whole life and never known the truth about where I came from, what has been hiding in my own blood?

"This was one of my favorite classrooms," I say, my nerves making me spew out useless words. "We used to read here on this couch about the world before the viruses."

Axel still says nothing as he joins me on the couch. I jiggle my leg nervously, afraid to meet his gaze. What if I see hatred in his eyes? Or worse, betrayal? What if he blames me for all the suffering he's endured? After all, he knew my grandpa, put trust in him. Can he find it in him to forgive me?

We might be made the same, but we've grown up on different ground. I've looked at the sky and wondered about worlds beyond us in awe, and he probably looked down at the Earth and thought only that we are responsible for his pain.

His sister has made it clear how she feels about us. I wish my alien blood gave me the power to read minds, because I'd give anything to know what Axel is thinking right now.

"I'm rambling when what I really want is to tell you that I'm sorry. I'm sorry that my family was responsible for so much of your suffering. If not directly, indirectly. I wouldn't be here if it weren't for the experiments they did on the moon. My grandpa might have had good intentions, but you suffered for us, so that humans could live on in some way. I am so sorry. If you can't trust me now, if you even did before... I'll understand. You don't owe me anything; you can take your family and go anywhere. You can walk away from us if that's what you need to do."

I take a deep breath and rub my sweaty palms against my jeans. I want to take back what I've said and beg Axel to stay, but that isn't fair.

None of the words in my mind feel like the right ones to say. So I bite my tongue and wait for him to say something. *Please, say anything.*

Axel shifts beside me, and I hold my breath, worried he will walk out and I'll never see him again.

"Can I show you something?" His voice is gentle as his fingers slip under my chin, tilting my face toward his. His silver gaze holds me captive there, the light in them unmatched. I've never seen eyes like his, and I doubt any would ever match their beauty. He might not live on the moon anymore, but the moonlight will always be in his eyes.

The lump in my throat is hard to talk around, but I fight against it. "Of course."

A smile touches the corner of his mouth, and I turn my body toward him. He takes both of my hands in his, the way he'd done that first time in the woods. I feel the faintest spark of our connection through the soft skin of his hands and watch him take a deep breath, and then, just like before, I feel myself thrust into his mind.

My body is freezing. The fireplace in the little cabin is lit, but the heat is barely touching my skin, and the small wooden chair I'm sitting on stabs uncomfortably into my sore muscles. Selena sits across from me; she's asking me questions that make me feel dishonest. I don't know how much I should tell her about where I've come from, but it makes me feel sick to lie. So I say very little, and I am intentionally vague. I take a sip of my water as I watch the gears turn in her eyes. She's gearing up for more questions; I can tell.

Her dark hair is messy—pieces of it have fallen into her face. Those pieces make me focus more on the dark blue of her eyes. Lyra has blue eyes, but they're not this shade; these are almost midnight blue, and I want to look at them more closely. She's not the first human I've ever met, but she's the first I've ever been so intrigued by.

"So how did you end up in the woods all alone?" she asks.

I set my cup down on the small table and shift in my chair, trying to get more comfortable. I give her another vague answer, telling her I don't know. That I only remember my sister talking with me after the crash.

I cringe inwardly when I realize I've mentioned the crash. She sits up straighter, her body on alert. "Oh my goodness, you were in an accident? Was she hurt? Your sister?"

Lyra. My head hurts as I try to remember the crash and the events afterward. It had been absolute chaos. We'd hit the Earth hard, our ship breaking into pieces on impact. Without our pods, we'd have been killed instantly. Our pilot was dead—I found one of his shoes, but not much else was left of him. Lyra had been helping the others out of their pods when I noticed a fire had started near the entrance to the woods. I'd argued with her, told her we had to put the fire out before we could leave... she'd been angry with me. And then... had she hit me, or had I passed out? Everything about what happened next is black and confusing.

I shake my fuzzy head, frustrated that I can't remember more. "No. I remember she was okay. I was trying to check over all of us... But then, I think I hit my head? The next thing I remember is waking up alone in the woods next to your things and then seeing you. I don't know where they are now."

Selena looks stricken—her cheeks are pink, and she's breathing more quickly. "Do you think your car was close by? Maybe we can find your family? It wouldn't hurt to have a few more people on our side—it's dangerous to be outnumbered out here. Maybe they're looking for you?"

"I wish I could remember, but we fell so fast..." *I can't seem to meet her eyes. My family might be half human, but I can't promise her they'd be on her side. Am I even on her side? The things humans have done to us over our lifetimes...*

"You mean... you were in a plane?" *She stares at me, wide-eyed.*

I've done it again. Said the wrong thing and let her in on more information than I'd intended. I can't tell her I'd come on the ship; she'd never understand. "Ah... yes. Aircraft." *I nod while I scramble for something to say. Technically, it was an aircraft, but the lie tastes sour on* my tongue. "It won't be flying again, that I remember. Absolutely destroyed."

Selena watches me too closely. "You said all of us; who else was with you?"

My family. The only members remaining. The only proof Ardor was ever a planet, that Ardorians existed in this reality. Everyone else... gone. I turn my face away to hide the tears that are falling, but I can't stop my body from heaving under the pain I feel. So I take deep breaths, in through my nose and out through my mouth. I have to get myself under control.

An icy chill rushes through me, and I fear I'm injured in places I cannot see.

"Axel? I'm sorry—you don't have to talk about it." Selena's voice is melodic, like a song. She's being kind, but I don't know yet if I can trust her.

I swallow back my emotions and turn the questioning back on her. "What about you? Why are you out here all alone?"

The story she tells me makes my blood rush in my ears. She'd run for her life, and now she's beating herself up for it. Her hands twist in her lap with guilt, tears sliding down her reddening cheeks. With every word she speaks, she reminds me that humans are not to be trusted.

"Violence. Hate. Greed." I shake my head. "That's all this species offers, isn't it?"

Her face softens then, her hands relaxing in her lap. "Not everyone is awful. I like to think most people are good. The bad ones simply make the most noise."

I'm not sure I agree with her. I've learned plenty about human history, and much of it is painful and dark. But I watch Selena, and she doesn't seem threatening or detached like the humans I've known—could she truly be different?

"*People should care for each other, family or not. They should not seek to hurt or overpower or get ahead at the expense of others.*"

Selena wipes her eyes. "*I think so, too. I think that's why I feel so bad about leaving my friends. I should have stayed with them...*"

A tremor rushes through me again, the cold penetrating so deep into my bones I'm not sure I remember what it feels like to be warm anymore. If those evil people had captured Selena as well, would I have survived even another hour out there, exposed to the elements? "*No, I think you did what was best. It would not have helped them for you to be captured as well, would it?*" I pat her arm, the heat coming off her a welcome distraction.

"*I hope so.*" She sniffles. "*I hope they're still...*"

She's worried her friends are dead, and they may very well be. I don't want to lie to her, so I do my best to distract her instead. "*And then you helped me, why? It would make sense after your experience to not help a stranger.*"

Her eyes meet mine. I want to see the truth in them, so I hold her gaze. "*I won't lie—I was afraid you might be one of them at first, but you were dying. I couldn't just leave you there. No one deserves that. And if I helped you and you turned out to be bad, at least I could live with myself, knowing that I did everything I could. Especially after leaving my friends behind like that.*"

She was afraid of me. She could have kept walking, and I'd never have known the difference. The fact that she'd stayed to help someone she didn't even know doesn't add up to the picture my family has painted of humans. Could they have been that off? It doesn't seem likely. But everything about Selena makes me question what I know about Earth and its people. *"You were afraid of me, but you helped me anyway?"*

"You needed my help. That was enough for me." She yawns, her eyes fluttering against exhaustion. It's been a long and troubling day for both of us. But surely I'm missing something—what does she hope to gain from helping me? She must have some ulterior motive. I ask her the question, and the disgusted face she makes in response gives me pause.

"Yes, you're right. I was hoping you'd be helpful in getting us out of this mess. Maybe be some big strong lumberjack with survival skills…"

She needs me to increase her odds of survival. That I can wrap my head around. I nod at her, letting her know I understand. *"We should rest—we can decide what steps to take next in the daylight."* I nod toward the one small bed. *"You may sleep there. I'll make do here."*

The wooden chair beneath me continues to dig hard into my back, and I know I'll have to move to the floor to have any chance of sleeping. My body continues to shake and shudder against the internal cold I feel.

Selena's eyebrows draw together, and she frowns. *"Don't be silly. That bed is small, but it's big enough that we can both sleep there. This is not the time to be chivalrous. We need the rest, and we're both mature enough to handle it, don't you think?"*

If I could feel any heat, all of it would be in my face. What she's suggesting… it's not right. I've never even shared my bed with a male—a female is absolutely forbidden. It would be uncomfortable for her; she's just being nice. I shake my head, the motion jerky and desperate. *"No, I couldn't ask you to share your space that way."*

The blood rushing in my ears drowns out whatever she says next. I catch something about it being for survival, but *my brain is slow from exhaustion and shock. Maybe I have a concussion, maybe sleeping is the wrong choice after all... but I find myself nodding my agreement anyway.*

I'm frozen in place as she moves about the small cabin, laying out blankets and adding wood to the fire. I'm unsure if I've made the right decision agreeing to share the bed with her but unable to find the words to take it back.

She takes off her outer layer, hanging it over the back of her chair. She has even more layers on—perhaps that's why she doesn't appear as cold as I feel.

"You can climb in first—you're bigger than I am, and I don't want you to feel like you're going to fall out of the bed." She smiles at me. If that is the response I get, perhaps falling out of the bed wouldn't be so bad. Maybe I should let her have the inside after all.

I remove my boots; my fingers are stiff from the cold, and it takes me a few tries to get the knots out. It feels good to remove them. I flex my icy toes in my socks and then force myself to climb into the bed before I change my mind. I press myself up against the wall, giving her as much space as is scientifically possible. Then I wait, staring at the ceiling, looking for strength in the shadows there. I hear her moving around the cabin, tidying things up, but I don't look at her. Instead, I close my eyes and focus on my own breathing. My body shakes violently—I can't seem to make it stop.

"Axel, are you still freezing?" The concern in her voice makes me ache. The tremors seem stronger now; it's nearly impossible to move anything on my own, as all my movements have become involuntary. My heart is racing, my breathing seems more difficult—I've never felt this before.

She turns to face me, her eyes searching my face.

"I am easily chilled." My teeth chatter as I speak, and the words sound disjointed even to my own ears. "It's not helpful on a night like this."

She offers to trade sides if the cabin wall is too cold, telling me she's warmer than I look. All I can do is shake my head—even if I tried, I'm not sure I could make the switch. My body refuses to cooperate.

She lifts her hand; it hovers near my face, and I stiffen. "May I?" she asks.

I don't know what she intends, but it's possible I'm dying, and my curiosity deserves to be answered. I nod my agreement as best I can. She places one soft hand against my cheek, and I hear her loud intake of breath.

Heavenly. If human heaven exists, I bet it feels like this. Her hand is impossibly silky and deliciously warm. I close my eyes in ecstasy, my hand reaching up to hold hers in place. I want nothing more than to feel this connection. "You're so warm." The words pass my lips like a prayer. And then my body convulses violently, over and over.

Selena jerks her hand away, sitting up in the bed. I immediately mourn the loss of warmth, but I do not wish to make her uncomfortable.

"I'm going to get you warm, okay? Do you trust me?"

I use all my strength to sit up beside her. Do I trust her? A voice in my heart screams an enthusiastic yes. I try to nod, but I'm shaking too hard. "Y-Yes..." Despite my fear, I manage to speak that one simple word.

"Good," she says. She unzips her top layer and removes it before yanking off more layers in one quick tug. She's less covered than Lyra is when we swim, and the pink garment she's wearing is too small, too much of her laid bare for me. I press my shaking hands over my eyes.

"*What are you doing?*" *My voice is an octave or two higher than usual.* "*This is not appropriate.*"

"*Relax, it's no different than a swimsuit top.*"

Lyra's swimwear had long sleeves and zipped up to her neck. "*I don't know what kind of swimwear you're talking about, because the females I know do not own those.*"

She's amused by my response, and then she tells me she's going to remove more clothing. I press my fingers harder against my eyes. She's asking me to remove some of my own clothing, telling me that as much skin-to-skin contact as possible is necessary for my survival.

Everything is telling me this is wrong. That I should deny her, and if I'm meant to die tonight, then so be it. But given the way her hand felt against my cheek, the warmth that had cascaded over me from that small contact, can I really deny myself this chance to live? To be warmed by her?

"*You want me to take off my clothes?*" *I can't help but repeat her request. I have to be sure I haven't misheard or misunderstood what she's saying.*

She's frustrated with me, and her words are clipped and harsh as she explains again why this is necessary. "*I'm really afraid that if we don't do something, I'm going to wake up next to your cold, dead body.*"

I pull my hands away from my face and chew on my trembling lip. If I die, Selena will be alone, and she may not make it to her destination. I want her to make it.

Feeling less confident than I want to, I resign myself to doing as she says. I unzip my hoodie and remove the rest of my clothes, leaving behind only my cotton undershorts and socks. Selena removes her own pants, and I feel my already racing heart kick up a notch. I lay back and stare at the ceiling. Selena does the same beside me.

This girl. She may need my help, but part of me doubts that. She found shelter, made a fire, had food and enough knowledge to get warm and keep herself alive. She owes me nothing, and yet, she refuses to let me die. This is more than I know how to comprehend. We take care of each other at home, but not like this, not in such an intimate way. Emotions I can't describe and don't know how to name swirl through me in intricate patterns as if I've discovered a whole new galaxy of feelings.

I reach for Selena's hand beneath the blankets, squeezing gently as her fingers interlock with mine. "Thank you," I say, and she turns to face me in the hazy firelight. The emotions are heavy, and I feel tears leaking from my eyes.

She squeezes my hand in return. "I'd like to think you'd do the same for me."

I'm not sure I would have made the same choices that she has, but I'd like to think so, too. I reluctantly drop her hand so I can turn to face her. "What do we do now? You're going to have to help me out here; I don't quite know how to handle this. I am surprised by your willingness to help me. It is both confusing and overwhelming."

Her hesitancy from before seems to vanish, and her mouth curls into a smile. "Next, we try to get as much of my skin touching yours as we can. I'm going to turn around and back up against you. You can wrap your arms around me like a hug—you know, big spoon, little spoon style? And then we try our best to sleep. If we don't rest, tomorrow will be really difficult."

I still feel wrong invading her space, but I know I'm going to do it anyway. I nod my agreement and follow her lead as she turns around and presses her body against mine. My stomach flips over, and my heart speeds up as the heat from her body slams into me like a hammer. She's a furnace, a living breathing flame. I sigh in relief as she threads her fingers through mine and presses our joined hands against her chest. It's the closest thing to a hug I've ever experienced—if hug is even the right word to describe it.

She shivers in my arms, and I feel guilty for robbing her of her warmth.

"You okay?" Her voice shakes. She wiggles against me, getting even closer. I'm not sure even the air could fit between us now. I've never felt this cared for in my life. I've never been as thankful for another being as I am at this moment. It's unexpected, and it makes me question everything I know.

"Yes, you feel wonderful." I let my honesty slip through my lips. I feel like I'm back in the anti-gravity rules of space, my body unbound by the laws of physics. This human girl breaks all the laws and rules I know.

"Goodnight, Axel," she whispers, her voice soft and sleepy.

"Goodnight, Selena." I hold her like the lifeline she is. I can feel her heart beating steadily beneath my fingertips, stealing more of my resolve with each beat. Humans are dangerous. They've told me that my whole life. Maybe they're right—Selena feels dangerous. But not in the way I've always been taught.

I blink back tears as I come out of Axel's vision. I'd lived the same memory, but it was beautiful to see it the way that Axel had experienced it. It's strange to see myself from that perspective, though. To feel the emotions and think the thoughts that Axel was thinking in those moments. This is not a weapon, his gift—it's a chance to understand someone on another level. "Why did you show me that?" I ask.

Axel runs his knuckles gently down the side of my face. "That's the first moment I knew."

"Knew what?"

"That what I thought about humans might not be true. That my limited knowledge might have been colored by the experiences my race had endured on the moon. That perhaps I could trust you after all. And I do, Selena; I do trust you."

I shake my head, wanting desperately to believe he means what he's saying. I open my mouth to speak, but he puts a finger to his lips, silencing me.

"I also wanted to show you that memory, because I believe it's the moment I first knew something else."

"What's that?" I ask, my own eyes lost in the swirling moonlight of his gaze.

He cradles my face in both hands. "That I love you."

My heart beats hard in my chest. Our lives have been filled with immeasurable loss, but this... us finding each other in the mess of it all is a true miracle.

He presses closer, our noses almost touching. "You made me realize I could love humanity after all. In loving you, I realized I could love all the parts of myself, even the human ones."

"I love you, too," I say, leaning forward to press my lips to his. As our lips meet, all the fight leaves my body. There will be more to talk about. We have plans to make and a future to fight for, but right now, at this moment, my world feels solid. Gravity has returned, and I have so much to live for.

Axel kisses me back, his soft lips dancing with mine as if that's what they were made for, and I allow myself to get lost in our love.

Chapter Thirty

Two Months Later

The generator fires up and hums loudly as Riley finishes gathering his tools. The school basement is not a place I've ever spent time in before, but it has been my second home lately. I've been tasked with monitoring repairs and helping to keep everyone on mission. Turns out I have a real knack for organizing people and helping things run smoothly.

I can't help the excitement I feel as I jump up and down at the wonderful sound of power buzzing away. "Ha! It actually worked!"

Riley, the always serious soldier, doesn't even crack a smile. "We have success. Give it a few hours, and then, if we have a true victory, I claim the first hot shower."

"I could kiss you for this one," Chase says, clapping a hand on Riley's back. "I'm glad we were able to source enough parts from what we brought with us."

"Thankfully, the solar panels didn't need much work. Someone will have to remove the snow from them regularly, though."

Liam groans from his chair by the toolbox. "By someone, I assume you mean me."

"Well, if you don't have any other skills worth sharing, then yeah, bro, that'll be all you." Chase tosses him the broom he's been using as a plow for the last week while Riley repaired what he could.

"I'll put you down as our snow removal crew indefinitely," I tease, winking at Liam.

"So when do we head out?" Garrett asks, his eyes somber.

"We"—Chase motions to Riley and me—"head out tomorrow morning. You, however, are not part of the equation. You have a family here that needs you."

Garrett shakes his head, opening his mouth to protest, but Liam beats him to it.

"What the heck—why am I out?" Liam swings at his brother with the end of the broom. Chase grabs it and yanks, knocking Liam off-balance.

"I'm guessing because you're needed for snow removal." I laugh, helping him right himself. Chase has already clued me in that Liam and Garrett will not be joining us.

"I thought we said no more goodbyes." Garrett pins me with a sad look, but I just smile at him, pressing a hand over my heart. This is not goodbye, and he knows that.

Over the last two months, we accomplished more than any of us thought possible. Axel easily won his old friends over, and they'd joined the Academy family as if they'd always belonged. We redistributed rooms, and since the Academy was built to accommodate well over two hundred people, everyone was comfortable with their room assignments and taking on their own chores and duties. Chase's soldiers have a range of useful skills and training and also fit right in around here.

With the generator and solar panels working, we'll now be able to make use of the greenhouse and science lab to get our own food growing. The stash of MREs and non-perishable foods from the army base will hold us over for a long while, but we are ready to get started on a more sustainable way of living.

We still don't know why the power went out.

Garrett and Kelly moved into the old headmaster's quarters. I think Garrett takes a lot of comfort in having his family in his dad's old space. While it still hurts him to have missed the chance to say goodbye to his parents, the fact that their last act was to care for Kelly and their grandchild gives him peace. Little Hank is crawling all over the Academy, and everyone dotes on the cute little chub.

Hanna, Evelynn, and I stayed in our old room. It was nice to sleep in my own bed and feel right back at home again. I hung up the photo of my family and finally retired my tracker. Letting it go was easy now that I have what really matters back.

The girls grilled me for weeks about my time alone with Axel—they wanted all the details. I've managed to keep most of it to myself. However, I was sure to tell Evelynn that first kisses don't have to be disappointing.

We have a great home base set up. The Academy is off-grid and easily secured with all the extra hands. Everyone here will be well taken care of, and this will always be home, but my grandpa confirmed what Chase and his men already expected. There are other academies besides ours. There are other kids like us out there, and if we're going to rebuild everything that's been lost, we need to find them.

We aren't relying on just my grandpa's word, either—we found evidence in the school files of correspondence between the schools. We will use those addresses first, and hopefully they will lead us to more locations as time goes on. It's a promising start and a lot more direction to go on than we had before.

Chase handpicked a small group of his men to accompany us. Riley, Tess, Marx, and Quinn will be the muscle, and Axel and Dax are coming to offer other perspectives. We wanted to bring Lyra with us, but we decided to let her have some more time at the Academy to come around. She has a knack for agriculture, and if she is willing to play nice with everyone, we are thankful to have her leading that project.

And me? I am simply happy to honor the memory of my grandpa and help build the future he always felt was possible.

"Did you hear me? I thought we said no more goodbyes?" Garrett waves his hand in front of my face to get my attention.

"Haven't you ever heard that saying, 'absence makes the heart grow fonder'?" I ask, pulling him in for a hug. He smells like Hank, and I can't help but smile thinking of the adventures in fatherhood that await him. He and Kelly are natural parents, and they give the rest of us a picture of what our future could look like if that's what we want someday.

Garrett leans back from our embrace and pulls a small piece of paper out of his pocket. I stare at the rectangle of sketchbook paper, my fingers lightly tracing the outside edge, careful not to smudge the pencil marks.

"So you don't forget where your home is." Garrett smiles, gently brushing my chin with his thumb. My eyes blur with tears as I stare down at the perfect sketch of all our friends around one of the cafeteria tables. I'd always wondered what was in those sketchbooks, but I'd never realized the extent of his skill. We're all there, and he's captured each one of our personalities in the simple lines.

"Thank you," I whisper. "I promise, I'll come home when this is all done."

"Don't think this means you get out of your auntie duties." He laughs, lightening the mood. "Seriously, though, be careful out there. Hanna and Evelynn will probably take it out on me if something happens to you. They're pretty mad you're not taking them with you. And I suppose I'd miss you, too, if you didn't come back."

"I'll make sure she's safe," Chase says, "and those girls are much more helpful here. We have a lot more to do around here if we're going to be self-sustaining. I hope they both have green thumbs."

"Are we good here?" I ask Riley. "This being our last night here for a while, I'd like to spend it celebrating with our family."

"All good. Get out of here," Chase answers for him. "Tell Axel we're leaving at first light."

I nod, relieved that there's at least one goodbye I won't have to make.

Axel's room is on the blue side of the school, and while the purpling rules no longer apply, I still feel my cheeks heat as I cross over the blue line. Mr. Mason and Ms. Kay, our last two teachers, are no longer with us. I can't help but wonder if Garrett and I entering the town somehow brought the virus to them. Not long after my group left school, they'd felt the first symptoms of the virus and fled campus for fear of infecting anyone else. If they'd only known the rest of us were immune, perhaps they wouldn't have had to die alone.

It's heavy, knowing how many people have died. It makes me feel like I owe the world, like I'm obligated to make sure my life serves a bigger purpose. I have a responsibility to live for all the people who are no longer with us, and I refuse to let them down.

Not all of it is sad, not if I allow my hope to speak to me. Sometimes, I think back to when I was a small child and my biggest dream was to travel the world and climb every mountain and see every ocean. I think the universe was already whispering to me then. Something out there already knew this would be my calling.

Axel's door is ajar—he's been waiting for me to return from my chores. I push the door open and find him sitting on the edge of his neatly made bed. He's writing something in a notebook, but he stops when he hears me knock gently on the open door. He smiles at me, that wide gorgeous smile I've come to know well, his silver eyes flashing with joy. I like seeing him in jeans and a t-shirt. He looks comfortable, like he fits in here and has always been one of us.

"What are you writing?" I ask, joining him on the bed.

"A letter to Lyra. I want her to understand. Maybe when we get back from this first mission, she'll be more willing to talk."

I rub Axel's back. It's been hard on him, the distance he feels from Lyra. They used to be close, and she's not ready to accept our reality for what it is yet. I want her to come around so I can get to know her, too, but mostly so that Axel can have his own family back.

"Even if she doesn't say it, I think she'll appreciate the effort."

"She needs to find a Selena." He smiles at me. "But she can't have mine."

I roll my eyes. "I'm not that great, but just so you know, you're stuck with me."

Axel shakes his head. "Someday, I'll make you understand. Before you, people always let me down. I didn't trust that someone could be who they say they are, that their actions could match their words. You showed me that, Selena. How loving someone could be as easy as breathing."

"You love Lyra, don't you?" I ask. His words are touching, but I want to understand his meaning.

"I love Lyra, but only because I've known her my entire life. It doesn't matter what she says, I know who she is. I understand her. I don't always know what you're thinking, or what you're going to do, but I trust you anyway. I love you without knowing all the facts. That's not something I thought was possible."

I swallow back my emotion. If I could love this boy any more, my heart would burst open. "Well, then I hope she finds her own Selena, too. Even if she's mean and would probably try to kill them."

"Let's hope her person is equipped to handle her hostility." Axel smirks, and I laugh because I can't quite imagine a person who could handle Lyra. "Are you almost ready to leave? Do you need me to help you pack anything?"

I shake my head. I've been packed for a few days. As hard as it will be to leave the school again, to walk away from Evelynn and Hanna, from Garrett and his little family, I know this is something I need to do.

This is my purpose, to bring all the immune together. To rebuild a world that we can be proud of.

"It's our last night here for a while. Evie and Hanna are putting together a little dinner thing tonight."

"I hope it's oatmeal," Axel says. "I think I could eat oatmeal every day for the rest of my life and never get tired of it."

I laugh. "Oatmeal is like sludge-of-the-Earth breakfast. Hanna found an old stash of macaroni and cheese, and if you're that impressed with oatmeal, this will blow you out of the water."

"Better than oatmeal?" Axel shakes his head. "I'll be the judge of that."

"There are so many things better than oatmeal. I hope that someday I can show you all of them. Especially pizza."

Axel presses a kiss to my lips. "I know you will."

"All our friends will be waiting for us in the commons," I say, standing up from the bed and tugging on Axel's arm. His silver eyes still stop me in my tracks, and I feel lost in his gaze.

Axel tugs me back toward him, wrapping his arms around me. "I don't know what the future holds, Selena. It's dangerous out there, and not everyone may feel the same way about joining forces. We might not like everything we find."

I nod at him because I know he's right. The road ahead will not be easy, but it can be good—I know it can. A greater purpose for my extraordinary life.

"But what I do know"—he kisses the tip of my nose—"is that you are the best person of all of us to bring everyone together. You're something special."

Tears gather in my eyes as I launch myself into Axel's arms and hold on tightly. It's been a long road already, and we're only getting started, but I have more hope and confidence in our future than I ever thought possible.

Someone knocks at the door, and I peel myself away from Axel. Evelynn pokes her head in, one hand barely covering her eyes as if she's trying not to see anything indecent. "Hey, guys, it's time to eat."

"We're coming." I laugh, grabbing Axel's hand and dragging him behind me. "Axel has never tried macaroni before, and he can't see how it'll be better than oatmeal."

Evelynn makes a gagging sound. "Oatmeal is gross. You'll love this." She takes my arm in hers, I loop Axel's arm in on the other side, and we walk together the rest of the way.

In the commons, everyone is talking and laughing together, the tables full of our friends. It looks effortlessly normal, despite the journey it took us to get here. My heart feels so full it could burst as I take my seat. Things are going to be okay; I know it.

While this feels like the bittersweet end of our lives as we've always known them, it also feels like the beginning of our greatest adventure yet. Ardor is gone, the space station is destroyed, humans as a species are now forever altered, but even so, I feel in my heart that we are going to make the world proud. We're going to rebuild humanity into something great.

Because despite all our losses—all the death, destruction, and heartache—hope prevails.

We are the hope.

We are what remains.

Acknowledgements

First and foremost, I want to thank my readers. After I published Crimson Hearts, it was all of you who made me feel like the published author I always knew I could be. I am forever thankful for all of you. I could not do this job without you. I hope you loved this book as much as my last.

If you read my first book, you were probably surprised that What Remains was a slightly different genre than Crimson Hearts. After 2020 and the wild ride that was... I starting thinking about how much the world changed for us on a day-to-day level, and the fickle nature of humans when we are faced with problems that we feel are out of our hands. What began as a simple story about some immune kids at a private school, quickly warped into something far more adventurous. Thank you for coming on this ride with me. I hope you fell in love with Selena and the Ardorians (especially Axel), and I hope you're ready for more, because this will not be the last of their story.

Before I say anything else, I want to thank my amazing husband, Josh. When the imposter syndrome came knocking and I was doubting my choice to try a new genre, you never let me give up. And when I had a million questions, you used your rocket-scientist brain to help me work through all of it. I appreciate you more than you'll ever know. Thank you for believing in me for the last twenty-one years. I'm looking forward to seeing what the next twenty-one bring us. I love you.

Now, there are friends... and then there are my friends, Sommer Olson and Tiffanie Ruby. Thank you for being brave Alpha readers and pushing me for more chapters every week. Kelly wouldn't have her happy ending if it weren't for you two. I love you both like sisters. You're the best hype-team anyone could ask for and my favorite Bunco players. Thank you for loving Crimson Hearts, and now this book, and for shouting that love from the rooftops.

Best-Selling Author Kayla Grosse (Yeah, you earned that title!), can you believe it's been more than four years since our friendship began? Before either of us had published anything... Thank you for always believing in me and cheering me on, even when I write in your least favorite genre and without any spice. I am so proud of everything you've accomplished. Author-besties for life.

Sarah Mello, once again you've helped me take my book to another level. I fell in love with your writing in Westcott High and I will forever sing your praises. Thank you for all your help and insight, and most of all for your friendship. I cannot wait to read your next book.

A very special thank you to my BETA readers who always ask the hard questions and help polish my story even more. Thank you to Kelly Heirigs, Melissa Crump, K. Loren Bettridge, Nina Wills, Marissa Guzman, Ludmila, Lori Wise, Ashley Queen, and Jayden Tellado. My books are better because of your feedback, and I cannot thank you enough for your time and support.

Melissa Frey, editor extraordinaire, you are the real MVP. I enjoyed working with you so much on my first book, there was no question in my mind who I wanted this time around. Thank you for your tireless work making my words shine and fixing all that tedious tense shifting. I appreciate you for making me look like I know what I'm doing!

To my kids: Lincoln, Sophia, Kinley, and Declan. Thank you for forgiving me when I'm lost in the world of writing and have to be reminded five times that you asked me to do something. For asking me about my stories, and for being some of my biggest fans. You're the reason I want to be great at this, I want to show you how to follow your own dreams and enjoy the ride. I love all four of you, forever and always.

Finally, to all my friends and family who love and support me in this dream, I say thank you. There will never be enough words to express my gratitude, I love you all.

XOXO

-Nic